Praise for

"I'm personally excited about the work ... years of influence in the urban context fleshed out in ... I'm honored to support him."

—**LECRAE**, Hip Hop recording artist

"The story of Kai'Ro shows the effects of how one man's choice to relocate to his old neighborhood with the hope of the gospel makes a profound impact on changing his city for Christ."

—**JOHN PERKINS**, founder of Christian Community Development
    Association

"I tried to find something that my guys could relate to and identify with, and at the same time help to teach the Bible. I thought, let me try *Kai'Ro* with the boys. Imagine about 17 young guys listening to me read the book . . . the guys ate it up! They loved it so much that, at the end of each chapter, they wanted me to keep reading."

—**ALONZO BROWN JR.**, Common Ground Ministry, Montgomery, Alabama

"I wanna be like Kai'Ro because he cares about what God, his only King, thinks about him."

—**JAQUARIUS**, 13 years old

"My favorite character in the book is Kai'Ro because he wants to change his life around, even though his friends didn't want to change their lives; it made me want to be like Kai'Ro."

—**RONDALE**, 12 years old

"This book gives hope for those who messed up. God takes the burden of our sins and changes our lives."

—**KENDAL**, 17 years old

"KAI*RO" RETURNS

by JUDAH BEN

MOODY PUBLISHERS
CHICAGO

Scriptures are based on the author's paraphrase of the Holy Bible, English Standard Version.

Scripture quotations are taken from *The Holy Bible, English Standard Version.* Copyright © 2000, 2001 by Crossway Bibles, a division of Good News Publishers. Used by permission. All rights reserved.

Rap lyrics in chapter 21, "War of the Words" were written by Sho Baraka expressly to be used by Judah Ben in *Kai'Ro Returns.*

Edited by Kathryn Hall
Interior Designer: Design Corps
Cover Design and Image: Geoffrey Sciacca

Library of Congress Cataloging-in-Publication Data

Ben, Judah.
  Kai'Ro returns / Judah Ben.
    pages cm
  ISBN 978-0-8024-0665-1
  1. Bunyan, John, 1628-1688. Pilgrim's progress—Adaptations. 2. Christian fiction. I. Title.
PS3602.E6557K33 2013
813'.6—dc23

                                                    2012048541

We hope you enjoy this book from Moody Publishers. Our goal is to provide high-quality, thought-provoking books and products that connect truth to your real needs and challenges. For more information on other books and products written and produced from a biblical perspective, go to www.moodypublishers.com or write to:

Moody Publishers
820 N. LaSalle Boulevard
Chicago, IL 60610

1 3 5 7 9 10 8 6 4 2

Printed in the United States of America

To my mom and dad.
You not only introduced me to the King,
but you showed me by example how to follow His footsteps
down the Heavenly Highway and wherever He might lead.

CONTENTS

COMING HOME

STORYTELLER: One night as I was up late watching television, I nodded off on my couch and drifted into a deep sleep. I found myself alone on a hill. It was a cold night. In the distance, I saw before me a dark city. Its buildings rose up out of the ground and appeared to leer and lean like shadowy monsters. A grayish-red cloud hung around the city like a halo of fire.

Occasionally, something would flash in the cloud like streaks of lightning only to be followed by deep groans of thunder. A few dull yellow lights shined dimly from various windows in the buildings beneath.

I was drawn in closer along an old cracked strip of black-top until I was just inside the city. Hard brick walls lined the road, sprawled with graffiti of angry words and pictures. Random piles of trash lay strewn about the streets. Along the sidewalk was a succession of old sagging houses. Some of them were burned out and others merely boarded up. Mangy grass grew knee high in most of the yards. Dogs barked, paced and growled behind chain-link fences.

Every now and then, on a distant block, I heard the staccato cracking of gunfire. The sounds of police sirens blared through the night air like the cries of howling ghosts. I saw to my left a large man standing in his doorway, hollering and cursing at a woman on his porch. She yelled back at him before he struck her twice. The woman kicked and screamed as he dragged her by the hair back into the house.

I was pulled along further until I came upon a house that was on fire. The looming orange flames leaped and danced in the air. No one seemed to care as this building burned to the ground. The houses on either side were charred skeletons of homes that used to be there.

Throughout the night, cars with shiny rims and tinted glass rolled slowly down the dark streets. The drone of bass announced their coming and the rapid fire from their tweeters assaulted my ears as they passed by. Many of the street lights along the road were broken. Those that were working cast an eerie light upon the ground. I was drawn along quickly until I spotted a large sign pulsating from the tallest building. It read in bright red letters: CITY OF DOOM: HOME OF THE FALLEN.

Every once in a while I saw a few men leaning against buildings, smoking cigarettes. There were some women in short and tight fitting clothing, with faces covered in heavy makeup and eyes full of pain. They stood beneath the street lights and leaned into car windows as vehicles stopped on the corner.

As I was pulled along further, I saw that many of the businesses along the street were boarded shut. Their signs were old and tattered with chipped paint. "Sorry, we're closed" signs hung in the few remaining windows where the stores weren't already closed permanently. In some of the alleyways, I saw men and women slumped against the wall or sleeping in cardboard shelters.

I grew increasingly saddened and weighed down by all that was before me. Everything was cold, grey and lifeless. Yearning to awake or be swept away from all that I witnessed, I felt hopeless, overwhelmed and alone.

But then I saw it. In the distance was a strange beam of light. At first, it looked like a spotlight from a building top being cast down on the pavement. As I stared upwards, I could see that this light's source was actually something far above the buildings. In fact, it came from way beyond the dark clouds that blanketed the city, piercing them like a sword.

This unusual beam focused directly onto the street, quite a distance from where I was looking. And then suddenly, I realized that it highlighted a single image. I strained my eyes to see what but could only make out a shape. Yet, as the light drew closer, I could see that it was shining on a man. The glow around him appeared to shoo away the shadows, creating a gracious and favorable appearance to everything it touched.

The man I saw was wearing a baseball cap that shielded his face. Thick clouds of white vapor emerged from his mouth in the cold night air. He was tall and thin. A cross hung from a silver chain around his neck. Clothed in a white T-shirt and baggy jeans, he came closer and closer.

Then he stopped and appeared to look straight at me. I could see in this man's eyes an intense and raging fire and then I recognized his face. It was Kai'Ro. He was coming home and it appeared that he had brought a sliver of Heaven with him.

WELCOME BACK

STORYTELLER: I watched as Kai'Ro moved from beyond the shadows of the tall buildings and headed into a neighborhood just on the edge of downtown. The early morning mist twisted around his ankles like coiling snakes. He seemed especially nervous and I spotted a lump in his throat.

KAI'RO: (quietly to himself) My King, please give me the words and the strength. Being back here brings a lot of bad memories, and I feel more than weighed down and afraid. I trust You are here with me, for You've promised You would not abandon Your servants.

STORYTELLER: As Kai'Ro continued down the main road, the first glowing colors of dawn started to emerge. I watched him walk until he came to the intersection of CAPTIVITY COURT and BAD TIMES BOULEVARD. He glanced at the street sign for a moment then took a right and started walking down the Boulevard.

    The houses along this street were especially rundown. Most of the yards were littered with trash and overgrown with weeds. Old cars were parked along the curbs. In several spots along the road there were pools of busted window glass. The sun continued to rise in the sky, but its light still struggled to push through the cloudy haze above the city.

Kai'Ro moved slowly and eyed each house that he passed with a sorrowful expression. Occasionally, he turned his eyes upwards towards Heaven as if he were searching for a sign or an answer. Then, stopping in front of an old gray house, he stared at it especially hard. A faint light glowed behind dark curtains in one of the rooms. The grass in the yard was nearly a foot high.

As Kai'Ro walked up the cracked driveway, he spotted beer cans and cigarette butts tossed on the ground. Cautiously, he stepped onto the rotting patio and stood there for over a minute, with his chin slumped on his chest. I could tell he was having doubts. But then the flicker of fire emerged in his eyes once again.

Emboldened, he slowly raised his arm, extended his finger and pressed the doorbell. Slender fingers pulled back the curtain behind the small window near the top of the door and two large brown eyes appeared. They widened when they saw Kai'Ro standing on the patio. I heard the click of two locks and the door was pulled open as far as the lock-chain would allow. The face of a beautiful woman appeared.

KAI'RO: Evangeline...

STORYTELLER: The woman pursed her lips and narrowed her eyes at him.

KAI'RO: I...ah...

STORYTELLER: Kai'Ro pulled off his cap, rubbed his chin and let out a deep sigh.

EVANGELINE: What is it, boy? Why you here?

KAI'RO: I came back to tell you that I made it down the Highway I was telling you about. It was amazin', girl. I came back to tell you...

EVANGELINE: You told me in that note you left me, you wasn't comin' back!

KAI'RO: I wasn't plannin' on comin' back...not at first. But things changed...I changed.

EVANGELINE: You changed? You look the same to me.

KAI'RO: I'm not talkin' 'bout how I look. Of course I look the same, but on the inside...how I live...that's all different. That part is all new. The ol' Kai'Ro...you won't ever see him again. I ain't the same no more. I ain't hustlin' no more. I'm not runnin' the streets no more. This is a new dude standin' here before you right now. I'm changed. I'm brand new!

EVANGELINE: So, why you here? You came back from your lil' trip just to show up and say to me "Hey, I'm brand new"? C'mon, you think I care?

KAI'RO: I understand you're mad. I was hopin' you'd give me a chance to talk with you.

STORYTELLER: Evangeline continued to glare at Kai'Ro through the crack in her door.

EVANGELINE: You ain't the only one 'round here who changed, Kai'Ro.

KAI'RO: What'cha mean?

STORYTELLER: Evangeline slammed the door shut. I could hear her unfastening the chain lock before she swung the door open wide. With her hands on her hips, she stood there in a pink tank-top and some light blue sweat pants. Kai'Ro's eyes dropped from staring at her face to her belly, which was protruding with a small bump. He was speechless.

EVANGELINE: Yeah, that's right, boy. I'm pregnant!

STORYTELLER: Kai'ro sucked his lips in and stared at her belly in shock.

KAI'RO: Who...who's the daddy?

STORYTELLER: Evangeline smirked and leaned her face into Kai'Ro's.

EVANGELINE: I ain't been with no other man, Kai'Ro. You this baby's daddy! Now what're you and your King gonna do about that? You gonna run now. Aren't you, boy? Go on, run!

STORYTELLER: Then, to my surprise, Kai'Ro took a step forward and grabbed Evangeline in a powerful hug. She looked confused as her face rested on his shoulder.

KAI'RO: (whispering) I'm not gonna run, Evangeline. I'm back and I'm not gonna leave you alone with this child.

STORYTELLER: He held her with a tight grip until I saw Evangeline's face soften slightly. It took several minutes before she wiggled free from Kai'Ro's embrace.

EVANGELINE: But you already left me once. How am I 'sposed to believe you gonna stay this time?

KAI'RO: Because that's what a man does. A man owns up to his mistakes when he makes 'em. But, by the King's grace, he tries to make it right.

EVANGELINE: Make it right? What's that mean? You said you ain't hustlin' and dealin' no more, so how you 'sposed to provide for this baby?

KAI'RO: Gotta get a job then.

EVANGELINE: (laughing) A job? Kai'Ro, you ain't never had a job. You mean, you're gonna go out and get you a *real* job...like a nine to five?

KAI'RO: If I got to. Yeah.

EVANGELINE: So you just expect me to welcome you back 'cause you got religion now?

KAI'RO: No. It ain't like that.

EVANGELINE: How do you know if I even wanna keep this thing?

KAI'RO: Whatcha mean?

EVANGELINE: I haven't decided if it's a baby or a burden.

KAI'RO: That ain't no debate, girl. That's a human life in your belly. In fact, that baby is made in the image of the King. It ain't no *thing* . . . it's a one-of-a-kind treasure.

EVANGELINE: My two girls Mess and Drama told me to do somethin' with this baby. They told me to get rid of it.

KAI'RO: Why would they tell you somethin' like that?

EVANGELINE: They told me no man would want me knocked up or with a kid. They told me to get rid of this thing and start over. You know that's what Drama did like two years ago.

KAI'RO: Yeah. I remember that.

EVANGELINE: Honestly, I was thinkin' 'bout what they said. I mean, there's no way for me to keep this baby by myself.

STORYTELLER: With her head hanging down, Evangeline stared at the floor.

EVANGELINE: I don't know, Kai'Ro. I been thinkin' 'bout goin' to the clinic just to talk to somebody about it.

KAI'RO: You talkin' 'bout the Choice for Murder Clinic?

EVANGELINE: C'mon, boy, that ain't what that place is called. It's called My Choice Clinic.

KAI'RO: They can call it what they want, but it ain't no *choice* but murder. Don't you know Diablo loves puttin' a positive spin on somethin' awful? He's got folks thinkin' it's a choice to murder their own young. Now that's crazy. Since when did people ever think they should have a choice on whether or not a baby lives? There's only one choice and that choice is life! There ain't no debate 'bout this.

EVANGELINE: You right. There ain't no debate. For a debate, you got two equal voices. Right? Well, you got no voice on this. You can't just show up on my porch after being gone as long as you been gone and then try 'n tell me what I gotta do with my body!

KAI'RO: That's what that baby would say too. If that baby could talk, it would tell you that you can't do whatever you want with its body either!

STORYTELLER: Kai'Ro sighed and hung his head.

KAI'RO: Look, I didn't come back to make you or anybody else do nothin'. I came back for a coupla reasons, but one of them is because the King sent me back to introduce this city to Life.

EVANGELINE: Whatcha mean?

KAI'RO: Before I gave my life to the King and lost that doggone burden, I was choosin' nothin' but death. I mean, every decision I was makin' was bad and harmful to me or somebody else. I was robbin' from folks to make money. I was lyin' to get what I needed. I was dealin' and hustlin' and not carin' at all that I was killin' relationships and murderin' trust with other people.

    Now I know any and every action outside of a relationship with the King is sin and it's destructive. It doesn't matter if you're murderin' a baby or tellin' a lie...either way, you're spreadin' sin. And sin kills.

EVANGELINE: You sound like that crazy Preacher man who got inside your head.

KAI'RO: Preacher was the only man who was in his right mind in this whole city! You right. His words sounded like craziness to me at first too. But the more I listened, the more it made sense. He was spreadin' Life. He was pointin' me to freedom. To hope...to Life!

    The more I listened to him, the more I realized that I was on a road to death. I was promotin' and producin' death with every decision I made. When I looked hard at the City of Doom, it became obvious to me that this whole city is dyin'. Preacher told me that the King offered me Life for eternity and life for today. But then he said, when the King comes back, He's comin' back as Judge. He's gonna judge us all accordin' to our deeds. I knew then that I was in trouble. I didn't wanna be judged and I didn't wanna be bound up in death the way I was. So I left to find Life and the freedom it brings.

STORYTELLER: Evangeline's arms were folded across her chest. She stared into Kai'Ro's face as he spoke.

EVANGELINE: Well, you're sayin' that you found this Life and freedom. And you're claimin' that the City of Doom's got nothin' but death. So why didn't you just stay away with your Life and freedom?

KAI'RO: To be honest wit you, I was plannin' on it. But then the King redirected my steps. He showed me that the Life that He offered to me was meant to be shared with everyone. It'd be like me discoverin' a cure to a terrible disease that me and the rest of the world had. Once I was cured, I could choose to keep that cure to myself, or I could choose to share it with everyone I found. How could I keep somethin' so amazin' to myself?

EVANGELINE: (shrugging) You know that nobody here wants to hear that mess, right? I mean, people are gonna clown you when they hear you talkin' out the side of your neck like that. The Kai'Ro they remember had everybody's respect. Whoever this dude is that's standin' in my house right now is either a fake or he lost his mind. I don't know which one it is . . .

KAI'RO: (smiling) I understand your doubts, Evangeline. A lot of folks ain't gonna believe me. I know that. I did a lot of dirt in this city and I'm gonna have to make some mends. I'm just here 'cause the King sent me back. I think He wants to use me somehow to show the people of this city His love and to point 'em towards Life. I got a lotta mixed feelin's 'bout this place.

But I also feel like I got a fire shut up in my bones like that cat Jeremiah. I just gotta tell people about how great this King really is.

EVANGELINE: Well, good luck with that.

STORYTELLER: Evangeline opened the door for Kai'Ro. Before stepping outside, he gave her a tender smile and put his hat back on his head. She gently closed the door.

In my dream, I saw her pull back the shade and watch Kai'Ro as he headed back down the block. Once he disappeared around the corner, she stepped back and slowly placed her hands on her face. Evangeline stared at the wall, lost in her thoughts.

LIL' ONE 3

STORYTELLER: I watched as Kai'Ro walked slowly down the sidewalk away from Evangeline's house. On his face I spotted a look of deep concern.

The sun had now risen in the morning sky. Suddenly, car alarms went off and vehicle windows shook mercilessly from the explosive bass of an approaching vehicle. A jet black Impala on 24s was rolling by slowly.

Kai'Ro turned his head just slightly and looked over his shoulder as the car drew closer. He fixed his eyes on it as it passed him by. Then the Impala screeched to a halt. KaiRo hesitated and looked to his left and right, as if he was contemplating whether he should run. The driver's side window rolled down slowly and a face emerged. It was a young man wearing a St. Louis cap that was pulled low over his eyes.

LIL' ONE: What up, bruh?

STORYTELLER: Kai'Ro stood his ground and stared at the driver.

LIL' ONE: Man, whatcha doin', dawg? Come over here and talk to ya bruh.

KAI'RO: Lil' One? That you?

STORYTELLER: The door of the car was thrown open and Lil' One stepped out. Wearing a beater and some sweats, he had grown tall and skinny. A thick silver chain hung from his neck and he had on some bright red Js. Lil' One flashed a big smile and held his arms wide, anticipating a hug. His forearms were covered with tattoos.

KAI'RO: (smiling) My lil' bro. Man, what's up, dawg?

STORYTELLER: In semi shock, Kai'Ro stepped towards his little brother and the two embraced.

KAI'RO: Man, look at you. I ain't been gone that long, and you've grown like three inches, son. Now you're...

LIL' ONE: As big as you.

KAI'RO: (shaking his head in disbelief) Yeah, dawg. I can't believe it.

LIL' ONE: You back checkin' on ya ol' girl or somethin'?

KAI'RO: Somethin' like that...I'm actually checkin' in on my old city. That's what's up.

LIL' ONE: For real? Man, you dipped outta here so fast nobody even knew you was gone. Then you roll back into town and no one even knows you're here. So, what happened? You got tired of chasin' that religion nonsense? Coulda told ya that was a dead-end road.

KAI'RO: I ain't chasin' no more. I *found* what I was lookin' for and I brought it back with me.

LIL' ONE: (shrugging) Yeah, well maybe we can talk 'bout that some time. Look, let's jump in my ride and I'll roll you back to the crib. Here, got an extra chicken biscuit. Ya look hungry, dawg.

KAI'RO: Shoot, man, I'm starvin'.

STORYTELLER: The two brothers jumped into the car and started rolling down the block. When Lil' One tossed Kai'Ro a biscuit, he didn't hesitate to unwrap the paper and take a bite.

KAI'RO: (chewing) Who's ride is this?

LIL' ONE: (grinning) This whip is mine, playa.

KAI'RO: C'mon, dawg. A new Impala...leather seats...fully loaded. This ain't yours.

LIL' ONE: I'm a businessman now. Bought this from Doc like a month ago.

KAI'RO: You work for Doc Destruction? Man, when did you make *that* stupid move?

LIL' ONE: Stupid? Hold up! Whatcha mean, stupid? Workin' for Doc was the best move I ever made. I'm pullin' in like three Gs a week. Besides, you made your dough hustlin'. So who are you to talk? Yo new religion made you a judge now?

STORYTELLER: Kai'Ro sighed and looked at his brother. Lil' One had an angry scowl on his face, as he gripped the steering wheel.

KAI'RO: Look, you right. I got no right to call you stupid. And you right 'bout me bein' in no position to judge either. I owe you an apology for livin' that kinda life and for showin' you that pushin' weight was how a man was 'sposed to make ends meet. I'm responsible for that mistake.

STORYTELLER: Lil' One pulled out a Black & Mild from his pocket and lit it up.

LIL' ONE: Want one?

KAI'RO: Nah. Ya hear what I'm sayin'? I made some big mistakes. Bein' a playa ain't all that. We need to talk 'bout this, for real.

LIL' ONE: Yeah? Well, I don't wanna talk 'bout that mess right now.

KAI'RO: (sighing) How's Ma?

LIL' ONE: She's straight.

STORYTELLER: The two brothers rode on in silence for a while. Lil' One turned right down ADDICT AVENUE. Kai'Ro stared out the window, sucked in his lips and stroked his chin. A few guys in blue tall-Ts nodded at his brother's ride as they rolled by. A girl in some short-shorts and a tight tank top was pushing two small kids in a stroller. The cracks in the sidewalk were crammed with weeds and forced her to navigate carefully. Lil' One pulled his ride down a short driveway and the two got out.

FIEND: What up, Kush Man?

STORYTELLER: Across the street, a young man stood wearing a sleeveless shirt, some shorts and flip-flops. He was washing down his Mercedes.

LIL ONE: What up?

KAI'RO: Kush Man, huh?

LIL ONE: That's what they all call me now...I like it.

STORYTELLER: In my dream, I watched as Kai'Ro looked up at his old house. The roof was covered with dead branches and it looked like nearly half the shingles had blown away. There was a lot of trash strewn about the tall grass in the front yard. Lil' One pulled out a big set of keys and started opening a variety of locks on the front door.

KAI'RO: Ma must really be feelin' unsafe, huh?

STORYTELLER: Lil' One and Kai'Ro stepped into the house. Inside, it was very dark. A small television in the corner was playing a music video. An old green couch was slumped against the wall with little sprouts of white stuffing gushing from the cushions. A dirty bowl sitting on an old table held a small mountain of cigarette butts.

KAI'RO: Yo. Where's Ma?

LIL ONE: Prob'ly in the bed. She sleeps most of the day. C'mon, let me show ya somethin'.

STORYTELLER: Lil' One led the way down into the basement. A single lightbulb dangling from the ceiling guided their steps. The first thing I saw was a long, dark leather couch sitting in the middle of the room. Seated on it were three young men, watching a basketball game on a large flatscreen television mounted on the wall.

LIL ONE: Lemme introduce you to my squad. Aye, y'all, get up and say w'sup to a real G, my big brotha, Kai'Ro.

STORYTELLER: As soon as Lil' One said Kai'Ro's name, all three young men stood up at once and turned to face him. One of them cleared his throat and tried to straighten his shirt.

LIL ONE: (pointing) That boy there, that's 2-Fake.

STORYTELLER: 2-Fake was fat. He was wearing a thick fake chain and a silly looking tattoo of a skull on his neck.

2-FAKE: What up, Kai'Ro . . . didn't know you was back in town . . .

LIL ONE: That dude there, that's my boy Lazy.

STORYTELLER: Lazy nodded. He was holding a big bag of chips in his hands.

LIL ONE: (nodding towards the third guy) And that's Addict.

STORYTELLER: Addict gave a half-smile that revealed some missing teeth. He was very skinny and had a strange looking scar on his cheek. A joint dangled from his lips.

KAI'RO: Man, you let these dudes smoke weed in Ma's basement?

2-FAKE: Hey, we don't just smoke weed down here, dawg. We sell it.

LIL ONE: (grinning) Yeah, that's what's up.

STORYTELLER: I watched as Lil' One walked over to a red toolbox. He opened it up and pulled out two Ziploc bags full of weed. Lil' One tossed a bag to Kai'Ro.

LIL ONE: Doc is movin' some of the best kush this city has seen in years. This stuff is way better than that trash you was sellin'. Ya know what folks are callin' it?

ADDICT: They call it "baked bread." And down here—

2-FAKE: This is the bakery.

LAZY: Just take a whiff. It's some sweet, sweet stuff.

LIL ONE: Folks are buggin' out to get their hands on this here weed. I got ADDICT AVENUE all the way down to HOPELESS HIGHWAY on lock. Doc's given that turf to me and my boys here.

STORYTELLER: Kai'Ro's eyes narrowed as he threw the bag back at Lil' One.

KAI'RO: There's no way you're turnin' Ma's house into some kinda crack den. I'm shuttin' this bakery down.

LIL ONE: Man, you trippin'. This bread I'm sellin' is puttin' *bread* on the table.

KAI'RO: Nah. It's puttin' bread in your pocket and puttin' rides in the driveway. This whole house is fallin' down 'round you. What about Ma?

LIL ONE: Ma's got everything she wants. The fridge is full and I pay for that cable TV she likes to watch so much.

KAI'RO: Our responsibility as sons is to guard her and keep her safe. A man takes care of his home and family and doesn't bring evil to his own doorstep. You're bringin' dangerous people to Ma's house. You're dishonorin' and disrespectin' her name. This is Ma's house! Now everybody knows it's where they can get some of that green. I don't believe this!

LIL ONE: You one to talk, Kai'Ro!

KAI'RO: You right! I fumbled the ball, dawg. I left you a bad example. I told ya that already. Look, I was no saint back in the day, but I changed. The King changed me and I despise all this stuff now. Used to love it...used to love the paper and the power this stuff brought me...but not no more...can't go robbin' poor folks of their last few dollars so they can literally watch their lives go up in smoke. Nah! This bakery of yours is closed.

LAZY: You gonna try and shut us down?

STORYTELLER: Kai'Ro took two steps towards the couch.

KAI'RO: I'm not tryin'. As of now, this bakery is closed—for good!

STORYTELLER: Kai'Ro calmly stared 2-Fake, Lazy and Addict in the eyes. 2-Fake swallowed hard and looked at the other two.

2-FAKE: C'mon, y'all. Let's dip outta here. I ain't tusslin' with this dude.

STORYTELLER: Just then, the doorbell rang.

KAI'RO: Who's that?

ADDICT: Prob'ly somebody at the back door lookin' for a taste.

STORYTELLER: Kai'Ro grabbed 2-Fake by the arm as he tried to pass by. He pulled the boy close to his chest.

KAI'RO: You tell whoever that is out there that this bakery of yours is closed. You tell them to spread the word to everybody they see that this place is shut down. Ya feel me?

2-FAKE: (hoarsely) Yeah. I feel you, dawg.

STORYTELLER: The three young men raced up the stairs, and Kai'Ro spun his attention to Lil' One.

LIL' ONE: Man, I don't believe this mess. I thought you was cool.

KAI'RO: Cool? You think this dope game is cool? Ya got a new name, Kush Man. Ya got a tight whip. Ya got a new reputation and a fat stack. So what? You really think that stuff is gonna keep you happy. I had it all too. You forget that. I went to bed at night with a Benz in the driveway, a stack under the bed, heat under my pillow and a honey to keep me company. But I woke up every mornin' feelin' like a starvin' dog.

LIL ONE: Yeah? So what you got now? Nuttin'.

KAI'RO: That's a matter of opinion, isn't it? Let me tell you what I got. I got hope for the first time. I got Life. Purpose. Meaning. Security. Love. When I die, I'm gonna live with the King whose pleasures are forevermore.

But let me tell you what I don't got. I got no worries. I don't gotta look over my shoulder no more. I ain't afraid to die no more. I got regrets, but no guilt. I fall asleep easy at night. I owe no man nothin'. I ain't no man's puppet. I'm a soldier in the King's army. I rep Him now and I rep Him loud.

LIL ONE: So you think scarin' my crew outta here is gonna end all this? Those three clowns still respect you enough to run. But word's gonna get back to Doc, and he'll look you up and make you hurt. Shoot! He might snuff you out completely. He runs the City of Doom and you're nothin' to him.

KAI'RO: He's just the biggest puppet on the string.

LIL ONE: Whatcha mean?

KAI'RO: This is Diablo's town. Doc Destruction is just a pawn in his game.

LIL ONE: Who's Diablo?

KAI'RO: Diablo is a mastermind demon. He's a patient beast who'll suck the blood out of you over a lifetime and you'll never even know it. His goal is to kill and destroy us all. You think Doc and his crew roll deep. You ain't seen nothin'. Ain't no one who can take Diablo out—except for One!

LIL ONE: Your King dude?

KAI'RO: That's right.

LIL' ONE: Man, you sure you ain't been smokin' some stuff yoself? Talkin' 'bout demon monsters and this King of yours makes me think you trippin', for real.

KAI'RO: There's nothin' more real than what I'm tellin' you. When I look at you right now, I'm lookin' at myself not too long ago. See, the thing is, I know where the road you're on ends. It ends in death and hell. Can't say it any simpler than that.

But you wanna know what's funny, bruh? You're livin' in hell right now. You ain't happy. You're miserable. You ain't gonna admit it to me, but I already know. I been further down this road than you are now. I know. Believe me, I know.

STORYTELLER: Lil' One looked at Kai'Ro and then looked at the bag of weed in his hand.

LIL' ONE: This stuff here has bought me more happiness than I knew a man could have.

STORYTELLER: Kai'Ro gave a weak smile and shook his head.

KAI'RO: Nah, bruh. That stuff *owns* you. It calls the shots. If the dope game ended tomorrow, your happiness would end one second later. You ain't free, lil' bro. You a slave. I'm a slave too. Not to no dope game...but to a game that won't end. And the joy from this game has got no limit.

STORYTELLER: Lil' One stared at Kai'Ro with a blank look, but said nothing.

KAI'RO: I aim to show you a better way. I know you brought me down here hopin' to recruit me to join ya in this business of yours. But I came back from far, faraway to recruit you.

STORYTELLER: Kai'Ro turned and started walking back up the stairs.

LIL' ONE: Where ya goin'?

KAI'RO: I gotta go find me a job.

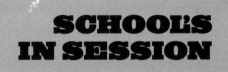

SCHOOL'S IN SESSION

4

STORYTELLER: Kai'Ro walked away from his old house and started down the street. By now, the sun was high in the sky and shone like a glowing orange ball behind the thick clouds overhead.

As Kai'Ro moved down the sidewalk, I saw in my dream three young men sitting on a porch in the front of a house. One of them was sitting in a rocking chair, smoking a Black & Mild. The other two were playing cards at a plastic table. They nodded at Kai'Ro as he drew nearer to the house.

KAI'RO: What's up, fellas?

SLACKER: (exhaling smoke) Nuttin' much. Chillin'.

STORYTELLER: Kai'Ro appeared like he was going to keep walking, but then he stopped as if prompted by someone. He turned suddenly up their sidewalk and came near the porch.

KAI'RO: Shouldn't y'all be in school?

SLACKER: (chuckling) Yeah. Prob'ly, but ain't nothin' goin' on there, for real.

KAI'RO: How old are you?

SLACKER: Fifteen. What's it to you?

KAI'RO: You should be in school, dawg.

CEASE: (shuffling the deck) Who're you? And why you care?

KAI'RO: The name's Kai'Ro. I'm only askin' 'cause I don't like seein' young dudes decidin' to be taught by some fools.

DESIST: What'cha mean, "Taught by some fools"? We ain't bein' taught by no fools.

KAI'RO: Well, the I way see it, y'all are choosin' to drop outta school. You're sayin' you don't wanna be taught by real teachers, and so you'd rather be taught by fools.

SLACKER: Man, we ain't bein' taught by nobody. I ain't been to school since the first day. We been out here chillin' most days, or just out cruisin' the block.

KAI'RO: Eer'body is bein' taught by some teacher. You just may not notice it. How'd you learn to tie ya shoes?

CEASE: My mama taught me.

KAI'RO: What about ridin' a bike?

DESIST: My homeboy, Wild.

KAI'RO: How'd you learn to read?

SLACKER: Ok, dawg. I can see where this is goin'.

KAI'RO: You learned how to walk and talk by somebody in your family. You learned how to shuffle that deck of cards and how to play that game 'cause somebody taught you how. Somebody taught you how to curse, how to dribble a basketball...the list goes on and on. Every one of us is bein' taught every day by somebody.

SLACKER: That's obvious, dawg. You ain't tellin' us nothin' new.

DESIST: For real, man...what's that gotta do wit school and wit gettin' an education?

KAI'RO: That's a good question. Those things that I mentioned ain't nothin' more than just the basics. Nothin' too special 'bout ridin' bikes and dribblin' a ball. But see, education is all about learnin' how to approach life and *how* to live it.

CEASE: What'cha mean?

KAI'RO: Take me, for instance. I dropped outta school when I was just a little older than y'all three. Prob'ly for some of the same reasons y'all mentioned. Crazy home environment...teachers who didn't care. See, I figured I'd just drop outta school for good. But I didn't realize somethin' important. The minute I decided to drop out, I was re-enrolled in a whole 'nother school. This school had teachers too, and I was learnin' a whole lot. But it wasn't no ABCs and arithmetic. I learned the ABCs of hustlin'.

I wasn't up late studyin' for no exams. I was up late dealin' on the corner. Instead of countin' numbers in my math class, I was countin' stacks of cash in the back alley. I didn't exercise by runnin' in no PE class. I got my exercise runnin' from the cops and duckin' shots. After droppin' out, I never got a high school diploma, but I graduated from my new school of thug-enomics with honors.

STORYTELLER: Having said that, Kai'Ro rolled up his sleeve and pointed to a gang tattoo and some brandings on his shoulder. Then he raised his shirt and pointed to two ugly scars on his stomach that looked like old bullet wounds.

KAI'RO: My so-called "honors" came with some strange benefits too. I became known as one of the hardest cats on the block, but I could barely read. Because of my rap sheet with the law, it made me cool with the fellas but made it impossible for me to ever get a good job. I earned mucho paper hustlin' drugs, but I paid the price 'cause I was also an addict and an alcoholic. Woke up mornin' after mornin' with a headache and no clue where I was.

The education I got gave me no real friends but a ton of enemies who wanted to merk me. I made a lot of money but didn't know how to manage it. I spent it as soon as I got it. Mainly, my education helped me learn that most cats can't be trusted. When stuff goes down, your so-called homies run and leave you alone.

STORYTELLER: Slacker cleared his throat. Cease shuffled his deck of cards.

KAI'RO: And check this. Through that education, I learned some very specific things: how to intimidate people with violence and threats. How to abuse women and how to use 'em up. I mean, it taught me how to go through 'em like fast food. I learned how to hide from authority. I discovered how to break my mama's heart and make her cry. How to medicate myself so I could just go to sleep at night. I was educated on how to look over my shoulder...and how to lie, cheat and steal. But after all that, you know what happened to all my teachers?

STORYTELLER: Slacker and Desist shook their heads while Cease looked puzzled.

KAI'RO: Most of 'em are dead. A few of 'em are locked up for life. One or two of 'em still roam the blocks, though. They act like they're OGs but they look ol' and raggedy. They move around the block like shadows. They sleep under bridges and bum coins off folks to buy cheap liquor. My guess is that you're gettin' educated by the same kinda clowns.

STORYTELLER: Kai'Ro stared off for a moment. The three on the porch cast a glance at each other.

KAI'RO: Then one day the student becomes the teacher. I had no idea that my lil' brotha was watchin' everything I did. He saw me havin' fun on the corner, while he toted that bag to class every day. He saw me makin' that paper, while he was in school writin' papers. Wasn't long before he checked out and took to the streets too.

CEASE: Why you tellin' us all this, bruh?

KAI'RO: Because when a student is full grown, he'll be just like his teacher. Like I said, most of the dudes who taught me on the corner are dead or locked up for life. That was almost me. My teachers were blind, dawg. They were leadin' a whole lot of young cats into a ditch, for real. I'm tellin' y'all that sittin' on this porch instead of sittin' in a classroom is gonna get you in a ditch in no time.

DESIST: What'cha mean by a ditch?

KAI'RO: Man, there's lots of ditches to fall into. Bein' jobless. Homeless. Gettin' a disease. Gettin' locked up. Beat up. Drugged up. Gettin' merked.

DESIST: So you sayin' that if you drop outta school, you automatically become a thug, a thief or some kinda menace to society? Just 'cause we givin' up on school don't mean that we gonna end up in a casket, in a jail cell or livin' under some bridge.

KAI'RO: That's true. Not everyone who drops out ends up in those types of ditches. But there's some other ditches that ya gotta think about too, like the ditch of "limited opportunities" and the ditch of "laziness." How many cats do you see just wanderin' 'round the community doin' nothin'? Hangin' out at the park, smokin' cigarettes and hollerin' at ladies? Grown dudes ridin' bikes instead of cars...ridin' 'round sippin' a can of Old E out of a brown paper bag. Livin' at Mama's house when they should have their own place. Growin' fat on the couch watchin' TV and playin' video games?

Most of these types of dudes are doin' nothin' 'cause there's almost nothin' for them to do. In fact, there's very little that they *can* do 'cause they got no education, trainin' or skills to make somebody wanna hire 'em. They end up wastin' their lives, livin' off the crumbs of what coulda been.

STORYTELLER: Slacker took a long draw on his cigar. He let the smoke out slowly and squinted his eyes.

SLACKER: Okay, but how's goin' to school gonna make a difference? You said you dropped out too. You know there's nothin' goin' on in these schools here that's gonna teach us anything.

KAI'RO: Yeah, but I think that's where there's a mistake in our thinkin'.

SLACKER: Ya know, we got some lazy no-good teachers up in our schools, and we got some fools on the block. So where are we 'sposed to go and who are we 'sposed to listen to?

KAI'RO: Had I asked that question you're askin' right there when I was your age, I'd be livin' with a whole lot less regret. Wasn't 'til I got locked up in jail for the third time that I finally realized I had gotten a lousy education from these streets and I was flunkin' out on life.

But, a good teacher pointed me to the true Teacher. The King of kings. After I was introduced to Him, I made it my life's ambition to learn what the King had to say. Now I try to follow how the King lived and surround myself with other cats followin' Him too.

CEASE: King? Who's that? You mean a "King" like one of these?

STORYTELLER: Cease pulled out the King of Hearts from his deck of cards.

KAI'RO: The King I'm talkin' 'bout is the *real* King of Hearts. His heart for you and me was so deep and so powerful. He left the most peaceful place in the universe to live the life of a poor teacher. All the dirt that we've done...He took the blame for it on Himself even though He'd never done anything wrong. And even more than that, He gave us the tools and the wisdom we need to live our lives no matter where we find ourselves.

See, if you roll with the King and follow His lead, you can make it even in the rundown school in ya hood. He'll fill you with that drive you need to crack those books and gain the knowledge you need to make it in life. He'll help you deal with the lousy teachers, but He'll give you the grace you'll need to respect 'em too. He'll direct you to the good teachers up in that school and open ya heart and mind so you can learn from 'em.

The King will give you the wisdom you need to avoid the ditches and the strength you'll need to overcome the obstacles that come ya way—'cause life is a beast.

SLACKER: True.

KAI'RO: At first this King only had like twelve students, for real. One of 'em became a traitor and betrayed Him. But the other eleven were used by the King to flip the world on its head.

SLACKER: (scratching his forehead and grinning) Dude, I ain't never heard nobody yo age talk like that before. You talk like you an ol' man or somethin'.

STORYTELLER: Cease and Desist chuckled a little bit.

KAI'RO: Yeah. What I'm sayin' prob'ly sounds funny to ya. I know. I just wanna pass on some wisdom and some hope to ya, if I can. I hope you'll listen to the words of an older brotha.

SLACKER: I already got an older brother, dawg. His name's Slug.

STORYTELLER: As if on cue, the front door of the house opened up and a very overweight slightly older guy teetered out onto the porch. He wore a dirty beater that showed half of his belly and some boxer shorts. Placing his hand over his bloodshot eyes, the young man squinted in the afternoon light. A nearly empty 40 was in his hand.

SLUG: What time is it, y'all?

STORYTELLER: Slacker looked at his brother and then back at Kai'Ro, but said nothing.

KAI'RO: (throwing up the deuces) Think about what I said, fellas. We all in school—one way or the other. The question is, who's ya teacher?

MAKIN' MENDS

5

STORYTELLER: Kai'Ro continued his walk down the street until he came to a small convenience store on the corner. It was called "MR. WEARY'S." The parking lot was empty. The blacktop was cracked with a few potholes, but otherwise it was clean. A faded "Open" sign hung on the door.

Kai'Ro opened the door and stepped inside. It was a small store with only three aisles containing canned goods, cleaning supplies, candy, snacks and various other items. A row of refrigerators holding cold sodas and energy drinks lined one wall. The floors reflected a worn but clean shine to them. An older man wearing a crisp white apron was stooped over, shelving some items.

MR. WEARY: Be with you in just a minute.

KAI'RO: No problem.

STORYTELLER: Mr. Weary finished stacking some cans and slowly stood up. I noticed him grimace and hold his lower back. After a long pause, he turned around. When he saw Kai'Ro, his face froze.

MR. WEARY: (angrily) I thought I told you to never step foot in my store again...

KAI'RO: Yes, sir, you did...

MR. WEARY: (marching towards his cash register) I'm going to call the police right now! After what you did to this place last time you were here . . .

KAI'RO: (holding up his hands) Mr Weary, I'm not here to cause you any more trouble. In fact, I'm here to apologize.

STORYTELLER: Mr. Weary paused with the phone in his hand. His wrinkled face tightened some more as he squinted at Kai'Ro. Slowly, he placed the phone back on the hook.

MR. WEARY: Apologize? Son, last time you were in here, I had to replace those two front windows there. Not to mention you and those fools you were fighting with tore up these aisles real bad. You almost killed two boys that night. Blood on the floors and mess everywhere! In fact, you almost killed my whole business. Took me over two years to pay off the damages. But what happened to you? You got like a month in juvenile?

KAI'RO: You're right, sir. I practically destroyed your business 'cause I was an angry and foolish kid. I was mad at everybody. I was mad at life itself. But you left some stuff out. Or maybe you didn't even know I used to steal from you almost every week too. I'd come in and buy a candy bar, but inside my pockets I had a whole lot of other stuff. Drinks, chips . . . sometimes cigarettes, if you weren't payin' any attention. The fact is, I was a liar, a thug and a thief. I lost track of how much I stole from you.

STORYTELLER: Mr. Weary looked confused and even a little nervous.

MR. WEARY: So, what's this all about? Is this some kind of game so you can case my place? You here to rob me some more? It won't work. I've got cameras now. See em?

KAI'RO: Mr. Weary, I'm not here to rob or harm you. I came in today to tell you that I am terribly sorry for how I wronged you. I am deeply ashamed for what I've done to you and this business. I'm hopin' that you can forgive me, sir.

MR. WEARY: Son, have you been doing some drugs? You feeling ok?

KAI'RO: I feel fine. I came to try to make mends. I know I can't win back your trust by just showin' up and sayin' I'm sorry. But it's the right thing to do. The King has forgiven me for all my dirt, but I still have a lotta folks that need to hear me apologize.

MR. WEARY: (scratching his head) Son, I don't think I've heard anything like this before in all my life. A lot of thugs and fools like you have made my life hell for over thirty years. Robbing from me. Cursing at me. Loitering outside the store and dealing dope in my parking lot. Spraying gang graffiti on my walls. I've never had a single one come back and apologize like this.

KAI'RO: Mr. Weary, I can't repay you for what I've done. I got no money. The fact is, I owe you a whole lot that I can never repay. Because of the King and the grace that He gave on the Cross, I'm a new man. You ain't goin' to see the old Kai'Ro that made your life so hard. That Kai'Ro is dead. You won't ever see him 'round here again. What you see before you is transformation. I'd really like to see this whole city transformed...I...

MR. WEARY: (chuckling) Son, you must be doing some drugs. Or maybe you got conked upside your head. Transformation? Of *this* city? This is the City of Doom, boy. You're lucky if you can just survive here. This city has gone to the dogs, the fiends and the monsters. The thugs running these streets today are like vampires, and they're sucking the blood out of all of us.

It's a miracle that my little shop is still here. Do you know how many times I've had to replace glass due to stray bullets? How many times I've actually been assaulted by teenage thugs with guns and knives? I've lost count, son! Look, I got almost no hope left for this city now. I'm tired of hoping and trying. I'm old, and I'm survivin'. That's all an old man like me can do now, is just to hang on and hopefully die in peace. I don't believe this city will ever see transformation or hope again. You're a fool if you think otherwise!

STORYTELLER: Kai'Ro looked discouraged. He closed his eyes and his chin dropped to his chest. Mr. Weary studied him hard with an angry fire in his eyes. His hands were balled up in fists on the countertop.

KAI'RO: Mr. Weary, I hear what you're sayin'. But think about what you just said a minute ago, how you didn't even wanna see me step foot in your door. Why? 'Cause I beat up two boys in that aisle right over there. I beat 'em with one of the flashlights you were sellin' until they stopped movin' and the flashlight broke into pieces. I took that fat boy that was runnin' his mouth that night and tossed him through that window behind me.

You didn't want me in your store today because you re-member Kai'Ro "the thug." And like I said, I stole right from under your nose many times. I used to rob from my mama, deal drugs, duck cops and fight every day. But the young man that is standin' before you right now is transformed. I'm changed. I am not the thug you used to know. That old Kai'Ro is in a casket. Dead and buried.

The one who stands before you now is brand new. I pursue peace now. I used to make war. I wanna work with my own two hands and never steal another penny. I used to bring chaos to this hood, but now I wanna rebuild it. I snatched hope from peoples' hearts and souls, but now I wanna help restore it. You need to understand that I have almost nothin' to give but the furious love I have for the city that raised me. I pray that the transformation you see in the face of the man before you will give you just a glimpse of what the King can do for our whole city.

STORYTELLER: Mr. Weary rubbed his hand over his mouth. His face softened slightly and he cleared his throat.

MR. WEARY: Did you say you were looking for work, son?

KAI'RO: Yes, sir.

MR. WEARY: I know I'll regret this in the morning, but I'm too old to keep all this up by myself for much longer. There's no one to hire around here but crackheads and drunks. I need someone to sweep and mop these floors each night. The restrooms need someone to look after them too. My back can't keep stocking these shelves either. There's a lot of boxes in the back that need to be unloaded. I can't pay you much...

KAI'RO: That's fine, Mr. Weary. I'll take whatever I can get at this point.

MR. WEARY: There's one more thing. I have a lawn business that I manage. I had a young man named Fickle who worked for me for about three months. But he just up and left me. Used to be that I could push a lawn mower and keep things going until help arrived, but I just can't...

KAI'RO: Well, I can cut grass, Mr. Weary. This is a real surprise! I didn't come in here lookin' for work...

MR. WEARY: I know. You came to apologize, right? As I said, I'm sure I'm going to regret this whole decision. Offering a job to a man who almost left this shop in ruins. You'll probably rob me blind or kill me when my back is turned. But if you're really a changed man, you can prove it to me by doing some hard work and helping out an old man. See that pile of boxes over there, son?

KAI'RO: Yes, sir.

MR. WEARY: Well, they aren't going to unpack themselves. Get started.

STORYTELLER: In my dream, I watched as Kai'Ro worked hard for his new boss. There was a surprising amount of boxes to unload, and he worked quickly and quietly. Mr. Weary was able to sit behind the register the rest of the day and help customers.

Kai'Ro worked well into the evening. He finished his first day by cleaning the restrooms and then sweeping and mopping the entire floor.

MR. WEARY: (counting the money from the register and shaking his head) So, where do you stay now, son?

KAI'RO: (chuckling) I haven't really figured that one out yet, to be honest.

STORYTELLER: Mr. Weary looked up from the small stack of cash in his hand. He whistled and shook his head again.

MR. WEARY: Now what kind of plan is that, son? You just roll back into town with no place to stay?

KAI'RO: The King told me to come back, and I just figured that He'd take care of me somehow.

MR. WEARY: Did this King of yours get you a hotel reservation or something?

KAI'RO: (smiling) Not exactly. No. But He'll provide what I need.

MR. WEARY: I've got an old pull-out couch in my garage you can sleep on for a little bit. But if you even think about coming into my house, I'll shoot you dead.

KAI'RO: (laughing) I—

MR. WEARY: I'm serious! I will shoot you dead!

KAI'RO: Yes, sir.

MR. WEARY: Now, let's lock this place down and get on out of here.

STORYTELLER: Mr. Weary pulled a large chain of keys out of his pocket. I watched Kai'Ro as he eyed some flowers in one of the refrigerated cases.

KAI'RO: How much is it for those flowers there?

MR. WEARY: Which ones? Those roses?

KAI'RO: Yeah, the yellow ones.

MR. WEARY: Two dollars each. Why?

KAI'RO: I got somebody who could use some flowers, that's all.

MR. WEARY: Boy, you got no where to stay. You broke. But you gotta buy some flowers. You are one confusing young man, you know that? I still don't know whether I should trust you or just call the police. I'm serious.

KAI'RO: I'll take three of 'em.

EVANGELINE AND THE ENEMIES

STORYTELLER: In my dream, I saw Kai'Ro walking down the sidewalk of BAD TIMES BOULEVARD. He was wearing a small backpack while pushing a lawn mower with one hand and carrying an old rake in the other.

It appeared to be mid-morning. As he walked along, I saw a dark Lexus approach him very slowly. The driver's-side window rolled down to reveal a man with a scowl on his face. He formed his hand into the shape of a gun and fired off an imaginary shot at Kai'Ro before peeling off down the street. I noticed the words "LIL PAIN" on the license plate before the car disappeared around the next corner.

KAI'RO: (shaking his head) That can't be good.

STORYTELLER: Kai'Ro pushed the lawn mower down the battered sidewalk until he came to Evangeline's house. When he walked up to her front door and rang the bell, no one answered.

In my dream, I saw two fingers pull back the shade from one of the side windows, but Kai'Ro didn't notice. Then I watched as he took off his backpack and pulled out a large black garbage bag. He opened it up and started walking through Evangeline's yard, picking up beer cans, cigarette butts and other trash. Her yard was a terrible mess. I watched as he raked and raked and scooped the trash with his hands before placing it in the bag.

6

When he was finally done, he fired up the lawnmower. I could see a pair of brown eyes peering through the shades. They were keeping an eye on his every move.

The grass was thick and tall and the cutting was slow going. As the day grew warmer, Kai'Ro mopped his face and neck with a white towel slung over his shoulder. The clippings filled nearly four bags. Kai'Ro tied all of them up neatly and placed the bags on the curb. Finally, he took a step back to admire his work.

Evangeline's yard looked beautiful amidst the long row of mangled homes with overgrown yards. He opened up his backpack and carefully pulled out the three yellow roses he had purchased, along with a small glass jar and a note. Using the hose, he put some water in the jar and then set the flowers just in front of her door. Then he reached into his pocket and pulled out a white baby's pacifier. Smiling, he carefully placed it around one of the roses. With his work done, Kai'Ro grabbed the mower and the rake and set off back down the sidewalk again.

When he was out of sight, I heard the front door unlock. Evangeline stepped outside and looked at the yard for a minute with a curious expression on her face. As soon as she spotted the flowers, she picked them up. After taking a moment to admire them, she held them to her nose and inhaled the sweet fragrance. The soft petals tickled her face and she closed her eyes while her lips curled just slightly into a smile. Carefully, she tore open the envelope and read the note inside:

Evangeline,

There ain't a whole lot I can do for you right now. I don't have much money and don't even really have much of a place to stay just yet. But the King has made it clear to me that I'm called to take care of you. That's something that He wants me to do. It's something that I want to do too.

I know that your life has got a lot of hurt and ugly to it, and I wish I could take all of that away. My hope is that when you see the change in your yard this morning, you will see something dirty and ugly made beautiful again. That's the King's goal in your life and mine. He takes the dirty and ugly in us, along with the dirty and ugly that we go through, and makes it beautiful again.

I bought you these three flowers for a couple of reasons. One, they remind me of you. You're the most beautiful girl I've ever met. I think if you were a flower you'd be a rose. But like these roses, you got no root. These roses, though they are beautiful, are going to die. The little bit of water in there will keep them alive for a while, but not too long.

You got no root either, girl. This life that you're living is going to dry up. If you're honest with yourself, I know you already feel the dryness in your life. I saw it in your eyes a few days ago. I felt the dryness of my soul too, until I found roots in the King. Now it's like I'm drinking from a river that won't ever run dry. I truly hope you'll admit you got that thirst and, just like I did, you'll go looking for the Drink that will satisfy you forever.

I also bought these three flowers because I believe the King brought the three of us back together again for a reason. Why'd I say three? Because you got number three growing in your belly right now. To be honest, girl, I don't know what the King is going to do and what the future holds, but I pray to Him and I ask you to please keep that beautiful gift of life growing within you. I don't know how just yet, but I will love, care for, protect and give everything I have for that miracle of life.

Do not snuff that life out! Don't listen to the liars telling you that baby is a blob of tissue. Those lies come from hell itself. If you can't do it, or if you feel unable to do this alone, then please know that I will love, care for, protect and give everything I have for you too. This is what a man does. He takes care of the mother of his child and his children. I will not run from this responsibility. Ever!

I understand you might want to have nothing to do with me no more. I hope that ain't the case, but please understand that even if you don't want that child—I do. If, by the King's grace, you will bring that child into the world but don't want him or her after that, then I will father it from there. I promise.

Evangeline, please leave this city and head out to the dirt road. I have prayed this for you for so long now. You know where it is. Admit you're thirsty. Admit you're burdened. The King will set you free. Please go now and find Life for yourself. The King has so much for you. You have a beauty within you that He longs to unleash for the world to see.

I love ya,

Kai'Ro

STORYTELLER: Evangeline's eyes started to brim with tears, as she held the letter to her chest. She pulled a rose out of the jar, removed the pacifier and held it in her hands. Then she suddenly spun around and went back into the house. I watched her as she walked into her bedroom and snatched a pink backpack from out of the closet. She hurriedly filled it with some clothing and a few random items.

Next, her attention was drawn to a small Bible tossed into the corner. Scooping it up, she dusted it off and opened the front cover. I saw these words inside: "The roadmap to Life everlasting. Read it, embrace it and follow it." It was signed by Kai'Ro. Evangeline stuffed the Bible in her bag and slung it over her shoulder. She placed the pacifier and Kai'Ro's letter in her pocket and put the jar of flowers on her dresser. Then she stopped and stood still.

EVANGELINE: Am I really doin' this?!? This is craaazy! King, I don't know why I'm doin' this. It's true that I've felt dry and burdened for a real long time, and I'm sick of pretendin' that I'm not. I don't wanna feel this way no more. If You're listenin', then You're gonna have to help me 'cause I'm so scared. I haven't read much of Your Letters and I don't really know where I'm goin'. So I'm just gonna run after You one step at a time. I pray that You'll protect me and send me the courage I'm gonna need. If You can change my old boy Kai'Ro into the man I just saw, then I figure You can change a girl like me too.

STORYTELLER: Evangeline caught a glimpse of herself in the mirror and paused. She straightened her shirt and placed her hands softly around the bump on her belly. Then she looked over at the jar with three flowers and smiled.

EVANGELINE: (taking a deep breath) Ok...ok...here I go.

STORYTELLER: Having gathered her confidence, Evangeline headed out the front door.

Then my dream suddenly took me down the road. Kai'Ro was pushing his lawn mower back towards Mr. Weary's house. Ahead, a large silver SUV was parked along the curb and three men in baggy jeans and red Ts were leaning against it. Kai'Ro slowed his pace. The men never took their eyes off of him as he drew closer.

KAI'RO: What up, fellas?

SLICE: What'cha say, fool?

KAI'RO: Nuttin'.

DICE: You some kinda lawn boy hero or somethin'?

STORYTELLER: Kai'Ro dropped his head slightly and kept pushing the mower until he was right next to them.

CUTTER: Hey, son, didn't you hear my boy's question to you? You tryin' to be hard up in this neighborhood? Well, this ain't your neighborhood, dude.

STORYTELLER: Cutter snorted and spit at Kai'Ro's feet. As he did so, Slice stepped in front of Kai'Ro with his arms folded across his chest.

KAI'RO: I ain't here to tussle with you, dawg. If you would please let me by here. I gotta get to work.

STORYTELLER: Dice burst out laughing.

DICE: This is Doc Destruction's neighborhood, son. And you the one gettin' in his way. The thing is, Doc don't ask people to get outta his way.

CUTTER: He just snuffs 'em out.

STORYTELLER: Slice suddenly jumped forward and attempted to shove Kai'Ro to the ground. Kai'Ro turned slightly and used Slice's momentum against him. With one deft move, Slice went flailing onto the grass. Cutter took a wild punch at Kai'Ro, but Kai'Ro ducked and drove his shoulder into Cutter's stomach before tossing him over his back onto the pavement. Dice came charging, but Kai'Ro grabbed him, pinned his arm behind his back and jammed him up against the SUV.

KAI'RO: Look, I don't want nobody to get hurt! Y'all just let me get my lawn mower and I'll be out'cha way.

STORYTELLER: For a moment, Doc's three goons looked startled. Slice and Cutter exchanged embarrassed looks, as they lay on the ground. Dice was wincing with his arm pinned behind his back. But just then a dark Lexus rolled around the corner along with another black SUV.

KAI'RO: (looking towards Heaven) What do I do now?

STORYTELLER: I heard the word *run* as if it were carried along by the wind. Kai'Ro released Dice from his grip and spun slightly to face the new arrivals. He turned to his left. A tall and muscular man dressed in a tight black polo shirt and black designer jeans stepped out of the Lexus with the words "LIL PAIN" on the back. Two very large men stepped out of the SUV and approached Kai'Ro. They both had long braids hanging down to their shoulders and their eyes were hidden behind thick black shades.

LIL' PAIN: (placing sunglasses in the pocket of his shirt) You must really be out of yo mind, boy. This is Doc's city. First, you try to shut down one of his bakeries, and now you're tryin' to hurt three of his soldiers. Now, that's just plain stupid.

KAI'RO: This ain't Doc's city and that house ain't no bakery. That's my mom's house. I don't recall Diablo givin' Doc this city and I know my mom didn't give him her house. So you're mistaken!

LIL' PAIN: Diablo? Who's that? Never heard of that clown.

KAI'RO: Well, then you're the clown. Diablo's got his talons sunk deep in this city. He's run it from the day they laid the first brick. He's the Father of Lies and a roarin' lion who seeks someone to devour. He lurks in the shadows, promotin' evil, feastin' on death, spreadin' disease and givin' birth to chaos. No sir, this is his city, and I've been sent back by the King to help reclaim it.

STORYTELLER: Slice, Dice and Cutter had surrounded Kai'Ro again, as Lil' Pain drew closer.

LIL' PAIN: Man, your brotha, Kush Man, said you'd lost your mind. I thought he was playin'. But he was shootin' straight. You done lost your mind, son.

KAI'RO: Yeah, I hear that a lot.

LIL' PAIN: So you serve a King, huh? Does He live in a castle? Wear a robe? A crown? Do you call Him "your majesty"?

KAI'RO: Nah. His presence fills all of creation. But He lives inside me too. He sent me as a messenger to bring light to a city strangled by darkness. I'm here to bring hope to the hopeless, food to the starvin' and clothes to the naked. When the King stormed the earth, that's what He did too. He couldn't stand for injustice. Where He found captives, He set 'em free. And where He found blindness, He provided light. He gave His whole life to bring light and hope to a darkened world.

LIL' PAIN: Well, this King must've been a stupid dude and He prob'ly wound up dead.

KAI'RO: Yeah. They killed Him.

LIL' PAIN: (laughing with the others) I thought so. What kinda sorry King is that?

KAI'RO: The kinda King that shrugged off death and put it in a choke hold. The kinda King that burst outta the grave like a rocket 'cause not even death could hold Him down. The kinda King who, when He rose up, shook the very gates of hell on their hinges. You see, my King *lives* and, when He returns, He'll rescue all those who have longed for His return. But He'll straight up crush those who get in His way! I'm here to warn ya and you'd be wise to listen.

LIL' PAIN: (growling) No, you listen, chump. You the one that needs to open his ears and listen. Doc Destruction has a message for you, so ya better open 'em real good.

STORYTELLER: With surprising speed, Lil' Pain drove his fist into Kai'Ro's stomach. Immediately, Kai'Ro fell to his knees, coughing and struggling to recover his breath. The others had bunched in so tightly that there was no chance for him to run now.

LIL' PAIN: Aye, Grizzly and Kodiak. Grab this boy up here and hold him tight, will ya?

STORYTELLER: The two large men, Grizzly and Kodiak, seized Kai'Ro's arms and held him in a tight grip. He struggled to free himself, but they were too strong. Lil' Pain hit him in the stomach two more times and then punched him across the face. Behind Kai'Ro, I saw one of the windows lower on the SUV that was last to arrive at the scene. In the vehicle I caught a glimpse of Lil' One's face, looking out at Kai'Ro. Lil' One's right eye was swollen and he had a split lip. Sitting next to him was a middle-aged man wearing an expensive charcoal gray-colored suit. He wore dark shades and a solid gold chain with a jeweled skull around his neck.

DOC DESTRUCTION: You see, boy, that's how I expect you to treat those who oppose the business. You crush them. You can't tolerate opposition if you want to grow and succeed. In this city, the strong survive and the weak are destroyed. You understand me, boy?

LIL' ONE: Yeah. I feel you.

STORYTELLER: Slice, Dice and Cutter now got in on the action and they worked Kai'Ro over with savage blows. By the time they were done, Kai'Ro was bleeding profusely from his nose and lips. Badly hurt, he hung in Grizzly and Kodiak's arms like a limp towel.

DOC DESTRUCTION: Ah'ight. That's enough. That's enough.

STORYTELLER: Doc's driver honked the horn twice. Lil' Pain nodded at the vehicle.

LIL' PAIN: Put our man down gently, boys.

STORYTELLER: Grizzly and Kodiak tossed Kai'Ro onto the pavement. Kai'Ro rolled over onto his back with his arms spread wide. He was still conscious, but barely.

LIL' PAIN: Listen to me real, real good. Doc just showed you some love and kindness. You pull another stunt even close to the one you pulled a few days ago, then we'll track you down and snuff ya life out.

KAI'RO: (barely a whisper) Ya can snuff me out, but ya can't snuff the message.

CUTTER: Man, what'd he say?

LIL' PAIN: He's delirious. Let's roll.

STORYTELLER: Doc's men got back into their vehicles and drove off. Kai'Ro, with great effort, rolled over onto his hands and knees. He spit some blood on the pavement and wiped the blood that was running from above his left eye. In his face, I spotted a look of despair mingled with anger.

KAI'RO: (shouting) So this is how it's gonna go, huh? Me 'gainst the world?

STORYTELLER: Just then, an old pickup truck came rumbling down the street. It was more rust than truck. Spotting Kai'Ro, the driver pulled up alongside the curb. Kai'Ro slowly raised his head. When he saw the driver, his face brightened slightly.

KAI'RO: Preacher? Is that you?

HEADIN' OUT

STORYTELLER: My dream then took me back to Evangeline. I saw her walking quickly down the sidewalk, as she headed towards the intersection of EXCUSES STREET and BONDAGE BOULEVARD. Her face was a mixture of excitement and worry. She looked to the left and to the right as if she hoped no one she knew would see where she was going.

To her dismay, just across the street, two young ladies spotted her and hollered out. They were both wearing really large hoop earrings, tight jeans and matching blue Chucks.

MESS: Hey, E., where you goin', girl?

EVANGELINE: Um...I'm just out walkin'.

DRAMA: Yeah? Walkin' where? The stores and stuff are the other way. We were 'bout to go get somethin' to eat. Wanna join us?

EVANGELINE: Nah. I'm gonna keep walkin'. I'll prob'ly catch up with y'all later.

MESS: (to Drama) Let's see what that girl's up to. This ain't like E. just to go on no walk like that.

DRAMA: (hollering) Hey! Hold up, girl. We'll go with you.

STORYTELLER: Evangeline let out a heavy sigh, as her two friends walked quickly to catch up with her. She stuffed her hands in her pockets and spun to face them.

EVANGELINE: Listen, I really don't think y'all wanna go with me on this walk.

DRAMA: Why? Where you goin'?

EVANGELINE: (kicking some pebbles with her foot) I'm leavin'. I'm headin' out on that Heavenly Highway.

MESS: You mean, that Highway Kai'Ro went down? Girl! People 'round here still be talkin' about ya boy and how crazy he is.

EVANGELINE: Yeah, I know. But the more I think 'bout it and the more I listen to what he said, the more I've come to realize that we're the crazy ones. It's like we're stuck in some kind of nightmare...some kind of lie...and we can't get out of it.

DRAMA: Don't be silly, E. Come on. You know what would make you feel a lot better about things? Some new shoes!

EVANGELINE: Listen, I tried to leave quick and by myself 'cause I knew you two wouldn't understand. I knew you'd try to change my mind. Well, I've made up my mind. My bag is packed and I don't plan on returnin' until I find Life and relief for my burdened soul.

MESS: What? This is craaazy! I can't believe you talkin' like this E. You used to curse Kai'Ro so bad for talkin' this mess. Now you talkin' just like him.

DRAMA: (turning to Mess) Look, we've been like sisters for years. I ain't sayin' I wanna go on no Heavenly Highway and find relief for my burdened soul, or whatever. But I'm willin' to walk with her for a little bit.

MESS: (rolling her eyes) Fine. Whatever. I just know folks are gonna talk about us as soon as they see us.

EVANGELINE: Y'all don't have to do this. I'm not makin' you come with me.

DRAMA: Well, it's kinda a nice day...can almost see the sunshine. It'll give us a chance to talk.

STORYTELLER: Evangeline and her two friends continued their trek down the sidewalk until they came to the intersection where a tall row of hedges stood before them.

EVANGELINE: This is it.

DRAMA: What's it, girl?

EVANGELINE: The dirt road is right on the other side of these bushes here.

MESS: For real?

EVANGELINE: That's what Kai'Ro said.

STORYTELLER: Evangeline placed her hands in front of her, ducked her head and plowed straight into the hedges.

DRAMA: Uh-uh. Ain't no way, E.

MESS: (sighing) C'mon, girl.

STORYTELLER: Mess grabbed Drama's hand and the two followed after Evangeline. They shrieked and squealed as twigs got stuck in their hair and pulled at their clothing.

EVANGELINE: See, that wasn't so bad, was it? Look how beautiful it is out here!

STORYTELLER: Mess and Drama were mumbling under their breath.

DRAMA: (pulling at twigs) I got some nature stuck in my new weave...

EVANGELINE: It's so green. So open! I can actually feel the sunshine on my face out here.

STORYTELLER: Evangeline spread her arms out and tilted her head back with her eyes closed.

MESS: Hmmmm. It ain't so bad.

DRAMA: It's hot to me.

EVANGELINE: (pointing) Look! There's the dirt road. That's the road we want.

STORYTELLER: The three young ladies set off together. Several comments were made about the peaceful and beautiful landscape. Stopping at one point, they admired a large field of bright pink flowers. A flock of geese forming a perfect "V" flew overhead, causing them to look up at the sky.

MESS: So, I know y'all heard 'bout Fast Girl and Playa, right?

EVANGELINE: No one wants to hear that, Mess.

DRAMA: I do. What's goin' on?

MESS: Well, you know how some people have seen Fast Girl talkin' to that boy Homewrecker?

DRAMA: Yeah.

MESS: Well, it turns out they wasn't just talkin'. Couple of girls I know saw Fast Girl comin' out of Homewrecker's house late last night.

DRAMA: What! Does Playa know?

MESS: Not yet. But when he does...ooooh...girl, it's gonna be on! Playa is goin' to kill that boy Homewrecker...prob'ly hurt that lil' tramp of his for messin' around too.

DRAMA: I can't stand Fast Girl. She'll talk to any boy that'll give her some attention. I could just rip the braids outta her head!

MESS: I know, right!?

DRAMA: What's wrong wit you, E.? You ain't said nothin' in a while.

EVANGELINE: I dunno. I'm just wishin' we could leave all that talk on the other side of the bushes back there. Why can't we just enjoy the peace and quiet for a little bit?

DRAMA: It's just talk, girl. What's wrong with talkin'?

EVANGELINE: Out here, that kinda talk just feels ugly. Like, it doesn't belong out here.

MESS: (whispering to Drama) What's she talkin' 'bout? "Out here"? What's that mean?

STORYTELLER: The three young ladies continued their walk down the dirt road. The sun rose overhead until it was directly above them. They went on in silence until they spotted a large building that I had seen in a dream once before. The sign read: "The House of Mockers."

DRAMA: Wow! What's this place?

MESS: Girl, I've heard of this place. They say it be goin' off up in this joint!

STORYTELLER: Just then, the doors opened up. A wave of music came flooding out as a tall and slender man in an expensive blue suit walked out to meet the girls. I noticed an extra large diamond in his left ear. Pulling a cigar out of his mouth, he smiled at them.

MESS: Guuuurrrl. Who is that?!

PARTYCAT: Ladies. Ladies. The name's Partycat. What brings you to The House of Mockers?

DRAMA: Nuttin'. We're just out walkin'.

PARTYCAT: Walkin'? Out here? What are some beautiful young ladies like you doin' walkin' 'round in the heat like that for? You should come inside. Get yourself somethin' to drink. Stay awhile.

DRAMA: Yeah. It's hot out here. I been sayin' that I could use a drink and some shade from this sweaty wilderness.

MESS: Me too. C'mon, E.

EVANGELINE: Nah. I'm gonna keep goin'.

STORYTELLER: At that point, two other men strolled out of the building. Like Partycat, they were dressed in nice suits. The men came out smiling, with their eyes fixed on the three young ladies.

PARTYCAT: Meet my two boys, Slick and Conniving.

SLICK: (whistling) Where'd you three fine ladies come from? I could see you walkin' from like a mile away. I just *had* to come out and say hello.

CONNIVING: This is truly a miracle. We have not one...not two...but three beautiful women come by at once. Must be our lucky day.

STORYTELLER: Drama and Mess giggled and elbowed each other.

PARTYCAT: For real, you need to come inside for a while. The party is jumpin'. You can be our dates for the evening. Drinks and whatever you want are on the House.

CONNIVING: We'll treat you right.

SLICK: We'll show you a good time.

MESS: (whispering to the other two) Do either of you know who these three boys are? I can't believe that Partycat and his boys are talkin' to us! They are actually invitin' us to be their dates this evenin'. This is so craaazy!

DRAMA: Those three dudes are soooo fine.

MESS: They are some of the richest cats around here too. C'mon, E., this is where it's at.

DRAMA: I might mess around and let one of those boys take me home tonight.

EVANGELINE: I ain't goin'.

DRAMA: C'mon, girl! When's the last time some dudes like these boys here have showed you any attention? They ain't thugs like the boys on our block. They ain't gangbangers who make their paper sellin' drugs. These guys are businessmen. They're classy. They ain't street—

EVANGELINE: They're just thugs in nice suits. All they wanna do is get with us and then dump us out with the morning garbage. For every girl that comes here in a day, I bet there's four or five goin' out the back door feelin' used up and ashamed.

MESS: Maybe all they want is to get with us and maybe not. Don't matter to me. What's the worst that could happen anyway? If I can get me some free drinks and dance with a fine man tonight, then that's cool with me.

DRAMA: Me too.

PARTYCAT: (checking his diamond encrusted watch) Ladies. Ladies. Time is ticking.

EVANGELINE: Thanks, but I'm goin' to keep movin'.

SLICK: Movin' where? I was hopin' to see you movin' on the dance floor with me.

MESS: She wants to go walkin' down some Heavenly Highway or somethin' stupid!

PARTYCAT: (chuckling) Heavenly Highway? Who put that nonsense in ya head, girl?

MESS: Her boy, Kai'Ro.

DRAMA: (to Mess) Will you shut up!

STORYTELLER: Partycat smirked and took a puff on his cigar.

PARTYCAT: Kai'Ro, huh? I haven't seen that clown in a while. Not since he wandered past here spittin' some of the same kinda nonsense. So you his girl, huh?

EVANGELINE: Kinda.

PARTYCAT: (looking at her stomach) Is that his bun cookin' in ya oven? Did he up and leave ya for his crush on that King?

EVANGELINE: No. It ain't like that. Besides, you one to talk. The way I hear it, you're like twelve babies' daddy. You got kids all over the place wonderin' who their daddy is. They say you like to party and play and then leave a mess behind.

PARTYCAT: (smirking) Is that what they say? I guess you countin' on Kai'Ro to be the "big man" and take care of that lump in your belly? I hope so. If not, you better lose the lump 'cause no man is gonna want a girl with a lil' thumbsucker to feed.

SLICK: C'mon, dawg. Quit wastin' your time talkin' to this knocked up piece of trash.

EVANGELINE: (taking offense) Excuse me?

PARTYCAT: Ya know, ya boy Kai'Ro used to be a name that stood for somethin' 'round town. Cats used to watch what they said 'bout him and 'round him. Most cats respected him and some feared him. Nowadays, you know what people call him? A clown...a fool. He had the world at his feet, but when he gave his life to chasin' that King of his, he lost everything he had.

EVANGELINE: Yeah? Well, Kai'Ro didn't see it that way. He felt like he was givin' up a life he could never hold onto, to gain a life he could never lose.

PARTYCAT: Ya boy's a fool. And if you go down that road, then you one too.

STORYTELLER: Partycat glared at Evangeline. He puffed his cigar until the tip was glowing orange and then released a thick cloud of smoke that danced around his face like tiny snakes.

CONNIVING: (to Mess and Drama) So, you two ladies wanna have a good time with us, or you wanna follow ol' girl here down her little imaginary highway?

STORYTELLER: Mess and Drama both had disappointed looks on their faces like someone just ruined their birthday party. I could tell they were about to make a decision. They looked at each other and then at the three men, before taking a final glance at Evangeline.

DRAMA: (sighing) Nah. We good.

MESS: What! Y'all for real?

DRAMA: C'mon, girl. We ain't stickin' 'round with some dudes who gonna dog E. like that.

SLICK: Wow! Y'all are some stupid, stupid girls. There're some honeys who would give their right arms to hang out in here with us and get some VIP treatment.

MESS: (under her breath) Yeah, and I'm one of 'em.

STORYTELLER: The three young ladies walked away as Party-cat and his friends continued to laugh and call them horrible names.

MESS: (angrily) I don't understand you, E. The *only* reason...and I mean, the only reason, I left that place is 'cause you my friend. But we're at a crossroad now. I ain't goin' any further down this road with ya. I'm not goin' to be the butt of jokes and called names just so I can chase some sort of dream that you're goin' after.

DRAMA: Me neither. I thought this was just gonna be a little walk you were goin' on. The E. I know would've gone in that club and had some fun. I can't hang with you if you're goin' to start makin' decisions that make us look bad with the fellas and other people. So we're goin' back to the City of Doom before people start talkin' about us. You comin'?

STORYTELLER: Evangeline looked very sad.

EVANGELINE: I'm sorry y'all had to go through all that back there. I was hopin' to go on this journey by myself 'cause I knew you wouldn't understand. The bottom line is that I don't like my life right now. I'm not feelin' the City of Doom. I feel like a caged animal there. My mind and body and soul are depressed every day.

When Kai'Ro started talkin' 'bout freedom and Life, I didn't believe him at first. Then I saw it in his face and in his eyes. He was at total peace. I've never seen that before. But I want it. If it's out here somewhere, then I plan on findin' it—even if it means I have to give up everything to do so.

DRAMA: Then you're goin' by yourself, girl.

MESS: (waving her hand in Evangeline's face) Bye.

STORYTELLER: Mess and Drama turned around and started their walk back towards the City of Doom. Evangeline stared after them for a moment but then spun around and continued her journey down the narrow dirt road.

THE INVISIBLE STRUGGLE

STORYTELLER: In my dream, I saw a bruised Kai'Ro. He was still bleeding pretty badly from the beating he had taken. Preacher got out of his pickup truck and helped him to his feet. He pulled out a handkerchief from his pocket and handed it to Kai'Ro to wipe his bloodied lip and nose.

PREACHER: I had a feeling the King was going to send you back here. I was looking forward to running into you again...but not like this. What happened?

KAI'RO: A whole bunch of dudes jumped me...some dudes that Lil' One is mixed up with. I tried to talk to my brother about sellin' that kush and purple haze. Told him and his homies that they needed to stay away from Ma's house. Looks like word spread to Doc Destruction and his goons.

PREACHER: Doc's boys beat you like a pinata. Didn't you ever consider running, son?

KAI'RO: Run? That word ain't in my vocabulary.

PREACHER: Well, it better be if you want to stay alive.

KAI'RO: The King didn't send me back here to run from danger and evil. He sent me back to stand up against Doc and those fools. How am I supposed to rep the King if I'm runnin'?

PREACHER: Sometimes the King calls us to rep Him by standing our ground and holding our turf. But sometimes we're called to flee like Elijah and run for our lives. Sometimes we stand because He called us to, but sometimes we stand our ground out of pride.

STORYTELLER: Kai'Ro was listening, but he was still very angry.

KAI'RO: Pride? What's that 'sposed to mean?

PREACHER: My hunch is that the King gave you a moment to run. A moment where you could escape.

KAI'RO: But I ain't scared. I ain't a coward. I can't let those clowns see me runnin' like that.

PREACHER: So, who's this about then? You reppin' the King or you reppin' your own image? The old Kai'Ro, true enough, wouldn't run from an army. He'd die swingin'. But that old Kai'Ro was one of the most arrogant young men to ever walk the streets in this city. There may be times that the King allows you to take a beating for Him...like what happened to you and Phanatik back in Babel-Bling. But He's not ever going to ask you to take a beating for your own pride and image.

STORYTELLER: Kai'Ro's face softened slightly and he hung his head.

KAI'RO: You right. I'm just frustrated. Back on the Heavenly High-way I felt like I could just keep on movin', ya know. I was dead set on movin' on until I came to the City of Light. I ran to that Cross to free myself up from all the drama and mess of my life and to find freedom from my burden. Ya feel me?

Since I've been back, I found out that my brother is neck deep in drug dealin'. My ol' girl, Evangeline, is pregnant with my baby and she's thinkin' 'bout killin' it. I got a job scrubbin' toilets and loadin' shelves and, everywhere I turn, people are hatin' on me and hatin' the King.

I've only been back for a few days. Already I feel burned out and beat down...literally. I'm startin' to wonder if comin' back here was a mistake. I mean, what's the point? For real...you're the one who told me that this whole place was goin' to be destroyed one day. You're the one who told me to get outta here. But now I'm back.

PREACHER: Son, I feel your pain. I do. I've been storming these streets for the King for nearly thirty years now. I've been beat down, cursed at and even spit on. Some of my own family have abandoned and rejected me completely. As you've already discovered, there's great sacrifice and suffering if you *really* want to follow the King. His mercies and the joy of His grace are never ending. But so is the resistance and the hostility of those who despise the King.

In regard to what I told you about leaving and this city being burned up...that's all true. The King said that He is going to return and He's going to destroy this world as we know it. When? I don't know. It's also true that everyone needs to flee this city and run to the Cross to find salvation. Anyone who stays here and never makes it to the Cross for salvation and forgiveness of their sins will be judged and burned up along with this city.

But I never said it was hopeless for everyone who lives here, and I never said that you or I should give up hope for this place. There are saints and soldiers who still storm these streets.

KAI'RO: Saints? Soldiers? Like who?

PREACHER: (smiling) Come on. Let me show you something.

STORYTELLER: Preacher and Kai'Ro threw the lawn mower and rake in the back of the truck. They both got inside and the pickup rumbled off down the road.

PREACHER: Look out your window for a minute. Tell me what you see.

STORYTELLER: Kai'Ro looked at Preacher and then out of his window at the scenery passing by.

KAI'RO: I see three dudes posted on the corner. Prob'ly dealers. Kids just wanderin' around. They should be in school. There's some goons in a Range. Doc's crew. I see a homeless cat pushin' a shopping cart. Prob'ly wasted himself on drugs and liquor. Girls hoverin' around the motels. They prostitutes. Burned out houses. Dudes sittin' on patios smokin' trees. Police cars parked in empty lots doin' absolutely nothin'. How much more you want me to see? I've seen this stuff all my life.

PREACHER: Open his eyes, O King, even for just a moment.

STORYTELLER: As soon as Preacher prayed, Kai'Ro lurched back from the window in shock. The scenery outside had changed. A small circle of young men on the corner were selling drugs. Behind them were two monstrous creatures with dark wings. They had blazing red eyes, horns on their heads and long talons growing from their fingers.

As the men exchanged the drugs and cash, the monsters mocked and sneered. I also saw a homeless man slumped against a wall. He was barely conscious. A monster stood next to him holding a long ugly chain that was fastened to the man's neck.

Next, the truck passed a house that was falling apart. Some teenage boys and girls were gathered on the patio smoking cigarettes. There were monsters in the yard and on the roof. Like menacing birds, they were everywhere and there were too many to count. Demons were flying in the air and some were gathered around houses and buildings. They had many of the people bound in chains. I was frightened by all that I saw.

KAI'RO: What is this? It's like the whole city is under attack!

PREACHER: This is the real battle, son. What you described to me a minute ago is only part of the struggle...a real small part. The war that matters is not with the flesh and blood. It's with the foul demons and with Diablo himself. You know that already, but sometimes you have to see it to believe it. Too often we lose hope with what we see on the stage in front of our faces. And we completely miss the fact that the real battle is going on behind the curtain...behind the veil of what our own natural eyes can see.

KAI'RO: Whoa! Whoa! What's goin' on at that house there?

STORYTELLER: The truck slowly passed a small house on the corner. A great light was all around it and even bursting forth from the windows. Tall, bright figures with drawn swords formed a perfect circle around the house. Some of these angelic beings were standing on the patio in front of the main door. Some of them launched from the yard like hurled spears and attacked the monsters that were lurking nearby. I saw horrific battles underway, as these bright beings tussled and slashed at the monsters while the dark creatures fought back with their cruel talons.

PREACHER: That's Sista Prayer's house. That woman is a soldier right there. She's almost seventy years old, and she prays, and she prays, and she prays for this city of ours. Over the years, I've watched her bring young women into her home. Women who are all used up through drugs and all kinds of abuse. She feeds them, protects them, and even helps some of them learn how to read and find work.

She's an amazing woman. I'm sure you realize that those bright beings are angelic warriors for the King. Her home is an earthly battle station. Those warriors are gathered to protect her. And, as an answer to her prayers, the King sends them to make war on the demonic monsters that ravage our city.

STORYTELLER: Moments later, they passed a small restaurant that was also brightly lit and surrounded by the angelic beings.

KAI'RO: That's Mr. Faithful. I used to buy his slammin' Buffalo wings and fries. One of the nicest dudes I ever met. He used to give me free food sometimes, and he was one of the few brotha's in my life that used to tell me to get myself back in school instead of runnin' the streets. Guess I should have recognized that he loved the King.

PREACHER: Mr. Faithful does a lot of stuff that nobody sees. Every Friday morning for the last twelve years, he's took a bunch of free food to the homeless shelter over on STARVATION STREET. But he doesn't just take them bread for their bellies. He takes them the Bread of the King. His Letters. His love. His compassion. Nobody pays him to do this, and no one goes with him, but he's making a big difference. Two of the guys who work in his kitchen used to sleep under bridges in cardboard boxes. Today they both have their own apartments. One of them is married and has a kid.

I could show you plenty more places, Kai'Ro. There's Mama Generous on COLD HEART COURT. You got Mr. Grace. He owns the shoe store on RESISTANCE ROAD. Then you got Mr. Justice. He's a successful lawyer in town who donates a ton of his time defending the poor and defenseless. Don't forget my little church, Sanctuary of the Saints. The King has soldiers all around town who have not bowed their knees to Diablo. We're not so alone after all, son.

STORYTELLER: Kai'Ro sat in stunned silence as they drove slowly down the road. Most of the homes and properties that they passed were surrounded with the monsters. On occasion, there were large fights as groups of angels and demons clashed. Eventually, the two men rode up to a huge open park. There was a long grassy field and then a row of cracked blacktop basketball courts surrounded by chain-link fences.

KAI'RO: Hmmm...THE FIELD OF DREAMS. Back in the day, I used to hoop here a couple of times a week.

STORYTELLER: The park was full of teenagers. Some of them were sitting on benches smoking and playing cards. There were tons of young men at the courts playing ball. Not only were there lots of people, but there were also lots of the dark monsters.

KAI'RO: Shoot! This place is swamped with them demons. It's like this is Diablo's turf, for real.

PREACHER: This city is Diablo's playground and has been for a long time. It's been overrun by him since the beginning. Life here is bad...real bad. But when you can see the *real* battle, you get an even better picture of the struggle.

STORYTELLER: As he said this, the scenery around them went back to normal and I could no longer see the demons and angels.

KAI'RO: I'm grateful that the King allowed me to see all of this. It's helped me realize what's at stake here. I already knew this wasn't Doc's town and that it belongs to Diablo. But it helps to get a look at things, for real. I'm also glad to see that the King has some other soldiers holdin' it down.

PREACHER: Every time one of the King's soldiers chooses to follow His lead and go to war, it brings just a little more light to this city. A long time ago, the King's soldier David said that the King's goodness and mercy would follow him wherever he went. This meant that wherever David went, goodness and mercy would remain behind—even after he had moved on. That's a beautiful picture.

As you know, the King Himself told us to pray that His Kingdom would come and that His will would be done here on earth, as it is in Heaven. Basically, that's a prayer that the light and grace of the City of Light would shine down and illuminate this dark world. The King uses His servants and soldiers to be lanterns in this fallen world.

KAI'RO: That's why He said that we're the light of the world.

PREACHER: Exactly. Your return has brought new hope and new light to this struggle. But be aware, son. Diablo knows that you're back too. And he doesn't like it.

The King has an ongoing plan to fill you with His Spirit and to use you for His glory. But Diablo and his minions have also got a plan—a plan to destroy you. Diablo is like a roaring and starving lion, and he is looking for someone to devour. Make no mistake about him. He's smarter and stronger than you in every way. On our own, we don't stand a chance against him.

KAI'RO: Yeah. I've tussled with that dude before. He don't play and he nearly killed me out on the Heavenly Highway.

PREACHER: Sometimes he aims for a kill shot, but his primary strategy is to wear the King's soldiers down over time. He uses smaller weapons like discouragement, depression, regret and fear to bring in the slow kill. Sometimes he'll try to sideline us by tempting us with wealth, success and status. If we're not careful, he'll make us forget that we're in a battle for the King.

In fact, he'll spend years getting a warrior off track and trying to cause you to give up hope and tuck tail. He wants to get you distracted from the war and start chasing after things. To him, a hopeless or unfocused soldier is as good as a dead one. That's why we must be steadfast and alert.

We're at war, Kai'Ro. All the time. Imagine if every day when you step outside, you knew there were snipers on the roof and assassins lurking in the bushes. And all of them were assigned to take you out. You'd have to be cunning, careful and wise just to survive.

It's good you've seen this today. This is how it is. The King has sent you His angels for protection and you're filled with His Spirit. You're cliqued up with the best of the best of the best. Still, you can't lose your concentration, and you can't lower your guard. Not for a moment. Our enemy does not sleep and he's relentless in his attempts to take you out.

STORYTELLER: Kai'Ro rubbed his bruised chin and winced.

KAI'RO: Can't believe I almost gave up hope after just a few days.

PREACHER: A lot of the King's soldiers have nearly given up. Just read His Letters and you'll see the cries and struggles of men and women who nearly gave up. There is always that tension. We just gotta remember this. The race is a marathon and not a sprint. The struggle isn't a conflict, it's a war. Remaining faithful until the end is my main desire, Kai'Ro. I'm getting old. I just want to finish well for the King.

KAI'RO: I appreciate you givin' me some Good News today...I needed this little ride.

PREACHER: (snapping his fingers) Man, I nearly forgot! Your old girl, Evangeline. She left!

KAI'RO: What'cha mean?

PREACHER: She's gone...on the Heavenly Highway!

STORYTELLER: Kai'Ro's face brightened and he grabbed Preacher's shoulder.

KAI'RO: You for real?

PREACHER: (laughing) That's right, son. She's on the Highway.

STORYTELLER: Kai'Ro threw his head back laughing and clasped his hands together.

KAI'RO: Oh, wow! This is fantastic news! Praise the King!

STORYTELLER: Kai'Ro stared out of his window with a broad smile on his face and shook his head in wonderment. When Preacher's old truck puttered up to Mr. Weary's store, the two men hopped out and unloaded the lawn mower from the back.

KAI'RO: Seems like the King always throws you in my path right when I'm 'bout to crash.

PREACHER: That's what brothers do. They pray for one another and hold one another up. Not a day goes by where I don't pray for you.

KAI'RO: You're more than a brother to me, Preacher. You've been like a father. From the beginning when I was falling off the path, you kept draggin' me back on it. When I was hustlin' and doin' wrong, you put a check on me in love. When I was in jail, you visited me. When I was beat down and out of strength, you helped me. And now when my hope was at its lowest, you challenged me and encouraged me in one conversation. I wanna thank you.

PREACHER: I'm proud of you, son. All that I ask is for you to stay the course.

STORYTELLER: Preacher balled up his fists and held them up as fire emerged in his eyes.

PREACHER: You keep fighting, and racing, and listening and growing. Teach those who need to be taught. Love the unloveable. Feed the hungry. Clothe the naked. Bring your light into the darkest of places. By the King's grace, I pray that your feet will go down every alley and into every side street that He calls you. I believe the King is going to provide a stage for you, a moment that will change some of the lives of this city forever!

STORYTELLER: Preacher grabbed Kai'Ro into a strong embrace and held him for a minute. Then he got back into his truck, waved and drove away. Kai'Ro watched him until he disappeared around the block.

SNIPER FIRE

STORYTELLER: Evangeline walked along the dirt road with her hands stuffed in her pockets. Her eyes were no longer focused on the beautiful landscape around her. Instead, she kept her eyes on her feet as they shuffled down the path. After a while, she came to some abnormally tall grass and promptly lost sight of where to go. Confused, she looked to her left and to her right, but the path was nowhere to be seen. It had vanished into the thick grass.

EVANGELINE: Oh, no. You gotta be kiddin' me! Kai'Ro never told me 'bout this mess!

STORYTELLER: She sighed a heavy sigh and then plunged into the grass where she imagined the path must be. The grass rose up high around her until she was lost deep inside of it. Then to her alarm, Evangeline stumbled and her left leg sank into some thick mud. Letting out a scream, she started flailing her arms and began losing her balance. Just in time, a strong arm reached out and tugged her up before she fell in completely.

HELPER: I gotcha! I gotcha! Watch your step now.

STORYTELLER: Evangeline looked stunned, as she stared into the face of a man not much older than herself.

EVANGELINE: Whoa. Thank you. Who are you and what're you doin' way out here?

HELPER: The name's Helper. I make it my aim to help folks from gettin' stuck here in the Swamp of Discouragement.

EVANGELINE: The Swamp of what?

HELPER: The Swamp of Discouragement. It's a pilgrim trap.

EVANGELINE: (eyeing her muddy shoe) It's so nasty...glad I didn't fall in, for real.

HELPER: Someone must've been prayin' for you 'cause a lot of folks just fall right in.

EVANGELINE: (smiling) Prob'ly Kai'Ro . . .

HELPER: I remember him . . . that poor boy fell in this Swamp up to his neck. He nearly drowned in ol' Discouragement. Praise the King I was able to help him out too. Look here, you need to follow me exactly. There's some big steppin' stones all the way through this Swamp. If you step where I step and do as I do, then I'll get you through with no problem.

STORYTELLER: I watched as Helper moved slowly but with great expertise through the Swamp. Evangeline could hardly see through all of the thick grass, but she did as she was told. And after a few moments, they were through the Swamp and out on the other side.

EVANGELINE: I appreciate you helpin' me through there...I can't swim and prob'ly would've drowned in there.

HELPER: (nodding at her belly) You both would have drowned. I will pray for you that the King will guide your steps from here. I would encourage you to go as fast as you can. There's still quite a bit of time left in the day. The Gate is not much further. If you make good time, you can pass through the Gate and then on to Mama Wisdom's cottage.

EVANGELINE: Mama who?

HELPER: Wisdom. She loves talkin' to pilgrims like you ... particularly the young ladies.

EVANGELINE: How will I know which place is hers?

HELPER: You'll know.

STORYTELLER: Evangeline thanked Helper again and then set off again on the dirt road.

EVANGELINE: (to herself) This ain't been too fun so far. Gettin' cussed by some dudes ... losin' my two homegirls ... nearly fallin' into a nasty swamp ... I'm startin' to think all that *joy* and *Life* talk of Kai'Ro's was a bunch of bunk.

STORYTELLER: I saw in my dream that the day was moving into the afternoon as the sun cast longer shadows across the road. Evangeline picked up her pace. After a while, she spotted a large Gate in the path just ahead. It was tall and foreboding—and it was closed. Evangeline stood there with a curious look on her face. At that very moment, I heard a sharp crack from up in one of the trees to the left of the path. Something struck the ground at Evangeline's feet, shooting pebbles and dirt on her shoes.

EVANGELINE: Oh, my! What was that?

STORYTELLER: Her eyes were wide as she looked around her but could see nothing. There was another sharp sound right before something tore through her backpack and spun her wildly off the road. Her mouth opened as if she wanted to scream, but she couldn't. Then more shots erupted from the top of a tree, landing all around her. In a panic, she took one step backwards, as if she was going to run away. But her instinct told her to run towards the Gate as fast as she could.

As the firing increased, Evangeline's feet and legs were completely hidden inside a cloud of dust and debris. When one of the shots kicking up from the ground suddenly hit her, the terrified young woman let out a loud cry and grabbed her knee. She was right at the foot of the Gate and the bullets were flying around her like hailstones. Determined to reach it, she limped the rest of the way and then started beating on the Gate and yelling at the top of her lungs.

GOODWILL: Who goes there?

EVANGELINE: (in a panicked voice) It's me... Evangeline!

GOODWILL: What brings you to the Gate?

EVANGELINE: Just please let me in! I've been hit and I'm goin' to die out here!

GOODWILL: That is true. What do you seek on the other side of this Gate? Do you come seekin' Life and the freedom it brings?

EVANGELINE: (at the top of her lungs) Yes! Whatever! Please open this Gate for me!

STORYTELLER: The Gate opened just wide enough for Goodwill to grab Evangeline's hand and yank her inside. Once she was on the other side, he slammed the Gate shut just as another volley of bullets struck against the heavy doors. Evangeline fell to the ground, weeping and holding her wounded leg.

EVANGELINE: What took you so long? I almost died out there!

GOODWILL: You've been *almost dead* on that side of the Gate since the day you were born, sister. Besides, I have no control over this Gate. The King opens the Gate to all who come to Him and are heavy burdened. I simply tug in the pilgrims. Now, let me see your leg for a minute.

STORYTELLER: Goodwill helped Evangeline to her feet and over to a nearby chair. He then got down on one knee and took a close look at her leg.

GOODWILL: You're fortunate.

EVANGELINE: Fortunate! How's that? I've been shot and it burns like fire!

GOODWILL: The King was watchin' out for you. Those snipers don't miss much. You got hit with a round of DOUBT, but it just grazed you. That burnin' you're feelin' is the poison. Each round is laced with some powerful stuff. But it looks like whatever is burnin' in your heart must be even more power-ful. Most of the time, a round of DOUBT will send a cat home limpin'. They hardly ever bang on the Gate like you did. Diablo is smart...he knew what to shoot at you. And it looks like he almost got you too!

EVANGELINE: (grimacing as Goodwill put some ointment labeled TRUST on her wound) I could slap Kai'Ro for tellin' me to go on this journey. That boy!

GOODWILL: (raising his eyebrows) Kai'Ro! You know Kai'Ro?

EVANGELINE: You could say that.

GOODWILL: I remember that dude...seems like he knocked on the Gate with more conviction than you.

EVANGELINE: (glaring) What'cha mean, conviction?

GOODWILL: He banged on that door like his life depended on it.

EVANGELINE: And how do you think I was bangin'? I was 'bout ready to knock those doors down!

GOODWILL: Yeah, but he was bangin' like that before the shots started comin'. He was desperate. He knew the only freedom for his burden was on this side of the Gate.

STORYTELLER: Evangeline watched as Goodwill bandaged her knee.

GOODWILL: Do you feel that same burden? I mean, what really made you come all the way out here? It's gotta be more than curiosity.

STORYTELLER: Evangeline looked like she wanted to snap on Goodwill, but she took a deep breath before speaking.

EVANGELINE: Burdened. Trapped. Miserable. You could call it a lot of things. I just feel sick, and ugly, and dirty and...weighed down. Yeah. I guess burdened is the right word. It's been sneakin' up on me more and more, ya know?

STORYTELLER: Goodwill nodded as he rose to his feet and sat down in a chair next to her.

EVANGELINE: When Kai'Ro first started talkin' 'bout his burden a while back, I couldn't relate. It just sounded like he was dealin' with guilt. I thought he was takin' things too seriously. At that time, he and I were sharin' a house. We was in love and I really enjoyed how things was goin'—most days.

GOODWILL: But then somethin' changed.

EVANGELINE: For Kai'Ro. Instead of stayin' up late watchin' TV like we used to, he'd read his ol' man's Bible. Then he started spendin' more time sleepin' on the couch. He was changin' slowly, and I didn't get it. Though he was still out hustlin' and whatever, I could tell it was botherin' him. He kept askin' me if it bothered me and, at the time, I'd tell him no. It really didn't. Anyway, after he left me for this King, I knew it was more than just a game to him.

GOODWILL: A game? It's hardly a game. Life out here is a battle, for real. Followin' the King is an everyday struggle—an all-out war.

EVANGELINE: So then, what's the big deal? I mean, things weren't this hard or this lonely back at the City of Doom. It's crazy to leave all I know and everyone and everything I loved so that I could come out here and be verbally abused, nearly drowned, and then get shot at by some dudes in some trees.

GOODWILL: (smiling) So, you prefer the slow boil, I guess?

EVANGELINE: Slow boil? What's that?

GOODWILL: You know. You can put a frog in a pot of water on the stove and turn the temperature up real slowly every few minutes. The frog, because he's cold-blooded, will adjust to the slow temperature change. That frog will hardly even notice. He'll keep adjustin' as the deadly heat sneaks up on him...until it's too late...until he boils to death.

People aren't much different. Most folks on the other side of the Gate are blind and don't realize that they're in the pot. Diablo's got 'em cookin' on the stove real slowly. They adjust in different ways, tryna make their lives livable. But they got no clue they're actually gettin' cooked. Then one day—bam! They're dead, boilin' in the water.

STORYTELLER: Evangeline looked confused.

EVANGELINE: So, how's it better out here? Ya still in danger.

GOODWILL: True. But see, once you're on this side of the Gate, you ain't in the pot no more. When you're in the pot, you just figure that your sorry, painful and empty life is all that there is. So, you do what you can to make your life work, even though your situation is bad.

EVANGELINE: What'cha mean?

GOODWILL: For example, most folks in the City of Doom have concluded that it's okay to lie, cheat, steal and kill, if necessary, to put bread on the table. *By any means necessary* is their anthem. But by livin' that way, they've also decided they need to live with fear, resentment, regret, chaos and pain.

Almost everyone in that town is worried about their property being stolen, about losin' everything...about getting merked. So, they adjust to the harsh reality of their lives, like the frog. They become greedier, more hateful, craftier and more aggressive. Based on their wrong thinkin', they make these bad choices to suit their toxic environment. They keep tryin' to survive as the heat gets cranked up. All the while, that city is boilin' worse and worse. Folks are dyin'. The city itself is dyin'.

EVANGELINE: So then, what's so good 'bout things out here?

GOODWILL: (smiling) For one, you embrace the beautiful Truth that life in the pot is not a real life. You realize there has to be more to life than what you see around you. Instead of acceptin' lyin', cheatin', hustlin', lustin' and killin' as a necessary part of your environment—you seek to *change* your environment for the better.

EVANGELINE: What's that mean?

GOODWILL: The King told us to pray that the City of Doom would start to look a whole lot more like the City of Light. He told us to pray that His will and His ways would be done on this earth as they are in the City of Light.

Well, the City of Light is a place full of peace, joy, kindness, grace and hope. That's where the King lives. It's where He came from when He entered this world where we live now. He promises that one day He's goin' to fix this broken world and make it brand new.

Until that time, followers of the King seek to make the City of Doom look a lot more like the City of Light. We seek to change the environment rather than become a victim of it.

EVANGELINE: Well then, I guess I was a frog in that pot. I wouldn't have said it like that, but I was. I didn't know I was boilin', for real. But I started to realize I couldn't stand my life goin' the way it was goin'.

GOODWILL: That's the startin' point. Just gettin' out of that doggone pot. The King has so much beauty and peace in store for you. If you keep goin'...

EVANGELINE: (sighing and placing her hand on her wounded knee) Yeah. I guess I gotta decide what I'm 'bout to do.

STORYTELLER: Goodwill folded his arms on his chest and leaned back.

GOODWILL: Look, I'm not goin' to lie to ya. There's danger down that road. There are cats that will do everything they can to drag you back to the pot. They love the pot. They're the biggest frogs in the pot, and they desire to keep everything in order so that they can grow fatter and stronger.

Diablo hates it when frogs jump off the stove. He will do what he can to get you back or to snuff you out. But know this, if you make it to the Cross, your burden will roll away. You'll have peace like you've never experienced before. The ugly and hurtful stuff that drove you out of the City of Doom will no longer have a hold on you. You'll be free, very free indeed. The death that you feel in your soul will be overwhelmed with Life! The pain that throbs in your heart will be replaced with joy! I know you noticed this in Kai'Ro when you saw him again.

STORYTELLER: Evangeline's mind drifted off and she smiled at the thought of Kai'Ro.

EVANGELINE: Yeah, I saw that look, for real. That wasn't the same Kai'Ro who came back to the City of Doom to tell me about the King.

STORYTELLER: Rather abruptly, Evangeline stood up and slung her backpack over her shoulder.

EVANGELINE: Thank you for talkin' to me and thank you for fixin' my knee. I'm gonna keep goin'. There's somethin' stirrin' inside of me that won't let me go back to that ugly pot on the stove again!

GOODWILL: (smiling) I'm glad to hear that, sista. Go quickly and you'll find shelter not too far down the Heavenly Highway.

STORYTELLER: Evangeline set out on her way again. The ointment that Goodwill put on her knee helped and she was able to move fairly quickly. Within a short period of time, she came to the Crossroads. Without hesitation, she took a sharp turn down the Heavenly Highway.

EVANGELINE: King, I thank You for savin' me twice today when You could've let me go. Please keep Your hands on me and give me the courage to keep followin' You. I'm goin' to need You for each and every step I take from here.

STORYTELLER: In my dream, I watched as she faded into the distance. The sun was still hanging in the sky, casting a rich orange light along the Highway.

To Evangeline's left, I spotted a large orchard of fruit trees. Evangeline paused a moment and then disappeared into the orchard and out of my sight.

YOUNG SLEAZY 10

My dream took me back to Mr. Weary's store. Kai'Ro was busy stocking shelves and putting some new drinks in the refrigerator section. Mr. Weary was behind the cash register, thumbing through a magazine.

Looking up, Kai'Ro glanced out the window and saw two young men on the corner. They were exchanging a small bag for a wad of cash. A frown instantly came across his face before he turned his attention back to the stack of boxes along the aisle, waiting to be unpacked.

Just about that time, a bright red convertible sports car pulled into the parking lot. The car was blasting music so loud that it shook the store windows. Behind the wheel was a young man in silver shades. He wore a white fitted hat that was cocked sideways and a white designer T-shirt with an expensive silver chain hanging from his neck. Two very beautiful girls were his riding companions.

After cutting off the stereo, he took a minute to gaze into the rearview mirror. Tilting his head slightly, it was obvious that he was admiring his reflection. The girl in the passenger seat leaned over and gave him a kiss on the neck. As the three got out of the car, Kai'Ro caught himself staring. Both the girls had on tight shorts and low-cut tank tops. I noticed they were wearing bright red lipstick and green tinted contact lenses. They looked like twins.

MR. WEARY: (looking up from his magazine) Who's that knuckle-head?

KAI'RO: Dunno.

MR. WEARY: Looks like he's got two bimbos with him too. One for each arm.

KAI'RO: Yeah.

STORYTELLER: Kai'Ro turned away from them but then slowly spun his head in their direction again. The bell over the door chimed when the trio entered the store. As though to make a fashion statement, the young man pulled off his shades and placed them on his collar. The girls giggled and immediately ran over to the candy display that was right behind Kai'Ro. The guy strutted down an aisle and looked at a display of chips. Mr. Weary stepped out from behind his counter and walked towards him.

MR. WEARY: Something I can help you find, son?

YOUNG SLEAZY: (with an arrogant tone) Nah. I dunno know. What kinda beer y'all sell here?

MR. WEARY: No alcohol here, son.

YOUNG SLEAZY: That's stupid.

STORYTELLER: The two girls continued to look at the candy as-sortment. One of them dropped a pack on the ground. As she bent over to pick it up, Kai'Ro snuck a glance. Then he bit his lower lip and looked away quickly. The other girl noticed and whispered to her friend.

KAI'RO: (under his breath to himself) That was whack. I made a covenant for my eyes not to look lustfully on a woman.

STORYTELLER: Just then, one of the girls walked up to Kai'Ro and tapped him on the shoulder. The word SEDUCTION was tat-tooed in small letters on her neck.

SEDUCTION: (in a tempting voice) 'Scuse me. Which of these two do you like better?

STORYTELLER: Swaying her hips to one side, she held out a pack of candies and a bubblegum sucker.

KAI'RO: Uh, those candies are good.

STORYTELLER: Seduction frowned.

SEDUCTION: Really? I like suckers.

STORYTELLER: She turned and winked at her friend who stepped up beside her. This girl also had a tattoo on her neck. It was the word SLAUGHTERHOUSE.

SLAUGHTERHOUSE: (in an alluring tone) Do I know you?

KAI'RO: Nah. Don't think so.

SLAUGHTERHOUSE: For real? I feel like I know you from somewhere.

SEDUCTION: Yeah, we know you. Wait a minute...

STORYTELLER: Seduction started to snap her fingers, as if she was trying to recall a memory.

SEDUCTION: What's ya name? It's comin' to me. Kylo? Nah, that ain't it. Kai'Ron?

KAI'RO: My name's Kai'Ro.

SEDUCTION: Kai'Ro! Yeah. That's it! You don't remember the two of us? Come on, boy! We went to school together.

SLAUGHTERHOUSE: I'm Slaughterhouse and this is my sister, Seduction. We're identical twins.

KAI'RO: (with a slight frown) Oh, yeah. I remember y'all now.

SLAUGHTERHOUSE: Yeah. We used to be up at the parties wit you. Seems like you used to be able to dance.

SEDUCTION: I remember Kai'Ro had those moves, girl!

SLAUGHTERHOUSE: And that money.

SEDUCTION: And that muscle. Where ya been, boy?

STORYTELLER: Seduction stepped forward and put her hand on Kai'Ro's chest. He pushed it away and stepped back until he was nearly stuck between them and the corner of the store.

SEDUCTION: I can't believe you could forget us.

SLAUGHTERHOUSE: Every man who's been with us remembers it for the rest of his life. (poking her finger in his chest) Oh yeah. You. Was. Definitely. *With*. Us.

STORYTELLER: Slaughterhouse then took her two fingers and walked them slowly up Kai'Ro's arm.

KAI'RO: (shaking off her hand) Look. I was with a lot of girls back in the day.

SLAUGHTERHOUSE: How 'bout you come to Young Sleazy's party this weekend?

KAI'RO: Nah. Don't think so.

SEDUCTION: C'mon! His pops is out of town. He's got one of the biggest and nicest cribs in the 'burbs. There's gonna be dancin'. Plus, he's got a pool...

SLAUGHTERHOUSE: And a real nice hot tub too!

KAI'RO: Thanks for the invite, but that whole scene ain't me no more.

SLAUGHTERHOUSE: What'cha mean, that ain't you no more?

KAI'RO: I mean, just what I said. I used to be at the parties and the clubs, wildin' out and all that. But I'm done with that mess now. That Kai'Ro you used to know is dead. I'm not the same man. I'm changed. I'm brand new.

SEDUCTION: So, you don't party no more? You don't like girls no more or somethin'?

KAI'RO: Nah! It ain't like that. But my appetite's changed. Now that stuff makes me sick. I got a hunger now for findin' one girl...the right girl...

SLAUGHTERHOUSE: You got two of the *right* girls standin' in front of ya now, boy.

KAI'RO: Nah. I don't think so.

STORYTELLER: Both of the girls frowned, stepped back and folded their arms across their chests.

SEDUCTION: What's ya problem, boy?

SLAUGHTERHOUSE: You sayin' we ain't fine? You sayin' we ain't good 'nough for ya?

KAI'RO: Nah. You don't get it. Y'all both fine. Any man can see that. But you ain't right. Not for me. The King's got me lookin' for a virtuous woman. I'm into fine. But more than that, I'm lookin' for a beautiful heart. A girl who loves the King. Loves His Word. Loves His ways. External beauty? Shoot! That's easy to find. But internal beauty? That's like findin' a real treasure.

STORYTELLER: Just then, Young Sleazy walked up and glared at Kai'Ro.

YOUNG SLEAZY: Yo. What up, homie? You makin' a move on my ladies here? You need that?

KAI'RO: Nah. It ain't like that, bruh.

YOUNG SLEAZY: Better not be. I'll beat the brakes off any boy talkin' to my ladies.

KAI'RO: You need to chill, dude. I said it ain't like that. Ya two girls came up and talked to me, and I told 'em I wasn't interested.

YOUNG SLEAZY: Talked to you, huh? C'mon! You think I'm some kinda fool. You think my two beautiful companions would come and talk to a raggedy clown like you?

STORYTELLER: Young Sleazy balled up one of his fists and took a step forward.

YOUNG SLEAZY: Is this fool botherin' you, girls?

SLAUGHTERHOUSE: I don't know yet. Kai'Ro's been talkin' non-sense.

STORYTELLER: Young Sleazy's face froze for a moment. He cleared his throat and relaxed his fist.

YOUNG SLEAZY: Kai'Ro? Thought I heard you was gone, lookin' for religion or somethin'.

KAI'RO: (smiling) Nah, homie. I didn't leave lookin' for no religion. I went lookin' for a relationship with my King and Creator. I found Him too and He was better than I imagined.

YOUNG SLEAZY: Heard you gave up the girls. The hustlin'. The money. The game. All that.

KAI'RO: That's true. And I don't miss any of it. In fact, I feel relieved and free, dawg. I feel like a convict losin' his chains and havin' the door to his cell kicked open. Shoot! I haven't felt this alive and free—ever!

YOUNG SLEAZY: Wooow! Some people had said you done lost your mind. They wasn't lyin'.

KAI'RO: Yeah, well. I never had your pop's money or grew up in a nice crib like you. But the lifestyle you're livin'? The players life, I had all that. It's played out. It ain't nothin', for real. I'm here to tell you now that the road you're on plain and simple leads to pain, emptiness and absolute destruction in the end.

That nice whip you got out there in the parking lot is like your life. It's tight. It's cool, but it's like you're cruisin' one hundred miles an hour towards a cliff. And at the end of that cliff is a bottomless hole full of flames and agony. I'm that flashin' road sign tellin' you to slow down and hang a sharp right turn before you gone for good, homie. That's real talk!

STORYTELLER: Young Sleazy smirked. He unscrewed the cap off a bottle of apple juice in his hand and took a sip. Just then, Mr. Weary hollered across the store.

MR. WEARY: Hey, Kai'Ro! You gonna gab with them all day? Those boxes won't unpack themselves.

SEDUCTION: What! You *work* here?

SLAUGHTERHOUSE: Ugh! You work in this nasty little place? I thought...ugh!

STORYTELLER: Seduction and Slaughterhouse rolled their eyes and took two steps backwards. Young Sleazy threw his head back and laughed.

YOUNG SLEAZY: Oh! Oh! This is classic! Kai'Ro is just a clown who stocks shelves and pro'bly scrubs toilets too.

STORYTELLER: A faint look of embarrassment crossed Kai'Ro's face, but he held his ground and stared at Young Sleazy and the two women.

YOUNG SLEAZY: So, wait a minute! Wait a minute! Lemme make sure I got this right. You just said that my life is like my car. Fast and cool and headin' towards a fiery cliff. You just said that, right? Ok. But here you are stockin' shelves at a raggedy ol' store. You got no girl. No money. No ride.

So, what's that make your life then? You like a busted-up skateboard with three wheels, or a rusted ol' bike with flat tires or somethin'. You said my life's headed off a cliff or some nonsense like that. Homie, your life is in the ditch right now! You're just a broke down, good for nothin' toilet boy. That's all you is. C'mon, ladies, let's bounce. I ain't talkin' with this fool no more!

STORYTELLER: Kai'Ro grimaced. It was obvious that he wanted to say something in his own defense, but he said nothing. Young Sleazy slapped three dollars on the counter, smirked at Mr. Weary and left the store with his two female companions.

Mr. Weary opened his mouth to say something but instead just shook his head. Kai'Ro let out a big sigh and returned to stocking the shelves.

THE ORCHARD

STORYTELLER: In my dream, I saw Evangeline inside a thick grove of trees. Hanging from the branches of these trees were large and delicious looking oranges and apples. The sun was still in the sky but starting to move slowly towards the horizon.

EVANGELINE: (to herself) Wow. I'm hungry. This fruit looks great.

STORYTELLER: She looked to her left and then to her right before walking over to the nearest tree and plucking an orange. Finding a nearby rock, she sat down underneath the shade of a tall tree and started to peel the large piece of fruit in her hand.

MAMA WISDOM: You look hungry, hon.

STORYTELLER: Evangeline jumped straight up with a start and nearly dropped her orange. She turned quickly to see who was speaking. Behind her stood an elderly woman with a basket full of oranges and apples in the crook of her arm. She was wearing old work gloves and a sun hat that rested neatly on the top of her head. A warm smile brightened her face, as she walked up closer to Evangeline.

EVANGELINE: I'm sorry. Uh, these must be your trees. I shoulda asked if I could have one.

MAMA WISDOM: Shush, child. Don't worry yourself with such nonsense. Sit back down and enjoy that orange. They're delicious this year.

STORYTELLER: Evangeline looked inquisitively at the older woman for a moment before sitting down again.

MAMA WISDOM: My name is Mama Wisdom and this is my orchard. What's your name, sweetheart?

EVANGELINE: Evangeline.

MAMA WISDOM: (holding her hands to her chest) Oh, my. That's a lovely name. Simply lovely.

EVANGELINE: Thank you.

MAMA WISDOM: Does it have a special meaning?

EVANGELINE: I'm not sure, ma'am.

MAMA WISDOM: Hmm. What are you doing way out here?

STORYTELLER: Evangeline looked nervously at the ground.

EVANGELINE: I'm searchin' for the Mountain of the Cross. I have a burden on my back that I just can't stand no more.

MAMA WISDOM: (smiling) Yes. I can see that.

EVANGELINE: You can see my burden?

MAMA WISDOM: Well, in a way, yes. I can see it in your eyes. You look weighed down, as if you have the entire world pressing on your shoulders.

EVANGELINE: It feels that way sometimes.

MAMA WISDOM: What has you feeling so weighed down, child?

EVANGELINE: I don't know. I—

MAMA WISDOM: It's guilt, isn't it? You feel weighed down by guilt and you don't know how to get rid of all that shame and pain.

STORYTELLER: Evangeline looked up from the ground and into Mama Wisdom's eyes. Her lip quivered slightly.

MAMA WISDOM: Perhaps it is guilt over young men? Guilt over how you've used your body for things that you're now ashamed of?

EVANGELINE: That's none of your business! Why you bein' so nosey, anyway? I just came here to eat. I best be goin'.

STORYTELLER: Evangeline stood up again, but Mama Wisdom intercepted her and put a strong hand on her shoulder.

MAMA WISDOM: You have a quick temper, child. I'm not one to meddle in anyone's business. I'm here to encourage you and perhaps enlighten you, if you'll listen. There's no real reason for you to continue down this road to the Mountain of the Cross if you aren't willing to be exposed for who you are and admit that you're sick, ashamed and a fake.

EVANGELINE: What do you mean a fake! I'm not a fake!

MAMA WISDOM: If you aren't a fake then what are you doing on this road, hon? The King is in the business of fixing people, but He can't fix what ain't broke. He heals the sick...removes shame from the ashamed...and brings a true identity to fake people. The burden that's on your back, weighing down your soul like a five hundred pound weight—you put that burden on yourself.

STORYTELLER: Evangeline sat back down but her fists were clenched beside her.

EVANGELINE: How did I do that?

MAMA WISDOM: Well, you were born sick and burdened. We all were. We got that from our great-great-great-granddaddy Adam. He chose to reject the peace and joy of the King in exchange for pain and a sin-filled burden. Then he passed it on to all his kin. As a result, we stay sick and burdened until we give our lives to the King and allow Him to make us brand new.

Sweetheart, up until the point you recognized that burden, you were only making yourself sicker by the choices you were making.

EVANGELINE: What choices?

MAMA WISDOM: Until you give your life to the King, *every* choice that you make is unrighteous and it usually harms you or someone else. According to the King's Letters, apart from Him, even on our best days—our best works are no better than filthy rags.

EVANGELINE: Ugh! That's nasty!

MAMA WISDOM: (smiling) It is nasty, but sin is nasty. Deep inside, I imagine you've started to feel nasty about your life or at least with the way your life is going.

STORYTELLER: Evangeline said nothing.

MAMA WISDOM: Talk to me about your baby.

EVANGELINE: (mumbling under her breath) You as nosey as my grandma.

MAMA WISDOM: Well, I'm not going to sit here and ignore the fact that you're pregnant, child. How do you feel about the mistake you made?

EVANGELINE: What'cha mean, mistake? I mean, I guess we shoulda used protection and been smarter.

MAMA WISDOM: I mean, don't you think you should have waited until you were married to have sex? Waited until your wedding night to share your body with your husband?

EVANGELINE: (laughing) Marriage? I don't know nobody who's gotten married lately in the City of Doom.

MAMA WISDOM: But I bet you know a lot of baby mamas. I'm sure you know a lot of girls who wander the blocks with broken hearts.

EVANGELINE: Yeah, but marriage is kinda old-fashioned. Most of the people who used to be married have got a divorce. But besides all that, sex is fun! It makes me feel good.

STORYTELLER: Mama Wisdom looked up into the orange tree to her left and studied the fruit for a minute. Then she reached up and plucked a medium-sized orange from one of the limbs and tossed it to Evangeline.

MAMA WISDOM: Here, try this one. You still look hungry.

STORYTELLER: Evangeline gladly accepted the fruit and rolled it around in her hands before she started peeling it. After pulling apart a slice, she popped it into her mouth and bit down. Instantly, she puckered her lips and spit the fruit out on the ground.

EVANGELINE: Ugh! That's sour 'n nasty!

STORYTELLER: Mama Wisdom giggled a little as Evangeline wiped her mouth with the back of her hand.

MAMA WISDOM: Funny, isn't it?

EVANGELINE: What? That wasn't funny. That was terrible.

MAMA WISDOM: Yes, it was. But it looked like the real thing, didn't it? It looked like a delicious orange, like the first one you ate.

EVANGELINE: That first orange was the best orange I've ever eaten. It was amazin'.

MAMA WISDOM: Hmmmmm. The funny thing is, the orange you just tried was just days away from being amazing too. The juicy-sweet part of the orange is one of the last things to develop before it becomes ripe for eating. I simply plucked it before it was ready.

EVANGELINE: So, why'd you give it to me then? Why not let it grow into a delicious orange?

MAMA WISDOM: I could ask you the same question.

EVANGELINE: Huh? What's that 'sposed to mean?

MAMA WISDOM: What about sex? The King tells us to wait until we're married to have sex. Sex is like an orange on a tree. It grows sweetest when it's fully developed and saved for the right time. But when plucked from the tree too soon, it produces bitterness and emptiness.

EVANGELINE: I don't know 'bout that. I'd say that sex anytime is pretty sweet. Just gotta make sure it's the right man. I ain't sayin' you need to be a freak. You need to keep your head and make a good decision.

MAMA WISDOM: Really? How many boys have you slept with?

EVANGELINE: (frowning) That's kinda personal.

MAMA WISDOM: How many?

STORYTELLER: Evangeline swallowed nervously and looked away for a moment.

EVANGELINE: Maybe four...five...six...I can't remember, for real.

MAMA WISDOM: And how many of those boys do you still care for?

EVANGELINE: I can't stand all of them, except one. I loved 'em all at the time, but they just up and left me for some other girls.

MAMA WISDOM: So, were they the *right* ones? You said that before you let a boy pluck you off the tree you need to be sure he's the right one.

EVANGELINE: I thought they were at the time.

MAMA WISDOM: So, how did you decide they were the right one?

EVANGELINE: I don't know. They were nice to me...gave me attention. A couple of 'em bought me stuff. They was fine too!

MAMA WISDOM: Let me rewind what you've shared with me. You've allowed six different boys to pluck you from the tree and enjoy you. Every one of them has left you. They've spit you out of their mouth and moved on to another piece of fruit. (pointing at Evangeline's belly) One of them left you with his seed, but every one of them left you with a broken heart.

STORYTELLER: In her defense, Evangeline looked like she was going to open her mouth, but she said nothing.

MAMA WISDOM: I've had hundreds and hundreds of girls over the years stop in this orchard and have a similar conversation with me. Most of these girls are broken inside. Some of them are pregnant with no daddy of the baby in sight. Some have diseases. A few are full of hate for men and don't want to be touched or near a man again. Some are addicted to being plucked off the tree and will give themselves to any boy who gives them a second glance. Now you tell me, doesn't that sound like bitter emptiness? Like that orange you just tasted?

STORYTELLER: Evangeline nodded with a little mist forming in her eyes.

MAMA WISDOM: The King desires some beautiful things for a man and woman. One of those things is sex. He made us to desire and want sex. But we need to wait until the timing is ripe. But that's not all. A man is called to serve and love his woman the way that the King loved and served His Bride.

EVANGELINE: Who was the King's bride?

MAMA WISDOM: (with a big smile) Child. *We* are His Bride. The King left the beauty and comfort of His home in the City of

Light to save us from destruction. Before the King came, everyone was living like a prostitute. They just gave themselves to anyone and anything that could give them pleasure and keep them alive. Then, because of His love for us, He came to show us life and pleasure everlasting that could only be found in a relationship with Him.

To create that relationship, He had to die a savage and horrible death on our behalf. By His example, His Letters tell all men that they should love their women the same way. They should serve their wives and be willing to give up their lives for their women. They should sacrifice and give everything they have to protect their women and to provide for them. Now, how many men do you know who'd be willing to do that?

EVANGELINE: I don't know any man like that. Well, maybe one. But—

MAMA WISDOM: But doesn't that sound wonderful? Imagine having a man who would serve you, protect you, provide for you and stay faithful to you—no matter what.

STORYTELLER: Evangeline was leaning forward, listening to every word.

MAMA WISDOM: See, the King promises to never leave or abandon His Bride. He's so committed that He stays faithful even when we wander off to other lovers.

EVANGELINE: Other lovers?

MAMA WISDOM: Even when we give our lives to the King, we still have a part of our heart that wants to chase other lovers. Money. Clothes. Popularity. Comfort. Ease. Other people. Sometimes we leave the arms of our King and run to the arms of these other things by giving them our attention, affection and our hearts. But the King doesn't give up on us. He pursues us because His love never fails for His Bride.

EVANGELINE: That sounds too good to believe.

MAMA WISDOM: That's because it is. His love is sweet and delicious like some of these wonderful oranges. He desires you to find that in Him. But He also desires for you to wait on the branches until the right man comes along. He wants for all of the men and women who follow Him to enjoy the sweetness of marriage the way He created it to be. There's sweetness in the waiting for sex.

And, girl, let me tell you something. (in a whisper) There's sweetness in the sex too. There is sweetness in the commitment and faithfulness to each other. Sometimes the King's people are too scared or ashamed to talk about sex and they act like it's a dirty thing, but it isn't. It only gets dirty when people have sex outside of the way the King intended. The King designed it as a beautiful part of marriage. Sadly, most people would rather have the quick fruit that leaves a bitter and nasty taste in their souls.

STORYTELLER: Mama Wisdom paused for a moment. Evangeline's forehead was furrowed with wrinkles, as if she were deep in thought.

MAMA WISDOM: Every once in a while, a storm will blow some fruit off of these trees and onto the ground before they become ripe. I collect that fruit and feed it to my goats and pigs. It's food fit for animals but not for people. In the same way, cheap and premature sex is for animals. Animals don't think. They just *do*. They don't wait. They just dive in and eat.

When we give away our bodies outside of the way the King designed, we are behaving no better than an animal. And sadly, we are missing out on all of the beauty the King originally intended for us. What I'm saying to you, child, is that you can choose to live off of those nasty oranges. They'll feed you and put something in your belly to keep you alive, but would you really want to live that way forever?

EVANGELINE: No, ma'am. That sounds terrible.

MAMA WISDOM: Has what I've been saying to you made sense?

EVANGELINE: I think so. But I'm gonna be real. I hear what you're sayin', but I have some doubts.

MAMA WISDOM: Such as?

EVANGELINE: Well, for one, I've never seen no man like the one you've been describin'. I'm not sure they exist. Sounds like a fantasy to me. In fact, I've never even seen a good marriage before. And the other thing is that I've been livin' off nasty fruit since I was fourteen. I've been lettin' boys pluck me off the branch way too easy. I'm not so sure that the King or the right man would want to have anything to do with me. Deep inside, I feel like that nasty piece of fruit over there.

STORYTELLER: Evangeline pointed to a bruised and shriveled apple lying in the grass. It was eaten through by bugs and squirrels.

MAMA WISDOM: Let me tell you something. First, you're never too bruised or ugly for the King. Don't sell yourself or His love for you short. When you recognize that you've messed up, you have to bring it before the King. He'll always be ready and willing to forgive you.

Secondly, a man who loves the King can always find beauty in the ashes. Now, it's okay to have some of those doubts. Finding a man like the King desires for you is definitely tough, but it's not impossible. I found a good man who loves the King and loves me. He guides, protects and provides for me every day.

The thing is, a lot of girls say they're waiting for the *right* man, but they're far too easily pleased. If you pray and seek for the right man, you'll know him when you see him. He won't be perfect like the King. No man is. But he'll have some unique characteristics to him. You need to be patient too. Don't give yourself to those silly boys who have no more sense and manners than a junkyard dog.

EVANGELINE: So, how do you spot this type of man?

MAMA WISDOM: Well, for one, he'll look and act and talk a lot more like the King than he will a man of this world. You'll know this because he'll talk about the King as if the King were his best friend. Real men aren't ashamed of their crush on the King. In fact, they should love Him more than they love you.

Then too, although he won't be perfect, he'll be kind. Patient. Protective. Compassionate. Gentle. Courteous. I see so many young men shoving girls around, hitting them and talking to them like they're trash. A real man would never do that. Silly and cowardly boys behave like that, but a man treats a woman like she's a treasure.

STORYTELLER: Not too far away, I saw an old man approaching the two women. He was heavyset and had on a pair of overalls. A long strand of straw hung out of his mouth.

PAPA FIX-IT: Excuse me, ladies. But it's getting dark out here.

MAMA WISDOM: Evangeline, I'd like for you to meet my husband, Papa Fix-It.

EVANGELINE: It's nice to meet you.

PAPA FIX-IT: (tipping his hat) It's too dark for you two to be out here. I've got three steaks waiting back at the house, and I can't wait to throw them on the grill. Got some greens and mashed potatoes too—

MAMA WISDOM: (smiling) And don't forget the apple cobbler. Come on, young lady. Please join us for supper. We can talk some more. We have a warm bed for you too.

EVANGELINE: I don't wanna be no bother.

MAMA WISDOM: Shush, child.

STORYTELLER: Mama Wisdom, Papa Fix-It and Evangeline walked through the orchard to a small but cozy-looking cottage. A steady plume of smoke billowed from the chimney. Inside, it was very inviting. Firelight illuminated the living room with a warm glow. All of the furniture looked handmade. A round oak table with six chairs sat in the middle of the dining room.

In my dream, I watched as Papa Fix-It put three large steaks on his grill outside the back door. Mama Wisdom invited Evangeline to cut some vegetables for a salad. The older woman cooked potatoes and greens on the stove and put a delicious looking cobbler in the oven.

By the time Evangeline finished the salad, she had a peaceful smile on her face. With pure contentment, she walked around the quaint and tidy home and admired the handmade quilts and other treasures. She took her time and studied the many pictures on the walls, the mantle and the shelves. The photographs were full of countless children, grandchildren and what appeared to be great-grandchildren.

After Papa Fix-It finished grilling, they came together at the table to share the meal. The kind gentleman prayed a blessing over the food and they began eating. With the firelight flickering off of their faces, Evangeline ate slowly and cautiously like she was slightly concerned that she might be doing something wrong.

Occasionally, Papa Fix-It said something funny. His shoulders would shake up and down as the wrinkles on his face retreated from his joyful smile. Mama Wisdom waved her hand at him and rolled her eyes while Evangeline struggled to contain her laughter behind a napkin.

When the meal was finished, Mama Wisdom pulled a steaming apple cobbler from the oven and they each enjoyed a large serving with a big scoop of vanilla ice cream. After dessert, she stood up and went to her rocking chair near the fire to take up her knitting. Papa Fix-It invited Evangeline to join him in washing the dishes.

PAPA FIX-IT: (as he washed the dishes and handed them to Evangeline to dry) Young lady, you have one of the most beautiful and joy-filled smiles I've ever seen.

EVANGELINE: Thank you.

PAPA FIX-IT: Some smiles reveal something wonderful from deep inside a person. They're like the sunshine when it first peeks over the horizon. Those first lovely oranges and yellows announce that the sun is coming and a new day is born. I never tire of watching the sun rise. Your smile reminds me of its beauty.

STORYTELLER: Blushing, Evangeline tried to stifle a smile from crossing her face as she dried a large serving bowl.

PAPA FIX-IT: Seems like there should be a man who'd want to spend the rest of his life with that smile of yours.

EVANGELINE: The rest of his life? That's a *real* long time.

PAPA FIX-IT: Is it? Look at me and Mama. We've been married sixty years. But it doesn't seem like that long.

EVANGELINE: Sixty years? Wow! That's a long time. I can't imagine spendin' my life with anyone for that long. I think there'd be so much fightin' and drama that one of us would kill the other.

PAPA FIX-IT: No relationship comes without some drama. There's no relationship that comes without death.

EVANGELINE: (placing the plates in the cupboard) What'cha mean?

PAPA FIX-IT: Well, believe it or not, me and Mama used to fight like cats and dogs back when we were youngsters. We used to fight over silly stuff like me leaving the toilet lid up or her not ironing my britches right. Sometimes it seemed like she'd nag me to death, and I'd spend all day out in the woods just talking to the trees. I declare they were better company than her nagging me all day.

MAMA WISDOM: (from her rocking chair) I hear you, you know?

PAPA FIX-IT: We used to argue about serious stuff too. We were nearly broke for our first five years of marriage. Poor finances put a real strain on us. During those years, we lost our first two babies due to miscarriage. That put more stress on us than you can imagine. Besides all that, our different opinions kept us wrangling over our dreams and desires. Sometimes we'd have a few good conversations in between our fights instead of the other way around. Broke a lot of dishes, though, and made a lot of emotional scars.

STORYTELLER: Papa Fix-It looked thoughtfully into the suds as he washed the silverware.

EVANGELINE: So, what happened?

PAPA FIX-IT: We had to start dying a little bit each day.

EVANGELINE: I don't get it.

PAPA FIX-IT: The majority of our fights and our drama was due to the fact that we were trying to force our wills, our desires and the way we thought things should be onto each other. I wanted Mama to be a certain way. I wanted her to do things the way I wanted them done. Some of what I wanted done was good, but most of it was due to my own flesh. I wanted Mama to do things a certain way because it made *me* happy. It was selfish.

Then I started learning that peace came about the most in surrender. By letting go of some of my own selfish desires, my wishes and my wants, I gave up trying to make her make me happy. That's the dying part. If you asked Mama, she'd tell you that she started learning the same thing.

But the King asks for more. He asks us to die to ourselves and our own selfish desires and to serve each other. When I was young, that whole concept sounded as foreign to me as speaking Chinese. *Serving my wife?* What's that supposed to mean? But then I learned that the King came to serve us and help us even when we're in rebellion against Him. When I started dying to myself and focusing on serving my lovely wife, I found this home starting to fill up with more peace than we could contain.

The funny thing is that Mama began doing the same thing for me. Serving. Sure, we still had our battles and our moments. But as the years rolled by, those petty, silly things that we used to fight over became things that we laugh about today. The tougher things became easier to struggle through with prayer and a willingness to work together. It's never perfect, but it's about as perfect as it could be on this side of the City of Light.

STORYTELLER: Evangeline placed her towel next to the sink and leaned back on the countertop.

PAPA FIX-IT: Is there a man for that baby you're carrying, or just another boy running from his responsibilities?

EVANGELINE: There's a man.

PAPA FIX-IT: Good. I'm growing weary with all these boys with mustaches and loud cars driving around, acting grown. They've got the self-control of a pit-bull when it's in heat...

MAMA WISDOM: Honey, hush!

PAPA FIX-IT: I'm just saying. So, is this man going to give you a ring, make you his wife and provide you and that little one with a home?

EVANGELINE: I don't know 'bout all that...

PAPA FIX-IT: If he's a *man*, he'll do it!

EVANGELINE: I think he'll be there for this baby...he's different...lost his burden when he gave his life to the King. He's a whole different man now. But I don't know 'bout marriage and all that...seems kinda old-fashioned. And like I told Mama, nobody gets married no more. Most of the married folks that I know ain't married now.

PAPA FIX-IT: Here, let me show you something. Mama, we'll be back in a minute.

STORYTELLER: Papa Fix-It grabbed a lantern, lit it and guided Evangeline outside. The moon was large and bright in the night sky. The pair walked towards a big brown barn behind the house. Papa Fix-It threw the doors wide open and clicked on a light. There were four large objects covered by tarps. It looked like they could be vehicles.

PAPA FIX-IT: You like trucks?

EVANGELINE: Yeah. I love trucks.

PAPA FIX-IT: What if I was to give you your very own four-wheel drive pickup truck?

EVANGELINE: (laughing) You wouldn't have to twist my arm too hard.

STORYTELLER: Papa Fix-It walked over to the first tarp and yanked it off. Underneath it was an old rusted pickup truck. The front windshield was spider-webbed with some ugly cracks. All four tires were flat. The driver's-side door had a massive dent in it. Both of the front lights were punched out.

PAPA FIX-IT: Voila! This is all yours! You can have it.

EVANGELINE: Um...no thanks.

PAPA FIX-IT: Why not? What's the matter?

EVANGELINE: Because...it's busted. It's ugly and messed up. I betcha it won't even crank up.

PAPA FIX-IT: Hmmm...

STORYTELLER: Papa Fix-It walked over to the next tarp and pulled it off. Underneath was a beautiful cherry-red pickup.

The paint job looked flawless. All of the windows appeared to be brand new. The tires were black and shiny with expensive silver rims.

PAPA FIX-IT: How about this one? Would you drive this truck?

EVANGELINE: (nodding) If you gave me the keys, me and that truck right there would be gone!

PAPA FIX-IT: (with a sparkle in his eye) But why?

EVANGELINE: Mr. Fix It, that truck right there looks so gooood. It's just beautiful. I mean, do you know how tight it would be to be rollin' the streets in that whip right there?

PAPA FIX-IT: What's a whip? Oh, never mind.

STORYTELLER: Evangeline walked up to the truck and traced her fingers along the sleek paint job. She stood up on the running board and peered inside. Just like the outside of the truck, the inside was equally spotless.

PAPA FIX-IT: Marriage is a lot like these trucks here.

EVANGELINE: Huh?

PAPA FIX-IT: You don't believe in marriage because all you've ever seen is the rusty and broke down version of it. That's all the world puts up in your face. Fatherless kids. Husbands and wives yelling at each other. Cheating on each other. Hurting each other. I don't blame you. Who'd want to drive a marriage like that? But what if the King had other plans?

EVANGELINE: Like what?

PAPA FIX-IT: Like this beautiful truck that you're looking at. Took me three years to turn that truck from an ugly piece of rusted junk into the beauty you see before you. The King is into making beautiful out of the ugly. He built a man and a woman to live together, to start a family together, to dream together...it's what He's *always* intended. Unfortunately, our sin and our selfishness has messed the whole thing up. We've turned something beautiful into a heap of rust and ugly.

EVANGELINE: So, what's your point?

PAPA FIX-IT: My point is that you, and a lot of young people like you, don't believe in marriage anymore because you've never seen it. Marriage is either an ugly rusted monster that scares them silly or it's like Santa Claus—too good to be true. I'm here to tell you that marriage can be and is supposed to be a beautiful, beautiful thing. In fact, the King said that marriage is the number one way that He shows the world His love for His people.

STORYTELLER: Evangeline placed her hand on the driver's-side mirror as she stepped down from checking out the inside of the truck. As she did so, the mirror snapped off and fell to the ground with a crash.

EVANGELINE: Oh! I'm so sorry. I didn't mean to . . .

PAPA FIX-IT: (laughing) Don't worry about that at all. I can fix it. Marriage is no different. Due to sin, sometimes stuff gets broken. But if we turn to the King, He can fix it.

STORYTELLER: The old man slung his arm over Evangeline's shoulder and turned her gently towards the door.

PAPA FIX-IT: Come on, child, it's time for us all to go to bed.

STORYTELLER: Papa Fix-It and Evangeline returned to the house. When they got there, Mama Wisdom had prepared a bed for Evangeline. After saying thank you and good night, she turned in for the evening. She was sound asleep five seconds after her weary head hit the pillow.

THE LOST BOYS

12

STORYTELLER: My dream took me back to Kai'Ro. It was morning. He was walking down the sidewalk with an old basketball under his arm. Eerie smog stained the blue sky with an orangish-red glow. Kai'Ro was wearing shorts and a sleeveless T-shirt. His feet were laced up in white and blue Js.

KAI'RO: King, when I saw this old place with Preacher the other day, I knew You had called me back here. If I'm gonna be a light, then let me shine where it needs the most. Shine through me today. I know it's gonna be tough.

STORYTELLER: After a short walk, he came to the FIELD OF DREAMS. The basketball courts were filling up with teenagers shouting, dribbling and squaring off into different squads. Kai'Ro jogged up to the nearest court. Two teams were already playing. He noticed four other young men leaning on the chain-link fence, watching the game.

KAI'RO: Y'all got next?

DOULOS: We need one more. Can you hoop?

KAI'RO: (with a confident smile) I can play.

DOULOS: My name's Doulos. This is my homeboy, Fast Talk. Those other two clowns, they're brothas. The tall African noodle lookin' dude, that's Motor Mouth. His midget lookin' brother, that's Annoying.

KAI'RO: They brothers, huh?

DOULOS: (grinning) Different daddies.

KAI'RO: I see.

DOULOS: Two different sizes. But both of 'em got big mouths. Got that from their mama.

KAI'RO: I'm Kai'Ro.

DOULOS: Kai'Ro? Cool. Well, I hope you can hoop and I hope you can fight if you gotta. We gonna be playin' the Lost Boys. Them boys are mean. All of 'em are super fast and super good. But you gotta be careful. They'll throw a bow in your mouth or in your ribs. Foul you like nobody's business and then curse you like an ugly dog if you call 'em for it. They like scrappin'. They're like sharks when blood's in the water.

STORYTELLER: Kai'Ro watched the game on the court. The Lost Boys were all wearing bright red shorts and matching all-black Js. Their shorts were sagging low. They were playing skins and all of them were covered in tats of half-naked girls, skulls and curse words. The other team looked intimidated and rattled by their aggressive play.

KAI'RO: What's the score?

MOTOR MOUTH: It's like eight to nuttin', dawg. These other clowns ain't gonna score a point. They ain't got no game.

STORYTELLER: About that time, three white Range Rovers drove by. Their windows were tinted thicker than midnight. As they rolled slowly past the park, the basketballs and energy drinks on the ground wobbled from the thunderous bass blasting.

KAI'RO: Whoa. Who's that?

DOULOS: You don't know who that is?

KAI'RO: I've been out of town for a minute.

DOULOS: That's Cut Throat and his clique. They the new competition in town.

KAI'RO: Basketball?

DOULOS: Nah, dawg. They Doc Destruction's new competition. Cut Throat's been movin' in on Doc's territory for the last few months. Pushin' product. You think Doc Destruction is a nasty dude? Shoot! Cut Throat makes Doc look like a saint. They been sparrin' over the turf, but the real fight is gonna go down at some point. So far, they kinda been sharin' the block, but that ain't gonna last much longer.

STORYTELLER: When he finished talking, a volley of shouting and profanity exploded on the court. The game appeared to be over but all ten players on the court were yelling and shoving.

INYAFACE: Get off the court, clowns! That's eleven to nothin'. Y'all need to go play over there on the kiddie courts. This court is for the real playas.

WHINER: Nah, dawg. You call that a steal? Y'all beat my boy down like you was goin' for his wallet. Then you shove me on the ground and score some cheap trey like that. That ain't happenin'.

CROSSOVA: What'cha gonna do, lil' man? You best get to steppin' before we hurt more than ya feelin's.

STORYTELLER: The Lost Boys moved towards their defeated opponents. The losers looked at one another for a second, mumbled some words and then moved on. One of the Lost Boys pointed to a piece of torn white fabric blowing around on the side of the court.

PUNISHER: Aye! One of y'all left ya lil' jockstrap.

STORYTELLER: All of the Lost Boys burst into laughter.

BRICK: So, who's next?

DOULOS: We gotcha!

STORYTELLER: Kai'Ro and his new squad ran out on the court. It was old blacktop and cracked in places.

INYAFACE: Doulos! You comin' back for another lesson?

DOULOS: Hey. Maybe I'm a slow learner.

INYAFACE: Nah. You just slow. I see ya brought yo same three clowns, but who's the new boy?

DOULOS: This is Kai'Ro.

STORYTELLER: The Lost Boys stared hard at Kai'Ro.

PROFANE: You pick 'em up at the homeless shelter?

PUNISHER: Doulos, you might be into charity or somethin', but we ain't. This is our court, homie. You need to get ya a squad before ya step on our turf again.

MOTOR MOUTH: How 'bout you just shut ya mouth and play some ball.

STORYTELLER: Punisher rushed forward but Annoying and Fast Talk stepped in between.

PUNISHER: Who ya talkin' to, son?

KAI'RO: Hey! I came to hoop. Y'all wanna play or not?

INYAFACE: Yeah, Gay-Ro, we'll play. Playin' to eleven. Ones and twos. Winners' ball.

KAI'RO: Cool. I'll be checkin' you then.

STORYTELLER: The Lost Boys took the ball at half court, as Kai'Ro and his new squad set up on D. Brick tossed the ball to Inyaface and then ran down into the low post. Brick was over six and a half feet tall and rippling with muscles. Inyaface faked a toss at Kai'Ro's face and smirked.

INYAFACE: Ima break ya ankles. I hope ya brought ya braces.

STORYTELLER: Inyaface faked hard to his left and then made a lightning quick crossover to his right. But Kai'Ro was even quicker and knocked the ball loose. He recovered the ball with one hand and then spun 360 degrees around a flailing Punisher before firing a rocket pass to Motor Mouth on a fast break. Motor Mouth delivered a nasty two-handed dunk that rattled the backboard and drew a couple of "oohs" from some spectators.

ANNOYING: That's one, clowns!

STORYTELLER: Inyaface unleashed a torrent of curse words and shoved Kai'Ro.

INYAFACE: You gonna claw me like some kinda girl?

FAST TALK: Girl? You the one whinin' like a baby. Shut up! Er'body here saw that was a clean steal! Play some ball and shut ya mouth!

STORYTELLER: Punisher recovered the ball and inbounded to Crossova. Annoying was all over him like a chihuahua yipping at a mailman's ankles. Punisher tried to dribble around him but Annoying was everywhere. Then Brick came up and blindsided him with a violent moving pick. Annoying went sprawling onto the concrete. Fast Talk switched over to help but Brick spun and cleared him out of the way with his shoulder. Crossova flicked the ball back to a wide-open Punisher, who drained an easy trey.

INYAFACE: Two to one, clowns!

DOULOS: We playin' basketball or football? Just wonderin'.

STORYTELLER: The entire Lost Boys squad laughed and jogged slowly back down the court.

DOULOS: Man, I ain't feelin' those dudes . . .

STORYTELLER: Kai'Ro placed his hand on his teammate's shoulder.

KAI'RO: Chill out, dawg. Just keep playin'.

STORYTELLER: Kai'Ro helped Annoying off the pavement. The wind got knocked out of him and he was having a hard time regaining his breath. Motor Mouth inbounded the ball to Doulos who tore down the court. He dribbled once between his legs, made a head fake and then rifled a pass to Kai'Ro who was cutting down the lane.

Kai'Ro went airborne from underneath Brick's outstretched arms and put up a beautiful reverse layup that kissed the backboard and rolled around the rim and into the net. As he came down, Brick laid into him with his shoulder. Kai'Ro landed awkwardly and fell backwards into the thick rusted metal pole, banging his head. He winced in pain and rubbed the back of his head. Glaring at Brick for a moment, he jogged back on defense.

KAI'RO: That's deuces.

STORYTELLER: Punisher slapped Brick in the chest and cursed at him.

PUNISHER: C'mon, dawg! You gonna let him score like that?

STORYTELLER: At this point, a small entourage of spectators and next-game hopefuls had gathered outside the fences to watch. The Lost Boys brought the ball to half court. Kai'Ro and his squad were playing tenacious defense. Fast Talk came down with a rebound from a missed shot by Crossova. He fired a pass to a streaking Doulos, who broke free from the pack.

Instead of rolling in for an easy layup, Doulos pulled up at the top of the three-point line and fired up a trey. The ball rimmed out and into the hands of Motor Mouth. Brick was on top of him in a hurry and tried to strip the ball free. But before he could do so, Motor Mouth fired off a pass to Annoying, who was wide open at the top of the key. He squared up and fired off a trey that fell cleanly through the chains.

ANNOYING: Yeah! That's what's up! That's four to two! C'mon. If y'all gonna leave me open like that, I'll rain treys down on ya all day long.

STORYTELLER: The Lost Boys were visibly angry. As they brought the ball down the court, Brick cleared a lane for Inyaface like a runaway semi through a parking lot full of Smart cars. Inyaface raised up for a one-handed dunk, but Kai'Ro poked the ball loose to Doulos. Inyaface came down and took a wild swing at Kai'Ro, but Kai'Ro was already tearing down court. Punisher made a desperate grab at Doulos that caught him upside the head. Doulos spun with one hand over his burning eye. With his other hand, he tossed a bounce pass to Fast Talk. Fast Talk fired a pass to Motor Mouth who drove home another savage dunk from the baseline. Annoying jumped in the air and pumped his fist.

ANNOYING: Ooh! Yeah, dawg...nice pass! It's gettin' nasty out here, y'all! Real nasty. That's five to two. We half way there to sendin' these Lost Boys packin'!

STORYTELLER: Doulos was livid. He was squinting badly and rubbing his eye with his fingers. He ran up to Punisher and shoved him. Punisher spun quickly on his feet and took a swing. Doulos ducked and took a swing of his own but Kai'Ro was there to intercept it with his forearm. He wrapped his arms around Doulos and dragged him backwards.

KAI'RO: Hey! Chill! Chill!

DOULOS: Man! Get ya hands off me! That's the second time he's done that to me, dawg! He's tryin' to claw my eyes out.

STORYTELLER: Annoying, Fast Talk and Motor Mouth stepped in between Kai'Ro, Doulos and the Lost Boys. Kai'Ro shoved Doulos up against the fence and held him there.

KAI'RO: Look! We can beat these dudes. But if you start playin' their dirty game, then no one's a winner! Ya feel me? If we gonna win this thing, then we're gonna win by puttin' eleven on the scoreboard.

STORYTELLER: Doulos continued to glare at Punisher who was smirking at him from a few feet away.

INYAFACE: Hey, Gay-Ro! You got ya girlfriend under control so we can finish this thing?

KAI'RO: (to Doulos) So, we cool? You ready to finish this thing?

DOULOS: (still salty) Yeah...we cool.

STORYTELLER: The Lost Boys huddled together at mid-court for a minute. I saw Punisher look up from the circle and steal a quick glance at Kai'Ro before ducking back. When play resumed, Inyaface took the ball up to the top of the key. Kai'Ro checked him again. There was a lot of jostling and cursing in the paint as Brick and Motor Mouth wrestled for position. Annoying continued to hound Punisher and chase him no matter where he ran on the court. Fast Talk and Crossova exchanged some shoves as they fought through the traffic.

Profane set a pick on Kai'Ro for Inyaface. Kai'Ro fought around it, but Inyaface had a step on him. Inyaface blew past Fast Talk and attacked the rim like he was on a mission. Kai'Ro came up behind him attempting to tip away the shot. When he did so, Punisher undercut him. Inyaface threw in an easy layup as Kai'Ro went crashing to the ground. Punisher raced by Kai'Ro, as he lay on the ground holding his left ankle.

PUNISHER: Gotcha, dude!

STORYTELLER: Doulos ran up to Kai'Ro and helped him to his feet.

DOULOS: You ah'ight, homie?

STORYTELLER: Kai'Ro closed his eyes and clenched his teeth, as he held his ankle.

FAST TALK: Is it broken? Sprained?

KAI'RO: Dunno. It hurts bad...

MOTOR MOUTH: Those clowns did that same thing to Dr. Trey like two weeks ago. Last I saw him, he was hobblin' around on crutches.

DOULOS: You gotta be careful if you go airborne, dawg. Punisher or Brick will clip you almost every time.

KAI'RO: I see.

ANNOYING: Man, forget this! If they wanna start that kinda mess, I can play that game. I'd love to put Punisher's leg in a cast for a minute.

KAI'RO: Nah. We ain't playin' that way.

DOULOS: What's wrong wit you, dawg? It's eye for an eye out here, if you wanna survive these courts. They're gonna keep beatin' you down if you don't fight back. Trust me. I been playin' with these cats for years.

KAI'RO: That's not how we're gonna win today. That's not how the King would want us to finish this thing.

FAST TALK: Who's the King? He ya coach or somethin'?

KAI'RO: Yeah, in a way. Let's finish this game.

DOULOS: You good?

KAI'RO: Fo sho! I'm good! Let's finish what we started.

STORYTELLER: Kai'Ro got back on his feet. Wincing a little, he applied pressure on his left leg. At the same time, he looked towards Heaven and whispered to himself.

KAI'RO: Ima need some help. Just give me a little more strength to finish this game, please. I want You to show out here today...not me...You!

STORYTELLER: Annoying brought the ball up the court. He faked left and then drove right. He was too quick for Punisher. He cut back into the middle of the paint and jumped as if he was going to take a jumper, but then he passed a dart to Fast Talker in the corner. Fast Talker head-faked Crossova into the air and dribbled to his left before draining a trey that crashed through the chains.

ANNOYING: Seven to three, baby! Oh, it's on! It's on now!

STORYTELLER: The Lost Boys moved quickly down the court on the attack. Profane worked the ball in to Brick. With two dribbles, he spun surprisingly fast for a big man and threw down a powerful dunk on Motor Mouth's head. Brick yelled at the top of his lungs and unleashed a flurry of profanity over his shoulder, as he jogged back down the court.

MOTOR MOUTH: Y'all are gonna have to give me some help with King Kong!

STORYTELLER: Doulos brought the ball up court. Profane was on him tight. He was snarling and cursing and taking swipes at the ball. Kai'Ro faked a jab into the paint but then shot back out behind the arc. Doulos hit him with a pass. Inyaface slashed his hand at the ball and hit Kai'Ro's forearm. The ball was jostled loose for a moment. Kai'Ro raced after it, but Crossova got there first and was loose on the break.

Annoying backpedaled as quickly as possible and forced Crossova to give up the ball to Punisher. Punisher leapt high into the air and threw down a violent dunk. But as he tried to hang on the rim to add to his highlight, his grip slipped and he fell down on his back. With a grimace, he rolled over on his side and placed both of his hands on his tailbone. Kai'Ro was the first one to his rescue and got down on one knee.

KAI'RO: You ah'ight, dawg?

STORYTELLER: Punisher turned his head and his eyes flashed with surprise as he looked at Kai'Ro.

PUNISHER: Yeah. Yeah. I'm ah'ight.

KAI'RO: C'mon then!

STORYTELLER: Kai'Ro helped Punisher to his feet and slapped him on the back.

KAI'RO: That was a nasty dunk, homie. Real nasty!

STORYTELLER: Punisher looked confused. He hobbled awkwardly down the court and back on defense.

PUNISHER: Appreciate that.

STORYTELLER: Kai'Ro called his teammates in for a quick huddle.

KAI'RO: Look! It's seven to five. We gotta put these boys away.

MOTOR MOUTH: Yo! Why'd you help that goon up? After what he did to you like five minutes ago, you shoulda let him lay there hurtin'.

KAI'RO: That's not how the King plays ball.

ANNOYING: Forget this! Who's this King, homie?

KAI'RO: Let's just finish this thing and I'll tell you all about Him, ah'ight?

STORYTELLER: Doulos brought the ball up court. His team passed the ball around, making the Lost Boys scramble and sweat on defense. Kai'Ro finally drove the lane and faked like he was going to the rim. But then he fired a behind-the-back pass to Doulos, who drained a trey.

KAI'RO: Good shot, dawg! Good shot!

ANNOYING: Oowee! Got em! We got em!

STORYTELLER: The Lost Boys looked like a nest of angry hornets. They were cursing and shouting at one another. The spectators watching the game were beating their palms against the fence and hollering. Kai'Ro looked completely at peace as he crouched down into his defensive stance.

Inyaface dribbled between his legs a few times and then behind his back. He faked a jab step and attempted a few crossovers. It was obvious that he wanted to humiliate Kai'Ro. But Kai'Ro wasn't deceived by any of his moves and stood his ground. Inyaface grew frustrated and attempted to charge past his defender. As he did so, he raised up his arm and drove his elbow into Kai'Ro's face, who fell to the ground holding his mouth. Inyaface raced towards the basket and laid in a shot. Irritated, Kai'Ro spat some blood on the ground and dabbed at his split lip with his T-shirt.

KAI'RO: (to himself) Help me . . . I'm 'bout to lose it, for real!

STORYTELLER: I could see some anger forming in his eyes and could tell that his ability to take this type of abuse on the court was fading. He slapped the ground with his hand and hopped back to his feet. Motor Mouth raced up to Kai'Ro and put his arm around him.

MOTOR MOUTH: I'm gonna set a pick so hard on that lil' dude that his grandkids are gonna be born dizzy.

KAI'RO: Nah. Chill out. Chill out.

STORYTELLER: With the game at nine to six, the Lost Boys became even more violent and dirty. There was a lot of shoving and elbowing. Kai'Ro's teammates looked like they were ready to come unglued and turn the game into an all-out brawl, but Kai'Ro kept encouraging them.

After moving the ball around the arc a few times, Doulos was finally able to fire off a fadeaway jumper and make it game point. The Lost Boys knew that their time was up. They charged down the court with Brick leading the way like a runaway train. Fast Talk got mauled and laid out on the blacktop like a pancake.

Profane had the ball and was bouncing around at the top of the key while Brick cleared players out of the way with his hip and elbows. He fired off a three-pointer that rimmed out into Motor Mouth's hands. Motor Mouth was quick to fire the ball to Kai'Ro before Brick could mug him with a violent foul. Inyaface was up tight on Kai'Ro, snarling and cursing and slashing at the ball.

As soon as Kai'Ro got to the top of the key, he faked hard to his right but then delivered a crossover back to his left with such amazing quickness that Inyaface lost control, buckled and fell to the ground. The eyes of many of the spectators widened and some of them put their hands over their mouths in shock. With Inyaface out of his way, Kai'Ro charged towards the goal. Punisher flailed hopelessly at him as he blew by.

At that point, Kai'Ro raised up with Brick and Profane in his way. They too jumped in the air to block his shot, but it was as if he were a missile that could not be stopped. He continued to rise through the air like a rocket leaving the earth with his elbows bent and the ball cocked behind his head like a weapon of mass destruction. Finally, with a thunderous explosion, he pounded the rock through the rim. He hung on tight and swung as Brick and Profane fell to the ground beneath him like so much wreckage.

Everyone outside the fence was going crazy, jumping and hollering. The Lost Boys looked shocked. Kai'Ro dropped back to the ground as his teammates embraced him, rubbed his head and slapped him on the back.

ANNOYING: I been out here playin' ball since I was knee high and I never...and I mean, *never*...seen nobody throw down a dunk that nasty!

MOTOR MOUTH: Boy, you still knee high! But that dunk was straight ridiculous, bruh.

STORYTELLER: Kai'Ro humbly thanked his teammates. But he was quick to run over to the Lost Boys who were exiting the courts, mumbling and swearing.

FAST TALK: Aye, dawg! Let those clowns go. We beat the brakes off them. This is our court now!

STORYTELLER: Kai'Ro ignored his teammate and ran up to his defeated opponents.

KAI'RO: Aye, y'all. Good game. Good game!

STORYTELLER: Brick turned around, spat on the ground and then walked away. Profane unleashed some vulgarities and kept going. Inyaface and Crossova dismissed him with a wave of their hands and continued walking. Punisher stopped to speak.

PUNISHER: Seems like I remember a Kai'Ro from back in the day...a loud-mouthed, arrogant lil' dude...wouldn't shut his mouth...loved to humiliate people and hurt 'em too.

KAI'RO: (grinning) Yeah, that was me.

PUNISHER: But you nothin' like that dude—not even a little bit.

KAI'RO: The dude you rememberin' used to play for a different squad back in the day. He used to be everything you just said, but that ol' Kai'Ro is dead. He's lyin' in a grave miles outside of town. The one standin' before you is rollin' for a new squad...got a new jersey...a new game...

STORYTELLER: About that time, Kai'Ro's teammates caught up to him and even some of the people watching the game gathered around to listen.

PUNISHER: It's funny 'cause I remember ya game, but I don't remember you. But I don't think I'll forget ya after today.

KAI'RO: Why's that?

PUNISHER: Nobody takes a physical beatin' the way you did out there and just keeps his cool, controls his team, controls the game and dominates. You showed me somethin' today that I ain't never seen before. That's why it's unforgettable. Anyway. I gotta catch up wit my boys. Y'all deserve to hold down this court today. Ya earned it. Oh, and I apologize for hurtin' ya leg. That was dirty. We cool?

KAI'RO: Yeah, homie. We cool. Maybe I'll see ya 'round.

ANNOYING: Y'all done with ya love session? We got to defend this court now.

KAI'RO: Nah, dawg. I'm done. My ankle is tweaked and I gotta get to work.

STORYTELLER: Annoying threw his head back and groaned.

FAST TALK: C'mon, Doulos. You hoopin' wit us, or what?

DOULOS: Nah. I'm done too. I wanna talk to my man here.

MOTOR MOUTH: Well, forget y'all then!

STORYTELLER: Kai'Ro and Doulos left together and headed back in the direction of Mr. Weary's store.

KAI'RO: Why aren't you stayin' to play, dawg? We all worked hard to win that one.

DOULOS: Because I wanna know how you learned to hoop like that?

KAI'RO: My game? What'cha mean? My dribblin'? My shootin'? My—

DOULOS: Nah. I ain't talkin' 'bout all that. Your game is tight, but how'd you learn to play under control like that? I never once heard you curse nobody...never saw you throw a bow or act a fool. I'm lookin' at you now. Your ankle is swolled. You got a split lip, some scratches on your knees and ya wrist. They beat you down and straight mugged you, but you just kept hoopin'. That's what I wanna know about.

KAI'RO: It's kinda a long story.

DOULOS: I got time.

KAI'RO: A few years ago, I was just like every knucklehead in that FIELD OF DREAMS back there. Like them, I was gonna be a rap star or play professional ball. I dropped out of school to chase a dream and didn't realize that you need more than athleticism and the ability to spit rhymes to make it in life. I was arrogant and a stupid thug that could hoop and rap.

That got me some cred on the block. But after a while, I started to look around. I didn't see no NBA scouts callin' my name...no agents tryin' to sign me to a record deal. My dream was turnin' into smoke, dawg. A lot of clowns hang onto that dream a lot longer than I did, but I wised up some. Got in with some dudes that were makin' a name for themselves on the block. Started makin' that paper. It's the same ol' story as a lot of dudes out here. In 'bout a year, I had a rep around town. I was livin' large and my name wasn't somethin' people took lightly. The squad I was rollin' wit was real deep.

DOULOS: So, then what happened?

KAI'RO: My team started gettin' whistled for lane violations and fouls.

DOULOS: What'cha mean?

KAI'RO: You know, I got locked up. Got me a record. Started gettin' in more fights. More scars. More enemies. Saw a coupla dudes on my squad get merked or locked up for good. It was around that time that I started to feel like I might be playin' for the wrong team. It didn't feel like we was doin' a whole lotta winnin'. I mean, the paper was still flowin' in. I was livin' like a king, but I started feelin' like a loser—like a doulos.

DOULOS: Like a *doulos*? I ain't no loser! What'cha tryin' to say?

KAI'RO: Doulos is an ancient word, dawg. It means "slave" or "bond-servant." You didn't know that?

DOULOS: Nah. Not for real.

KAI'RO: Well, yeah, I started feelin' like a slave to my pleasures. The hustlin', the liquor, the girls and the game. I thought I was controllin' those things, but actually they was controllin' me. I was a slave to my pleasures and my appetites. Those things mastered my time, my thoughts and my worship. I wasn't free at all though you'd say I was livin' like a free man.

My love for those things wound me up in the END OF THE ROAD JAIL. And you prob'ly heard what it's like up in that joint. It's about as close to bein' dead as a brotha can get. It was 'round that time, I started groanin' inside for freedom. Yeah, I wanted freedom from that jail, but somethin' inside my soul wanted to get loose. I wanted that more than anything.

STORYTELLER: Doulos stroked his chin with his hand and listened intently to Kai'Ro.

KAI'RO: My girl visited me a few times but outside of that nobody came. You start to see who ya real friends are when the drama goes down. Er'body scatters to the wind when stuff gets ugly.

DOULOS: That's real talk.

KAI'RO: So I got lonely, dawg. Started feelin' like givin' up on life. I was locked up like an animal and my soul was locked up too. But somebody musta been prayin' for me 'cause Preacher started comin' to see me. At first, I didn't wanna hear his noise, but he was speakin' words of Life and givin' me hope, homie. I mean, I felt my soul twistin' inside of me every time he started talkin'. He explained my situation to me and told me that I wasn't locked up 'cause I made some mistakes—but 'cause my entire life was a mistake.

DOULOS: That's harsh, dawg.

KAI'RO: Picture it this way. If life is a game of basketball, imagine gettin' whistles for travelin' and double-dribblin' every single time you touched the ball.

DOULOS: That would be whack.

KAI'RO: But see, that's our life outside of the King.

DOULOS: Yeah. You mentioned Him before.

KAI'RO: Preacher told me that the King made all of us for a purpose. But most of us have rejected that and have chosen to follow our own purposes. Those purposes are all fouls and lane violations. Every single one of our decisions and actions causes the whistle to blow. Every pass we try to make is a turnover. Every time we try to make a move, we get whistled for travelin'. Every shot that we score is against ourselves.

As sinners, it's like we're suited up in the wrong jersey and we're playin' ball *against* the King instead of *for* Him—the way we were designed. The problem is that His squad is unbeatable. Not only is He an opponent who can't lose, but He's also the Ref with the biggest whistle. And one day, He's gonna blow the whistle on this City of Doom and smash it for good. He's gonna smash it to hell!

DOULOS: Man! So where's the hope you was talkin' 'bout?

KAI'RO: Well, before the King blows that final whistle, He's made an offer based on somethin' He did a long time ago. See the Rule Book says that 'cause we're sinners we gotta die. There ain't no way 'round that. In fact, the Rule Book actually says we gotta go to hell. But the King decided that, instead of smashin' us, He'd allow Himself to get smashed in our place. So He came to this fallen world, took one of the most savage beatings a man could take and then was straight murdered for you and me. Only His death could satisfy that rule. Only His death could set you and me free.

DOULOS: Well, I'm grateful to that dead King. I'd rather He die than me.

KAI'RO: (smiling) But He ain't dead, dawg. He rose again and defeated death itself. See, Preacher explained some important things to me when I was in jail. One, you gotta admit that you're a sinner who deserves hell. That's the startin' point. If you can't admit that, then He'll never come close to extendin' His grace to you. And you won't really begin to understand what He did for ya. So, first ya gotta accept Him as Savior. But ya also gotta declare Him ya Lord. This is when ya become a new kinda "doulos."

DOULOS: What'cha mean?

KAI'RO: I'll get to that in a sec. You'll run into a lot of cats here and there that have heard of the King. And they're cool wit Him bein' their Savior. I mean, who wants to go to hell, right? But not as many people are cool wit Him bein' their Lord. They don't want a new master. They wanna get free from hell, but they still kinda enjoy all the fouls they were committin'. There's a part of them that still wants to be a slave to the old masters—pleasure, power, girls and stuff.

But see, if you wanna know freedom, my man, you gotta get a new Master. The King of kings. You allow Him to start callin' the shots, to start changin' your appetites and desires. And when you do, He teaches you how to dribble the ball without gettin' called for travelin'. He'll show you how to pass and make an assist to someone in need. You learn how to score points for His Kingdom—points that'll last for eternity. He gives you a new jersey and you become a part of a whole new squad.

That's the story behind my game, dawg. I play for the King now and no longer for myself. And the King plays through me. I'm a "doulos"—a servant to the King!

STORYTELLER: The two of them walked all the way to Mr. Weary's shop. Doulos stood at the door, scratching his head and squinting in the noonday sun.

DOULOS: Dawg, that's some of the realest stuff I've ever heard in my life. The stuff you been sayin' to me, my heart is soakin' up like a sponge. Ya think I could hang wit ya some and learn some more?

STORYTELLER: Kai'Ro smiled a big smile and put his hand on Doulos's shoulder.

KAI'RO: Meet me back here Wednesday at ten.

FIRE AND WEEDS

13

STORYTELLER: In my dream, I saw Evangeline. She was sitting on the edge of the bed, reading her Bible. It was early and the morning mist was still hovering around the cottage like a low-lying cloud. Mama Wisdom knocked gently at her door.

MAMA WISDOM: (slowly opening the door) Good morning, child. I hope you slept well.

EVANGELINE: (smiling) I slept great.

MAMA WISDOM: Spending some time with the King this morning?

EVANGELINE: (looking at her Bible) Yes. I'm tryin' to do that more often. Tryin' to see what He says in these Letters.

MAMA WISDOM: That's good. The more time you spend with Him each day, the more He will speak to you. He'll guide you and show up within you. Papa Fix-It has whipped up some grits and one of his famous omelets. Let's eat breakfast and get you on your way.

STORYTELLER: The three sat down and ate together. Afterward, Evangeline grabbed her bag and gave each of them a long hug.

EVANGELINE: Thanks, y'all, for takin' me in last night and for everything you said too. I've never met two nicer people.

PAPA FIX-IT: And we've never seen a more joyful smile.

MAMA WISDOM: Be careful on the road ahead. You are much nearer to the Mountain of the Cross than you realize. We've been praying for you this morning and we'll continue to do so. There may still be some dangers and some people who will try to drag you off the path.

EVANGELINE: I'll be careful. And thank you again.

STORYTELLER: Evangeline gave each of them one more hug and then set out on her way down the Heavenly Highway. It was a gorgeous morning. Birds chirped in the trees surrounding the path. Feeling at ease, Evangeline hummed to herself as she continued on her journey.

After a short time, she came to a beautiful field of bright pink and white flowers. I had never seen anything like it. The brilliant flowers were nearly waist high and their petals were large and radiant. Big lazy bees buzzed around and butterflies flitted through the air. Clearly, Evangeline couldn't resist stopping to admire the beauty of nature around her. So she stepped off of the Heavenly Highway and out into the field.

At a closer look, I noticed that certain parts of the field were dead and scorched. Other parts were overgrown with ugly thorny-looking weeds. Evangeline looked puzzled. She became even more perplexed once she spotted a young woman standing in the middle of the field. Just about Evangeline's age, the young lady was dressed in a dark miniskirt with a charcoal-colored hoodie. She wore large hoop earrings and white Chucks. Her eyelids were covered with thick eyeshadow and her lips were crimson red.

Like a scarecrow in the middle of a cornfield, she was standing motionless. Only her eyes moved about as though she was searching for someone. Then, without warning, the young woman came towards Evangeline with unusual swiftness. Evangeline looked alarmed but stood still, unsure of what she was to do.

EVANGELINE: Backstabber, is that you?

BACKSTABBER: Evangeline? Why are you way out here?

EVANGELINE: I could ask you the same thing.

BACKSTABBER: I just like it out here, girl. It's my kinda place.

EVANGELINE: It is beautiful and peaceful. I thought I'd stop and enjoy it for a minute before I headed to the Mountain of the Cross.

BACKSTABBER: So, it's really true?

EVANGELINE: What is?

BACKSTABBER: When I ran into Mess and Drama back in the City of Doom, they told me that you was headin' out here to that lil' Mountain of the Cross. Everybody is laughin' 'bout it, sayin' you and ya boy, Kai'Ro, are both crazy now.

EVANGELINE: Everybody? How does *everybody* know?

STORYTELLER: Backstabber shrugged.

EVANGELINE: I haven't been gone that long.

BACKSTABBER: Guess news travels fast. Speakin' of news, did you hear about Hurting?

EVANGELINE: No, what?

BACKSTABBER: She and I was talkin' a few days ago... and she told me to tell nobody... but she's been sleepin' 'round and now she's got an STD. Can you believe it?

STORYTELLER: When she said that, a small spark shot out of Backstabber's mouth and landed on Evangeline's collar. With a little tuft of smoke, it burned a hole all the way through the fabric.

EVANGELINE: No way! Who's she been sleepin' with?

BACKSTABBER: A bunch of boys. Hurting is trash, girl. You knew that!

STORYTELLER: As Backstabber continued to speak, a series of sparks shot from her mouth and started to drift on the breeze until they fell into the flowers. With a hideous sizzle, they burned through the petals and landed on the ground below. I also noticed some small weeds growing out of the ground at Evangeline's feet. Like tiny snakes, they coiled around her shoes. For some reason, Evangeline didn't seem to notice these strange things.

EVANGELINE: No! I had no idea that Hurting was like that.

BACKSTABBER: She ain't the only tramp either. Shoot girl, you heard what people sayin' about you too? Now that you knocked up, everybody's callin' you a slut.

STORYTELLER: As she turned her gossip to another young lady's business, more clouds of sparks blasted from Backstabber's mouth. The weeds at Evangeline's feet grew higher and stronger.

EVANGELINE: (angrily) Like who? Who's *everybody*?

BACKSTABBER: (smiling) Huh? Oh, I heard ya girl Mess say it. Fast Girl said somethin' 'bout you bein' a tramp...um...I know I heard some other people say it too. But—

STORYTELLER: Evangeline was visibly shaking. The sparks from Backstabber's mouth had now created flames. The beautiful flowers surrounding them had become stalks of fire. The weeds around Evangeline's feet were growing quickly up her knees and thighs.

EVANGELINE: My girl Mess said whaaat? Oooooooh! Next time I see her, I'm gonna slap the taste out her mouth, for real!

BACKSTABBER: (grinning from ear to ear) I know, right!

STORYTELLER: Just then, a yellow butterfly glided carefully around the rising flames that were close to engulfing them. It landed gently on Evangeline's shoulder and one of its wings softly flitted against her cheek. As soon as it did so, I watched her countenance soften and change. She sniffed once then twice as the smoke swirled around them. Finally, she spotted the flames and let out a small scream. When she tried to move, her legs were fully entangled in the strong weeds. Backstabber looked completely oblivious to the danger all around them.

EVANGELINE: Ugh! This gossip you're spreadin' is gonna kill us!

BACKSTABBER: (laughing) It's just harmless talk, girl. Why ya stressin'?

STORYTELLER: The flames were now a frightening wall around them and circling in tighter and tighter. Evangeline started to panic.

EVANGELINE: King! Help me! I'm sorry for listenin' to these lies and this mess. Help me before I burn!

STORYTELLER: As she cried out, one of the weeds around her leg grew yellow and brittle and suddenly snapped. She was able to free that leg. With desperate hands, she pried and tore at the other weed until both legs were freed. Still, the wall of fire was all around them and there was nowhere to run. Evangeline moved quickly back and forth looking for an escape like a kitten surrounded by angry dogs.

At last, the wind shifted slightly and created a temporary opening. Evangeline grabbed Backstabber's hand and yanked her to safety. They both fell crashing into the flowers. Gasping, Evangeline rolled over onto her back and heaved in big gulps of air. Backstabber jumped to her feet and brushed the dirt from her arms and legs.

BACKSTABBER: (angrily) What's your problem, girl? Folks are right when they say you crazy! I tried to defend you, but now I know they right, and I'm gonna let everyone know 'bout you. You crazy little tramp!

EVANGELINE: You mean, you didn't see the fire and the weeds and all that? We could've died!

BACKSTABBER: We was just talkin'. Catchin' up! How is talk gonna kill somebody? You lost ya mind!

STORYTELLER: Backstabber stomped off in a great huff. As she went, a cloud of sparks continued to rush from her mouth and fall around her. But I could no longer hear what she said.

EVANGELINE: (to herself) Who knew that talk could be so dangerous? I saw fire around me, but I felt it inside me too. When that girl was talkin' and tellin' me all that mess, I wanted to bring pain to everyone she was talkin' 'bout. Until she turned it on me, it felt good to stand there and just listen to those hurtful words. Strange how the weeds came out of nowhere and just held me there. That beautiful field is evil. It draws you in but then it won't let you go.

STORYTELLER: Slowly, she got to her feet and dusted herself off. Backstabber was a distant shadow on the horizon, heading back towards the City of Doom. Evangeline looked up and saw an old sign that was overgrown with those awful weeds. It read: GOSSIP GARDEN.

EVANGELINE: (shaking her head) No wonder Backstabber likes this place. King, thank You for showing me that little words can cause a big fire. I'm sorry for listenin' to such ugly words, and I'm sorry for the fires I've created with my own tongue. Please help me to hunger for Your words and to tune out the kind of words that caused that fire.

STORYTELLER: Evangeline got back onto the Heavenly Highway and picked up her pace. Very grateful for being rescued, she headed off in the right direction.

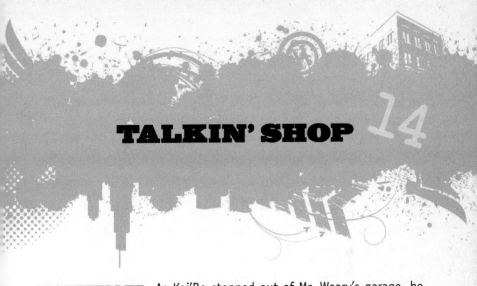

TALKIN' SHOP 14

STORYTELLER: As Kai'Ro stepped out of Mr. Weary's garage, he stretched his arms and yawned. It was morning and the sun was peeking through the smoggy brown skies. Kai'Ro placed a NY fitted on his head, cocked it slightly to the side and started walking down the block. After a short while, he made it to the parking lot of Mr. Weary's store. Doulos was standing on the sidewalk, munching on a Pop-tart.

KAI'RO: W'sup, homie?

DOULOS: Not much, dawg. Chillin'.

KAI'RO: Cool. So, you just wanna hang or what?

DOULOS: Dunno. I thought maybe we could talk some more or somethin'.

KAI'RO: Well, I gotta go get my hair cut. I'm 'bout to walk over to Close Shave.

STORYTELLER: The two friends headed down the sidewalk.

DOULOS: So, I got some questions.

KAI'RO: Shoot.

DOULOS: This King. You talk to Him?

KAI'RO: Every day.

DOULOS: How? I mean, where is He? Can you talk to Him like you're talkin' to me right now? Does He talk back? What's He say when He speaks?

KAI'RO: (laughing) Whoa! Dude. Chill. When the King rose from the dead, He left this world and returned to His home—to the City of Light. But He didn't abandon us. He left His Spirit to guide and to aid His followers. And not only that, He tells us that He lives within us—once we give our lives to Him.

DOULOS: So, He's in a city somewhere...and He's in you...I don't get it. Which one is it?

KAI'RO: It's both. He's not like you and me in the sense that His body can *only* be in *only* one place at a time. He's everywhere at once, dawg. His City of Light touches this earth every day. In fact, the King wants our fallen and broken world to look a whole lot more like His City. Every now and then, you catch glimpses of His City showin' up on earth.

DOULOS: How?

KAI'RO: In the little and great miracles that are all around us. When you see two enemies lay down their guns. Watchin' an addict break free from the drugs. Seein' a man marry his girl, take care of her, protect her and raise their family. Gettin' to see people back on their front patios again, sittin' in rockin' chairs, laughin', playin' games and watchin' kids runnin' in the yard.

Basically, whenever you see the peace of the City of Light bringin' goodness and change to our City of Doom. That's when you start to see daily miracles. But, like I said, if you give your life to the King then He's inside of you too. You'll start to see these daily miracles in your own life. Old habits startin' to die. Old appetites for crime, hate, violence and pleasure startin' to dry up and bein' replaced with a hunger for compassion, intimacy, unity, love and generosity.

This is when you know the King and His Spirit is startin' to change you. He makes our bodies His temple, His literal dwellin' place. That's why He tells us that our bodies are not our own, they were purchased with a price. The price was His death on the Cross for our sins. When we accept the free gift of His salvation, we also give Him our body in return.

DOULOS: So, how do you talk then?

KAI'RO: Well, the King listens to us, homie. I start every day with a prayer. I literally sit on the edge of my bed or even sometimes get down on my knees and just talk to my King. I worship Him and tell Him how great and how glorious He is. Then I ask Him to forgive me for my sins. Sure. He paid for the debt of my sins, but I'm still a sinner. I still mess up and hurt people and hurt myself.

I pray prayers of thanksgiving to the King too. That shows Him gratitude for wakin' me up, for puttin' a roof over my head, for puttin' food in the fridge and clothes on my back. Those are simple things, but there's a lot of cats who got none of 'em. So I close out by prayin' for other people.

DOULOS: Like what?

KAI'RO: Like prayin' for their needs, their fears, their pains. I pray that the King would rescue those who despise Him or just don't know 'bout Him. I pray for myself that I'd start to look and behave and think more like the King every single day. The ol' Kai'Ro needs to keep dyin' and the new Kai'Ro—the King's Kai'Ro—needs to grow more every day.

STORYTELLER: Doulos seemed especially interested. The look on his face was that of a child who just received some great news or a cool gift.

DOULOS: And He talks to you. Like, can you hear Him sayin' stuff to ya?

KAIRO: Hmmm...yeah, in a way. Sometimes He says stuff real clearly to me through His Spirit. There's been times where I'm 'bout to make a decision and I feel the Spirit grabbin' my mind or my conscience and pullin' me in a different direction.

DOULOS: What'cha mean?

KAIRO: Well, like at the game a few days ago. When those Lost Boys were beatin' me down, I had some moments when I wanted to cuss 'em out or throw a bow just to show 'em that I wasn't no clown. I almost got to fightin' with Punisher and every inch of me wanted to hurt Inyaface. But the Spirit kept calmin' me and remindin' me that I used to be like those dudes—angry and lost. He also reminded me that I needed to show the King to those boys. In that particular moment, showin' them the King meant showin' them my willingness to be meek and not vengeful.

DOULOS: Meek? Meek sounds weak, dawg.

KAIRO: Yeah it does, but meekness is really just "power under control." As the King's follower, you learn that any power or gifts that you have were given to you to glorify the King and to point people to Him. When we see our gifts as powers and things to benefit ourselves or to make ourselves look better, then we usually end up hurtin' someone or we just end up fallin' flat on our faces.

It's funny 'cause the King usually shows up largest in our weaknesses. But what I'm really sayin' is that I think the King called me to play ball hard and to do everything I could to win. But I needed to do it *His way* and not their way. They wanted to play loud and violent. I chose to play hard but humble and under control. I think that's how the King woulda hooped. He'd straight dunk on ya, don't get me wrong. But He'd somehow make ya feel good 'bout it in the process.

(laughing). All that chest thumpin' and f-bombin' mess that you see on the playground? Nah. You wouldn't see that out of the King. That kinda behavior is for clowns who think they somethin' but they really ain't.

DOULOS: So, is that the only way He speaks?

KAI'RO: No. He mainly speaks to me through this.

STORYTELLER: Kai'Ro pulled out his Bible from his back pocket and handed it to Doulos.

DOULOS: (flipping through it) Man, dude! This Book is lookin' raggedy. Pages creased and look at all ya notes and scribblins' and stuff.

KAI'RO: I got my nose in that Book daily, dawg. It's the King's Letters.

DOULOS: Letters?

KAI'RO: Yeah. The King inspired the words on those pages. By His Spirit, He spoke to the authors what He wanted them to write down. In those pages there's history. The history of the King's faithfulness to His people. There's poetry where the authors share their hearts, their pain, their frustrations, but also their love for the King. You gotta lot of teachin' in there too. The King's Letters teach ya how to follow Him, how to discipline ya mind, how to treat other people and how to look more like Him with whatcha do.

DOULOS: Wow! That's a lot of information, bruh.

KAI'RO: Yeah, but the King also opens up His heart to us in this Book and fills the pages with His love for us. Some dudes call the Book the "King's Love Letters" because of all the language in there 'bout His love for us. In a lot of ways that's true, but the King doesn't just want us to understand how much He loves us. That's part of it. He also wants us to take that same kinda love and unleash it on everybody we run into.

STORYTELLER: Doulos scratched his head and exhaled a big breath.

KAI'RO: What'cha thinkin'?

DOULOS: I'm just kinda confused in a way. I mean, when I look at you—I see me. I mean, we dress the same. We both like to hoop. But then, even though we look the same, we ain't the same. You don't talk like me, for real. When I look in ya eyes, I see some kinda peace that I just know I don't have. So when I look at ya, it's kinda like lookin' into a mirror and recognizin' the reflection lookin' back at me, but not the man inside. I've never, ever met nobody like you. I'm startin' to wonder if you from a different planet.

STORYTELLER: Kai'Ro burst out laughing and put a hand on Doulos's shoulder.

KAI'RO: Hey. I feel what ya sayin', playa. But I'm not from a different planet. I'm from right here in the City of Doom, and I've still gotta real sinful side just like everybody else. The difference is that my soul is brand new. My hunger for this world is dyin' more each day. I gotta desire to be with my King *now*.

When I read the King's Letters, I agree with Brother Paul. I like to put it this way, "To live is for the King, but to die is gain!" That's how I feel. When I wake up, it's time to go hard for the King. But if He decided to take me home to be with Him today, I'll be honest, I'd be so excited. Let me put it like this. I feel the urge to participate with my King in bringin' the City of Light to this City of Doom. He's called me to do this and so I'm here in obedience to His calling.

Like I said, every part of me is actually longin' for the day when He calls me out of this City of Doom to join Him in His City of Light. So I ain't from a different planet. Nah, but I'm longin' to live wit Him in a different world. Ya feel me?

DOULOS: (smiling faintly) Sounds cool, but it sounds crazy. I'm not gonna lie. So, real talk, what gives you this hunger to obey the King and one day to follow Him to His City?

KAI'RO: Like I said, after what He did on the Cross for me and my sin, I feel real driven and grateful to follow after Him and serve Him. But that ain't all. I'm startin' to understand more and more each day that I was built for the King's purposes and the King's glory.

DOULOS: Can you break that down for me? I mean, I understand some of what you said about usin' ya gifts. But what'cha mean, you was *built* to serve Him?

STORYTELLER: Kai'Ro stopped for a minute and looked around. Then his eyes widened.

KAI'RO: See that car across the street with the flat tire?

DOULOS: Yeah. What 'bout it?

STORYTELLER: Kai'Ro pulled a pencil out of his pocket and handed it to Doulos.

KAI'RO: Ah'ight. Here, take this pencil and go jack that car off the ground so we can change the tire.

STORYTELLER: Doulos wrinkled his forehead and smirked.

DOULOS: Nah, playa. That'd be stupid!

KAI'RO: Why?

DOULOS: This pencil ain't strong 'nough to lift no car up. It'd break right in half.

KAI'RO: Why isn't it strong 'nough?

DOULOS: 'Cause it's made out of wood, and it ain't designed to lift up heavy stuff.

STORYTELLER: Kai'Ro's eyes flashed and he raised his eyebrows.

KAI'RO: So, you're sayin' this pencil ain't made to help change tires?

DOULOS: No. C'mon, dawg, a pencil is made to write stuff down and then erase it if ya have to.

KAI'RO: You just answered your own question, homie.

DOULOS: Huh?

KAI'RO: You just said that a pencil wasn't designed to lift up cars. And if you tried to use it for that purpose, it would break. Then you said that a pencil was designed to write stuff down and erase when necessary. Right?

STORYTELLER: Doulos nodded.

KAI'RO: It's the same with us, dawg! The King made us just like He made that pencil. He made us for a purpose. We was designed to give Him glory and to participate with Him in bringin' His Good News to this fallen world. When we operate outside of our design and start doin' other things, we—

DOULOS: We break.

KAI'RO: Exactly! That's my life's story. I spent almost my whole life tryna operate outside of my design, tryna do things I wasn't built to do. You can put it any way ya want. I used my hands for hustlin' and hurtin' people instead of for helpin'. Used the mind the King gave me to create schemes to rob and hurt folks instead of how to make my community a livable place.

Over time, my life was gettin' stressed...it started crackin' and splinterin'. I woulda told ya then that I could hold things together and all that, but it woulda been a lie. Deep inside, I just knew that I was 'bout to break, for real.

DOULOS: I think I'm startin' to see.

KAI'RO: Once I started rollin' for the King, it was like I gave the pencil of my life back to Him. It's like I literally put myself in His hands so He could use me however He wanted. What I found out was, He wanted to use my life to keep writin' the story He was busy writin'.

DOULOS: Story?

KAI'RO: Yeah. The ongoing story of how He's gonna make this ugly, fallen and battered world whole and beautiful again. Bruh, I tell ya, when He started usin' me that way, I never felt more alive. Like I had a purpose and a real reason to wake up every mornin'. The stressed and broken feelin's in my soul were gone and I felt at peace for the first time in my life.

STORYTELLER: As Kai'Ro finished speaking, the two young men walked up to Close Shave.

DOULOS: Ya know, dawg. You've given me like a feast of ideas that I gotta chew on. But I think everything ya sayin' is true. I feel like I've spent my whole life stuck down in a hole, but I didn't know it. Not only have you showed me that I'm in a dark hole, but you've tossed me a light and a rope and ya slowly pullin' me out. A lotta folks need to hear this. I mean, they really need to hear this.

STORYTELLER: Doulos stared off for a moment. Then a big smile started to cross his face.

DOULOS: Dawg! I got it! But I gotta know somethin' first. Can you rap?

STORYTELLER: Kai'Ro grinned.

KAI'RO: I can spit better than I hoop. Why?

DOULOS: There's a big ol' rap battle off of MT. CARMEL COURT in 'bout a week. Shoot! Er'body's gonna be out there. It's a bunch of Doc Destruction's boys on that stage. You got Doc's right-hand man, King Ca$h . . . that pretty boy, Young Sleazy, Lil' Pain and maybe some other cats. It's a chance for the whole City of Doom to hear what this King's put on ya heart. But it ain't gonna be easy. Every one of Doc's dudes can straight flow. They may murder you on that stage.

KAI'RO: (chuckling) Or, they may just straight murder *me*.

DOULOS: Yeah, you right. It's pro'bly a bad idea.

STORYTELLER: Kai'Ro looked at his new friend.

KAI'RO: No, Doulos. This might be just what the King wants.

THE HOUSE OF MIRRORS

15

STORYTELLER: After Evangeline left GOSSIP GARDEN, she was able to pick up her pace on the Heavenly Highway. The sun rose quickly behind her, casting her long shadow down the road. It was a cloudless day and grew quite hot. Evangeline held her Bible in one hand as she tried to read from it while she walked along. This went on for some time until the heat from the sun grew so intense that she was forced to hold the Bible over her head to provide some shade.

Within a short period of time, Evangeline spotted a city in front of her. Looking up, she saw the city flag snapping in the wind. It seemed strange to her that on the flag was a picture of three large birds gobbling up seeds from the ground. An attractive looking billboard on the side of the road also caught her eye, as she read: WELCOME TO BIRDVILLE: HOME OF TRUE SIGHT.

Evangeline paused and stared at the black and yellow flag and the fancy billboard with an inquisitive look on her face. I watched her as she studied the city and its surroundings. Suddenly, her eyes widened and a great smile spread across her face. Just beyond the City of Birdville was a small mountain and, at the top of the mountain—there stood the Cross.

EVANGELINE: There it is! That's where Kai'Ro lost his burden ... and it's where I'm goin' to get rid of my doggone burden too! But why is this city here? What's *it* all about?

STORYTELLER: Evangeline was dismayed to see a long, tall wall stretching for miles in either direction. Clearly, the only way to the Mountain of the Cross was through the city itself. A bit hesitant to move forward, she looked directly to her left and saw a thick patch of woods that ran along the Highway up to the wall beside the city. From the tops of the trees, I spotted a small plume of smoke rising in the air.

EVANGELINE: (thinking out loud) If this city is right at the foot of the Cross, it can't be so bad. It's hot out here anyway. I can get me somethin' to drink before I make that climb up the Mountain. Maybe somebody can even help me find the best way to reach the top.

STORYTELLER: As Evangeline was talking to herself, I noticed a man with strange glasses walking towards her from the city. Behind him were four armed men who looked like police officers. They too were wearing the strange glasses. Then I saw a tall and slender woman just on the edge of the woods. Shrouded in a dark cloak, she called to Evangeline in a shrill whisper.

PERSPECTIVE: Child, you are in great danger here. Come to me quickly before they are able to speak with you.

STORYTELLER: Evangeline turned to face the woman in the woods. Perspective's face was almost completely covered by her hood. Evangeline looked frightened as she glanced at her and then back to the men who were quickly approaching.

PERSPECTIVE: My child, time is of the essence. If you do not come to me now, I can do nothing to help you.

STORYTELLER: Evangeline noticed one of the men unfasten some cuffs from his belt. Another one of the guards had his hand resting on the handle of his baton. She turned to the woods again, but the woman was quickly fading back into the trees. After an instant of hesitation, Evangeline sprang off the road and plunged into the trees. As she did so, the men swiftly crossed the Highway and leapt into the woods as well.

The trees were extremely thick and dark. Moving like a shadow just a few paces in front of Evangeline was the mysterious woman. Evangeline raced after her as fast as she could. The men were right behind Evangeline, calling to her to turn around before she was bewitched, but she would not listen.

To her surprise, what seemed like seconds later, she burst free from the trees and out into a small and wondrous meadow. The sunlight was nearly blinding. The field was covered with an array of beautiful flowers. In the middle of the meadow sat a whimsical cottage with a small stream trickling beside it before it disappeared into the woods again.

Not knowing what to expect, Evangeline stood in awe and took in the peaceful scene before her. Turning to face Evangeline, the mystical woman pulled off her hood.

PERSPECTIVE: Hello, child. I am Perspective. For your sake, I am glad that you chose to follow me.

STORYTELLER: Perspective was an older woman but surprisingly beautiful, like antique furniture that is aged but delightful to look at. Her skin was a dark mahogany; her eyes were green and lustrous.

EVANGELINE: (with concern) But are we safe from those men?

PERSPECTIVE: We are now. Be silent, child, and look behind you.

STORYTELLER: Evangeline turned quietly in the direction where Perspective was pointing. The five men had wandered through the woods after Evangeline. But now they stood on the edge of the trees looking lost and utterly confused by the sunlight that was pouring down on the meadow.

BLINDMAN: (frustrated, with his hands covering his face) Where did she go? She was right in front of us! I can't see anything in this confounded darkness.

FOOLS GOLD: Perhaps the witch got her. There's no way to find her here in this darkness. We'd waste the day and probably injure ourselves falling down or running into objects.

BLINDMAN: (cursing) You're right! Let's get back to the Highway. That horrible witch won't capture any more pilgrims today...at least, not while we're on the road.

STORYTELLER: With that said, Blindman and the policemen drifted back into the dark woods and disappeared.

EVANGELINE: What just happened? Those dudes were like ten feet away from us and they couldn't see? Were they blind?

PERSPECTIVE: (smiling) In a way...yes. This little meadow was set apart by the King. The light that shines here is no ordinary light. Men like Blindman and his guards can't see here at all. To them, the light is a great and oppressive darkness. They are afraid of it and will go no further.

EVANGELINE: But what about the woods? They were right behind me, callin' to me and one of 'em almost grabbed my arm.

PERSPECTIVE: The woods are dark to you and me, but they can see perfectly in them. Those glasses they wear cause them to see darkness in the light and provide light for them in darkness. As a result, they don't see things according to the way the King has set it up. In fact, you could say that they look at life completely opposite of the way the King sees it. But rest assured, it was the King who brought you to safety and would not allow them to capture you.

EVANGELINE: But how did you see me comin'? How did you know that I'd follow you? Why do they call you a witch?

PERSPECTIVE: So many questions, child. The King has stationed me here to save pilgrims before they enter that city. I am often watching from the edge of those woods, and I call to pilgrims all the time. Some listen, as you did. Some ignore me. And sadly, some don't even hear me though I call to them at the top of my lungs.

The men in Birdville say that I am a witch because they claim that I call people out of the light and into the darkness to destroy them. But as I've said, this is actually the opposite of what I do.

On the contrary, Birdville is one of Diablo's greatest traps on this Highway. Right at the foot of the Cross, it serves as a place where Truth and light are snatched just moments before salvation arrives.

So many pilgrims enter that city and never come out of it again. The seeds of Truth that are sown in their hearts, as they travel along the Highway, are gobbled up by the birds of Diablo before they can take root. Instead of receiving life, they are left in that city to rot with nothing. They are blind but claim they can see. It is a horrible, horrible place.

EVANGELINE: Don't you ever worry that Blindman and his guards will hunt you down one day?

PERSPECTIVE: (laughing softly) They will never find me, child. Not in a million years, unless they *really* want to see. Come along now. Let's have something to drink and a snack. You look like you could eat.

STORYTELLER: When Perspective opened the door to her cottage, I saw a charming and breathtaking sight, as large glass windows filled the room with light. Bright potted plants were everywhere, while butterflies flitted through the air. In the sitting area, there were two modest sofas, a small shelf of books, and a wooden table with four chairs.

When she removed her cloak, Perspective hung it on a coat rack. Underneath, she wore a sparkling white dress.

PERSPECTIVE: Would you like some tea and some cake, child?

EVANGELINE: I don't like tea that much, but I'm hungry and thirsty. So, sure. I guess.

STORYTELLER: An interesting sight towards the back of the living room caught Evangeline's eye and drew her there. Along the wall were four large, full-length mirrors. Each of them was different in style. The first mirror looked like something you would find in a clothing store. It was encased in a shiny silver frame and illuminated with bright lights.

Perspective placed the tea kettle on the stove and looked over at Evangeline from the corner of her eye. A smile curled on the edge of her lips as she watched Evangeline admire her reflection in the mirror.

EVANGELINE: Wow! I look good!

STORYTELLER: Although the reflection in the mirror resembled Evangeline, it was somehow an enhanced version of her.

EVANGELINE: I wish my hips looked like that! Oooh. And what about those curves too? And that makeup...where can I get that makeup? I look too fine!

STORYTELLER: Evangeline turned slowly in the mirror, enjoying her reflection from every angle. She pursed her lips, struck a few poses and took a few more looks before turning to Perspective.

EVANGELINE: Where did you get this mirror? I'd love to hang this thing in my bedroom back home, for real!

PERSPECTIVE: (cutting the cake) Would you really? Is that really you?

EVANGELINE: Well...no...but...

PERSPECTIVE: It's who you wish you could be, though. Right?

EVANGELINE: Well, sure. Who wouldn't wanna look like that? Every man in the world would go crazy when I walked in the room, if I looked like that.

STORYTELLER: Perspective placed two plates with slices of cake on the small wooden table in the center of the room and walked over to Evangeline.

PERSPECTIVE: So, you're not really happy with who you are now?

EVANGELINE: (frowning) Not really. I mean, sometimes I think I'm beautiful...I guess. But yeah, I could change some things. So what's up with this mirror, for real? How did it do that?

PERSPECTIVE: All of these mirrors will reveal something about you. Some of it you'll want to see. Yet some of it might cause you to look away.

EVANGELINE: So then, what's this one about?

PERSPECTIVE: It's called the MIRROR OF YOUR PROJECTED SELF. If you could, it's how you'd like to see yourself each day.

EVANGELINE: Hmmm...well, I'm not gonna lie. I'd look that way if I could.

PERSPECTIVE: But you already try to look that way. Don't you, child?

EVANGELINE: What'cha mean?

PERSPECTIVE: Look in the mirror again.

STORYTELLER: Evangeline stared into the mirror once more. Right away, a look of shame flashed across her face.

EVANGELINE: Hey! That's my Spacebook page! Those are my pictures...wait...how?

PERSPECTIVE: Look at those pictures for a moment and read what you say about yourself. Are those things so different from what the mirror showed you at first?

STORYTELLER: In my dream, I saw what the mirror revealed. There were several pictures of Evangeline taken from unique angles. Most of them revealed a lot of skin. In one of the pictures, she was hardly wearing anything at all. Her Spacebook name was "Lil' Sexy22."

PERSPECTIVE: Is that who you *really* are? Are those pictures *really* you? Is your name *really* Lil' Sexy22?

STORYTELLER: Evangeline opened her mouth but no words came out. She looked at Perspective then at the mirror again.

PERSPECTIVE: Child, some of what's on your Spacebook page is who you really are. But most of it is who you'd like for people to *think* you are. These pictures and the name you've given yourself project to everyone who visits this page that you are all the things they see here. Look at this. You call yourself a "lady gangsta" and "queen of the clubs." You say a lot of other stuff about you that I won't embarrass you with. But let me ask you again, child, is that who you *really* are?

EVANGELINE: A lot of that stuff is just talk, for real. That's how we do things on Spacebook. We kinda put stuff out there for people to look at and read. But a lot of it really isn't true, I guess.

PERSPECTIVE: Is that who you want to be, though? Do you *want* to be Lil' Sexy 22, the "lady gangsta" and the "queen of the clubs"?

EVANGELINE: Um...

PERSPECTIVE: Let's look at this other mirror now.

STORYTELLER: Perspective took Evangeline by the arm and placed her in front of the next mirror. Like the first one, this mirror was surrounded by bright lights. The frame was gold with dollar signs and jewels embedded in it. As it was with the first mirror, the reflection that appeared was an enhanced version of Evangeline. But in this reflection she was decked out in some very nice clothes and heels. Her hair was done up perfectly. Diamond earrings hung from her ears, and diamond rings and bracelets were on her fingers and wrists.

EVANGELINE: Wow! Looks like I'm ballin'.

STORYTELLER: Her reflection was suddenly joined by a handsome man in a dark suit. He kissed her reflection on the lips and then took her image by the hand. They looked amazing together.

EVANGELINE: Who's that boy right there? I don't think I've ever seen him before, but he's too fine!

PERSPECTIVE: Just keep looking.

STORYTELLER: Next, the mirror revealed her and the man standing in front of a monstrous mansion. There were four luxury vehicles in the driveway. The lawn was manicured to perfection and a large outdoor pool decked the backyard. Two small children were running and playing happily in the yard.

EVANGELINE: That's what I'm talkin' 'bout. There's some places like that in the City of Doom, but I've only dreamed 'bout livin' in one. A man like that dude right there and a crib like that could really make a girl satisfied, for real.

PERSPECTIVE: Do you think so?

EVANGELINE: I don't see how they couldn't. You got money like that and you got your problems solved, for real. There ain't a whole lot that could go wrong with that kinda security.

PERSPECTIVE: Keep watching.

STORYTELLER: Perspective gently tapped the frame of the mirror and some new images started to appear. The first was an image of Evangeline and her man standing back to back with their arms crossed. A look of anger covered both of their faces. Another reflection revealed her man in the arms of another woman, and then another woman, and then another. Next, the mirror revealed a moving truck with furniture from the mansion being loaded into it.

In the following scene, there was a picture of Evangeline somewhat aged. She was wearing nice clothing, but none of it was as expensive as before. Then the mirror started flashing more images rapidly. First, a picture of a child in a hospital bed with tubes in his nose. Evangeline was leaning over his bed with tears in her eyes. Sadly, a church scene with the child in a coffin followed.

Then Evangeline was with her other child in a smaller house unpacking. Her husband, much older now, was at his office flirting with his secretary. Next, Evangeline was in the principal's office with her child. Her man now remarried to a new woman, Evangeline was much older. Her former beauty almost gone, she was much heavier and more wrinkled. Her child was now a young man in the military. In the last scene, Evangeline was sitting in a chair alone and watching television.

EVANGELINE: OK, enough. Enough. What's this all about? Is this mirror sayin' that bein' rich is bad and that every good-lookin' man is goin' to up and leave his wife for a prettier face. I don't buy that!

PERSPECTIVE: Take it easy. This mirror is from Birdville. They have one in almost every store in the city. It's called the WORLDLY PERSPECTIVE MIRROR. It shows you everything you'll need to be happy in this life. Money. Beauty. Clothing. A good-looking man who can make you happy. The perfect home with two perfect kids . . .

EVANGELINE: Right, but you gotta agree, those things can make anyone happy.

PERSPECTIVE: Sure they can, sweetheart, for a time. There's nothing wrong with being rich or successful. In fact, it's good to try to become successful. Those things aren't evil in and of themselves. But the WORLDLY PERSPECTIVE MIRROR lies and blinds us to the Truth, just like everything else in Birdville. The mirror wants you to believe all of the things that it shows you will make you happy.

At first, the mirror didn't show you everything. Did you notice, it wasn't until I touched it that the other reflections started to appear? Those last images weren't showing you what *would* happen, but what *could* happen. Their purpose is to reveal that this life and the stuff it offers is too unpredictable.

Yes, there are some good handsome men out there, but even they can let you down. Beauty is wonderful, but it's not forever. Even the most beautiful among us will one day look like a prune, like a shell of our former selves. Then too, money itself is fleeting, and it's not always enough to save a sick child or to rescue someone who's made a bad decision. The lie that this mirror projects to us is this. If we simply put our trust in a few basic things, we will be happy and satisfied. It may be our career, our looks or our wealth.

But here's the thing. Only the King can truly satisfy us and support us because His love and His provision for us never fail. Our confidence must be based on Him above all else. Those earthly things will fade, die or be taken from us at some point. We must not for even one second assume that they will make us truly happy. And we must not pursue them above our love and desire for the King. Does this make sense to you?

EVANGELINE: I think it does. It's amazin' what can happen when you see your reflection and it shows you havin' all of those things. Right away, it grabs your attention and causes you to forget about the King and what He has to offer.

PERSPECTIVE: (clapping her hands together) Aha! You have spoken a marvelous Truth there, my child! Yes, that's the lie of Birdville. Many who arrive there have only come to pass through on their way to the Cross. But if they are not careful, they become blinded to the love of the King, blinded to the reality of the burden of sin on their back and blinded to the fact that *only* He can save them from destruction. Let's look at these other two mirrors here.

STORYTELLER: Evangeline moved to the next mirror. This one seemed old with a weatherworn wooden frame. There was dust along the edges and it had an ugly spiderweb of cracks near the center of the glass. Evangeline stared into it for a minute but then stepped back with a shocked expression on her face. Horrible words in red started to cover her reflection. In thick dripping letters, they looked as if they had been painted on the mirror.

LIAR, SLUT, IDIOT, TRASH, STUPID, UGLY, NASTY and other terrible words showed up. One right after the other, they kept coming until almost the whole mirror was covered with them. Evangeline's face appeared right in the middle of the crack on the mirror, leaving her reflection jigsawed and strange.

EVANGELINE: Why? Why are all those words comin' out on this mirror? What does this mean?

STORYTELLER: Perspective offered a weak smile but said nothing for a moment, while Evangeline stared at her marred reflection.

PERSPECTIVE: Have you heard those words before, child?

STORYTELLER: Evangeline shook her head, as her eyes grew a bit misty.

EVANGELINE: What is happenin' to me? My head is hurtin'!

STORYTELLER: The red words slowly faded away but the image that remained was hideous. Evangeline's face was covered in warts and scars. Her hair was a tangled mass and hung down in her eyes. The nails on her fingers were long and dirty like the talons of a vulture. Her teeth were a yellowish-green ghastly color. The eyes in her head were bloodshot. An ugly hump was on her back and folded her over like a hunchback.

EVANGELINE: (placing her hands over her face) Ugh! I can't look at this no more.

STORYTELLER: Perspective placed her hand on Evangeline's shoulder.

PERSPECTIVE: This is the most difficult mirror of them all. But you must look at yourself, for there are both great lies and great Truth in what you see.

EVANGELINE: What do you mean? I see nothin' here that looks like the truth.

PERSPECTIVE: This is the MIRROR OF SIN AND UGLINESS. Those words that you first saw were drawn from your own mind and heart.

EVANGELINE: I don't understand!

PERSPECTIVE: You would probably never say any of those words about yourself. But deep in your mind and heart, you've come to believe them about yourself. Perhaps you've been called those names by someone close to you. Or maybe you've just labeled yourself that way because of what you've done. I can see from your belly that you're not a virgin anymore.

EVANGELINE: I lost my virginity almost five years ago.

PERSPECTIVE: And since then, you have labeled yourself in your mind as a tramp. That may be the first baby that you're carrying, but I'm confident that it's not the first time you've been with a young man. Tell me something. Did you finish school?

EVANGELINE: No. I dropped out in my junior year.

PERSPECTIVE: That explains the words like *stupid* and *idiot*. Again, these words are buried deep down inside of you like the roots of a great tree. You may not even be aware they are there. But they are way below the surface, poisoning what little self-esteem you have. If you are honest with yourself, there are parts of your life that disgust you and parts of your past that you wish you could change. There are things you believe about yourself that would make you deeply ashamed and afraid if others were to find out.

This mirror is very powerful and it showed you something about yourself that is incredibly real. Remember in the first mirror, you saw what you wanted to see—your projected self. Beautiful. Captivating. Seductive. That mirror showed what you *wished* you looked like on the *outside*. This mirror in front of you now shows what's really going on *inside* of you. It's revealing some of the horrible things you *think* about yourself even though those things aren't actually true. As you can see, this is a much different perspective.

EVANGELINE: Well, what is this ugly monster of myself that I see in the mirror?

PERSPECTIVE: That is you in all of your sin. Every evil thing you've done along with every evil thought and desire you've had is revealed in the image in front of you. It is truly hideous. The hump on your back is the burden of your sin—an ugly mound of guilt and regret and hopelessness. The strange thing, child, is that this mirror shows a much better reflection of who you are than a regular mirror. What is on the inside of us is who we *really* are.

EVANGELINE: I didn't realize I was that disgustin'.

PERSPECTIVE: Oh, yes. You're actually much uglier, child. This mirror can only show us so much. Let me tell you that Diablo hates this mirror, and he would desire to draw your attention elsewhere.

STORYTELLER: Perspective pulled Evangeline to the left again, in front of the MIRROR OR YOUR PROJECTED SELF. The ugly and hideous reflection immediately disappeared and was replaced with the beautiful and shining reflection she had enjoyed before.

EVANGELINE: (sighing) That looks a whole lot better.

PERSPECTIVE: Looks better. Yes. But do you *feel* better now that you've seen yourself as you truly are?

EVANGELINE: No. This reflection feels hollow now. It feels fake. Like puttin' makeup on an ugly pimple. You can hide it a little, but you still know it's there.

PERSPECTIVE: Ah, yes. A great example! Now let us look at this final mirror, shall we?

STORYTELLER: Perspective guided Evangeline to the last mirror. Labeled the MIRROR OF REDEMPTION, it was very plain with nothing fancy about it. At first, the reflection revealed Evangeline just as she had been in the MIRROR OF SIN AND UGLINESS—utterly hideous. But the more she looked, some of the warts started to dissolve away. The scars slowly vanished. Her bloodshot eyes returned to their normal color. The talons on her fingers fell to the floor and her nails were clean once again. The tangled hair righted itself. Then finally, the ugly burden on her back shrunk and disappeared until she looked completely normal.

EVANGELINE: (smiling) It's me again!

PERSPECTIVE: Wait for it, child...wait for it...

STORYTELLER: The mirror in front of Evangeline rippled like a pond after a stone is cast into it. A small, faint light began to shine in the very center like the light at the end of a distant tunnel. I couldn't tell if the light was coming closer or if Evangeline was somehow being drawn towards it. But either way, her reflection in the mirror was encompassed by this great light until it burst forth from the mirror and filled the room like sun fire.

I could no longer see into the mirror but was nearly blinded from the glow it produced. The room itself shook and groaned as if it were in the center of an earthquake. I could sense something extraordinary had occurred. Then there was a final great flash and the mirror became still and returned to normal.

Evangeline stood there with her jaw hanging open. She did not move. She did not blink. She was nearly frozen in awe. Her eyes were wide open and a single tear meandered slowly down her cheek until it fell to the floor.

PERSPECTIVE: Oh, my!

EVANGELINE: (in a faint whisper) Is that really how He sees me?

PERSPECTIVE: Not yet, but at the Cross that's how He'll see you. If you trust in Him as your Lord and Savior, then He will remove your ugly sins and cover you with His beautiful righteousness.

EVANGELINE: And He did all of that for me? I mean, went through all of that to make me beautiful again?

PERSPECTIVE: Yes. He gave it all and died an ugly and painful death to give you His beauty.

EVANGELINE: (crying softly) I somehow knew that ugly reflection in the mirror was me. I saw it back at the Orchard too...me...an ugly piece of fruit. I recognized that reflection even more than I did the beautiful one in the first mirror. It was me, the part of me that I don't like. It made me think the King wouldn't want to love a stinkin' monster like me. But after what I just saw, I know I was wrong. He loves me and He longs to make me beautiful.

PERSPECTIVE: Yes. You were wrong, child. But isn't it so wonderful to know that you were wrong?

EVANGELINE: (grinning from ear to ear) Oh, yes! I've never been so glad to be wrong in my whole life.

PERSPECTIVE: Something tells me that the King has a man for you. Like the King, he will be a man who will see you for who you really are—and love you anyway. That's what true love is.

STORYTELLER: Evangeline's eyes lit up with hope. In that instant, the teapot on the stove gave its shrill whistle.

PERSPECTIVE: Come, child, let's enjoy some tea and cake. Then I will show you a route to the Mountain of the Cross.

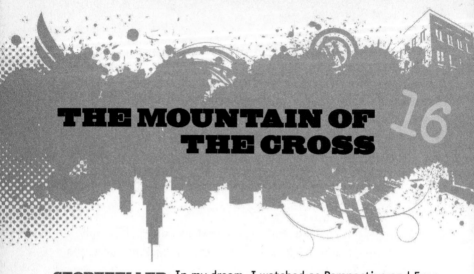

THE MOUNTAIN OF
THE CROSS

16

STORYTELLER: In my dream, I watched as Perspective and Evangeline talked over tea and cake. Evangeline's face had softened remarkably. I saw a peace in her eyes that had been missing before.

PERSPECTIVE: Well, child, it's about time for you to be on your way.

EVANGELINE: How am I 'sposed to get to the Cross? I don't wanna go through Birdville and face Blindman and his guards.

PERSPECTIVE: There is another way.

EVANGELINE: But the Heavenly Highway goes right into the city. There were walls on either side that stretched as far as I could see. Am I 'sposed to jump the wall?

PERSPECTIVE: (laughing) No, don't be silly. There is a way beneath the Highway. A tunnel runs directly below and passes straight through to the other side of Birdville.

EVANGELINE: A tunnel?

PERSPECTIVE: Yes. It's the Tunnel of Humility. Few travel through it. But I believe, after what you've seen today, your heart is prepared.

EVANGELINE: What does that mean?

PERSPECTIVE: You came into this house today full of pride and disillusionment. Your heart was not ready to submit to the King. You wanted relief of your guilt and burden, but you did not wish to accept the fact that your heart is ugly and fake. You were not ready to admit that you are utterly stained in your sins. You did not understand that you bring nothing good to the table.

A heart full of pride is not ready for the King or the Cross. In fact, child, I am quite sure about this. Had Blindman gotten his hands on you, you would have taken his offer of sight and remained blind in your pride for the rest of your days.

EVANGELINE: I have seen my ugliness in the mirror. And I'm willin' to accept it for what it is. I admit that I need this King. I want the beauty and the grace He's willin' to give me.

PERSPECTIVE: (smiling) Then you are ready for the Tunnel. Come with me.

STORYTELLER: Perspective put on her cloak and Evangeline grabbed her backpack. The older, wiser woman then led her outside to a well that was behind the house.

PERSPECTIVE: This is it. The entrance to the Tunnel. The well is the only way down.

EVANGELINE: Down there? Are you for real?

PERSPECTIVE: This is the only way at this point, child. Blindman will seek to bind you up if you go back to Birdville. He used to talk to pilgrims like you and try to reason with them. But now he locks them up if they're unwilling to forget their need for the Cross. This Tunnel is dark and long but, if you stay the course, you will come out on the other side.

STORYTELLER: Evangeline placed her hands on the edge of the well and peered down into its long dark throat.

EVANGELINE: I can't even see the bottom. How am I 'sposed to see where I'm goin'?

STORYTELLER: Perspective reached into her cloak and pulled out a small thin candle. She handed it to Evangeline and directed her to a large bucket above the well.

PERSPECTIVE: This will light your way. It is a very special light made by the King Himself. If for any reason it goes out or you lose it—just cry out to Him.

EVANGELINE: I can't believe you're askin' me to go into a nasty hole in the ground. I think I'd rather just take my chances with Blindman and see if I could duck and hide my way through town. I'm sure—

PERSPECTIVE: You're still so sure of yourself. Maybe you aren't ready yet.

STORYTELLER: Evangeline looked at Perspective and then at the well.

EVANGELINE: No. You're right. I need to do this.

PERSPECTIVE: Put your trust in the King. He has told all of us that if we will humble ourselves, then He will lift us up. This Tunnel will attack and remove any remaining pride that's within you.

STORYTELLER: Evangeline climbed up onto the stone wall of the well and stepped carefully into the bucket that was strung to a rope and pulley. She clung tightly to the rope and stared down into the dark hole beneath.

EVANGELINE: Go ahead and lower me. I'm ready.

STORYTELLER: Perspective turned the crank on the pulley and slowly lowered her down into the well. Almost instantly, Evangeline looked up at Perspective with a panicked look in her eyes.

EVANGELINE: I got nothin' to light my candle!

PERSPECTIVE: You are fine, child. Look!

STORYTELLER: As Evangeline disappeared into the thick darkness, the candle in her hand suddenly lit up into a bright white flame. The deeper she went into the ground, the flame grew brighter and brighter.

The throat of the well was solid rock. The faint creaks of the pulley could be heard as she went down. After several minutes of descending, she finally hit the bottom. The well was almost completely dry. Behind her was a wall of rock. In front of her was the Tunnel, although it actually looked like a long, dark cave. It was very quiet aside from a few faint drips of water that fell from the ceiling. Evangeline held her candle in front of her and took a deep breath.

EVANGELINE: (to herself) C'mon, girl, you can do this. You know you can.

STORYTELLER: As soon as she said this, the candle in her hand flickered and dimmed until it was just a faint spark on the edge of the wick.

EVANGELINE: Ah, that's right. No more pride. I can do this by Your strength, O King. Please give me the courage to make it.

STORYTELLER: The candle burst into flame again and created a wide circle of light that illuminated a good distance in front of her. But beyond the circle was pitch blackness.

Evangeline took some careful steps and started her journey through the Tunnel. Eventually, she came upon several deep holes in the ground. Standing over one of them, she gazed down into it with her candle. Then suddenly, she stumbled backwards. The hole was deep and the bottom was littered with bones. When she turned to the left, her light revealed some words chiseled into the wall. They read: BEWARE! THE PITS OF PRIDE. THOSE WHO FALL HERE RARELY RISE AGAIN.

EVANGELINE: Oh, my goodness! Those people fell to their doom down there. Perspective was right. This Tunnel is not for the proud. Thank the King for this candle or I would've fallen in there head first. I would've been gone, for sure.

STORYTELLER: Just then, a strange howling sound bounced along the walls.

EVANGELINE: Prob'ly just the wind...

STORYTELLER: Evangeline went on like this for some time. The Tunnel was very level and the ground was sandy with few obstacles. The ceiling arched high above her and the walls to either side were spacious. Evangeline could have easily stretched out her arms with plenty of room on either side. After a while, she started grinning and I noticed a sense of confidence to her stride.

EVANGELINE: This really ain't so bad...I don't know why I was bein' so scary.

STORYTELLER: But again, as soon as she spoke those words, a sudden wind rushed down the Tunnel and blew out her candle. Now she was left alone in absolute darkness. I could hear her breathing and her feet scratching along the floor, but I could see nothing.

EVANGELINE: C'mon, girl. Stay calm. Keep ya head. Don't get scared...

STORYTELLER: Her breathing sounded louder. Then from somewhere, I thought I heard a low, growling sound.

EVANGELINE: (with a trembling voice) Ahhh...what was that? King! Please give me some light! I can't see where I'm goin'. I can't make it!

STORYTELLER: The Tunnel was filled with light again when her candle flashed back to life. As soon as it did, I spotted an abnormally large dog crouched in the shadows just outside the circle of light. He had razor-edge teeth like a shark and his eyes were red like burning coals. Around his neck was a thick collar and a tag that read: THE HOUND OF HUBRIS.

Evangeline let out a shriek and waved the candle back and forth like a small sword. When she did so, the Hound growled and barked. His bark bounced along the walls like thunder. But the light obviously bothered him and he retreated deeper and deeper into the shadows.

EVANGELINE: Wow! Perspective didn't tell me about that crazy dog or all the dangers down here. Besides, this candle won't let me say nothin' about myself.

STORYTELLER: Evangeline went on in silence. The mysterious candle seemed to be having an effect on her. She walked on until she spotted what appeared to be a small circle of light in the distance.

EVANGELINE: Finally! The end of this doggone Tunnel. That's gotta be the end. I knew I could do this!

STORYTELLER: After she spoke this time, Evangeline started jogging down the sandy floor towards the light. And, very quickly, her candle went out. Then I heard her cry out and fall to the floor. Everything went dark again, as the light in the far distance was drowned out by the darkness of the Tunnel.

EVANGELINE: Oh, no...oh, no! My candle. Where is it?

STORYTELLER: I could hear her scuffling around on the ground frantically pawing and clawing the sand for her lost light. She did this for quite some time. Occasionally, I heard a thump and then a cry of pain as she continued her desperate search. Then there was a long silence. I started to fear that she had knocked herself unconscious or fallen into a hole. But then I heard a faint sniffling sound, and I knew she was crying.

EVANGELINE: I'm lost. I can't see. I can't get outta here...

STORYTELLER: The silence of the Tunnel was only broken from time to time by sudden gusts of rushing wind.

EVANGELINE: Oh, my King! Please help me! I can't make it even one more step without You. I'm afraid and I need You now more than ever!

STORYTELLER: I thought I saw the faintest of glows approaching her from out of the darkness. It was tiny and moved slowly. As it drew closer, I was surprised to see that this light was actually a very small child. He could not have been more than five years old. The closer he came, the faint light around him exposed Evangeline. She lay there on the ground curled up in a ball with her arms around her knees. When she looked up and saw the child, her eyes widened. The small boy extended his hand to her.

CHILD: Follow me. I can get you out.

EVANGELINE: You? Who are you? You're just a baby...why're you down here?

CHILD: Come on. I will lead you.

EVANGELINE: I can't let no baby lead me! There ain't no way you could get me outta here.

STORYTELLER: The boy's face saddened and he started to walk away. Evangeline was alone in the darkness again, and she cried out for him to come back.

EVANGELINE: Wait! Wait! You can lead me out. I can't go any further by myself.

STORYTELLER: When the boy reappeared, Evangeline took the child's hand and slowly stood to her feet. The small boy smiled at her and started walking. The light around him barely exposed the ground in front of them, but he walked with great confidence. Evangeline looked down and kept her eyes on him as they went. Her face was full of wonderment and surprise as she followed her unusual guide.

Once again, the circle of light appeared in the distance. As they walked, it became brighter and brighter. Clearly, they were coming to the end of the Tunnel. The closer they came, the light around the boy disappeared. The Tunnel started to gradually ascend as they were coming out from underground.

Pretty soon, Evangeline had to shield her eyes against the bright sunlight that was pouring in from outside. She turned her head to say something to the boy, but her hand was hanging empty at her side. Looking around for a moment with squinting eyes, she tried to find him. He was gone.

After a few moments, her eyes started to adjust. She was in an open field and behind her was a tall brick wall. In front of her was the Mountain of the Cross.

EVANGELINE: Perspective was right. That dark Tunnel got me to the other side. It took a candle, a baby and a big ol' slice of humble pie—but praise to the King! I'm here!

STORYTELLER: A small dirt trail crisscrossed up the side of the Mountain leading to the Cross on the top. Evangeline stared at the Cross and her eyes were brimming with wonder and awe.

EVANGELINE: So this is where the King died for me...for my burden...my sin...my ugliness. This is where He died to set me free, to clean me up and to make me worthy. I can't wait to get up there and thank Him!

STORYTELLER: Without hesitating, Evangeline set off on a sprint up the dirt trail. I was amazed with what speed and ease she ran, despite the fact that she was bearing a heavy burden. Nearly halfway up the hill, there was a loud snapping and tearing sound and her burden fell from her back. It rolled like a boulder down the hill until it disappeared into the mouth of an open grave.

She ran towards the Cross like a woman running from a burning building into fresh air. Yet the look on her face was that of a woman who had just found an indescribable treasure that was hers to keep. When Evangeline reached the foot of the Cross, she fell to her knees and wrapped her arms around it. Her shoulders were heaving up and down as she wept tears of joy. Clinging to the Cross, she wouldn't let it go.

EVANGELINE: Oh, thank You! Thank You! Thank You! Why did You do it? Why do You love me? When I've been so ugly to You...You've been so wonderful to me. You have my *whole* heart. You have *all* of me!

VISITOR ONE: Rise to your feet, child of the King. Rise and hear wonderful things.

STORYTELLER: There were three angelic beings surrounding her. Evangeline wiped her eyes and stood up.

EVANGELINE: I'm so glad, so glad that I made it. I mean, I'm so grateful that the King brought me this far.

VISITOR TWO: Every pilgrim's journey is different. Some make it up this Mountain as you did, running. Others crawl on their hands and knees, but the King draws each pilgrim to Himself.

VISITOR THREE: The King desires to give you the beauty of His grace. Your ugly sins and your burden are no more. Behold, they are dead.

STORYTELLER: The Visitor pointed to the open mouth of the grave.

VISITOR ONE: You are covered now by His righteousness. The stains of your past exist no more.

STORYTELLER: I watched as Evangeline was suddenly clothed in a radiantly beautiful white dress. She twirled around once and then twice, admiring its splendor. One of the Visitors then handed her a Scroll.

VISITOR THREE: When you arrive at the City of Light, give this to he who guards the Gate and the King will bid you welcome.

EVANGELINE: Thank you.

VISITOR ONE: Your name is "Evangeline" and it means *Proclaimer of Good News*. The King desires to use you as His megaphone to shout to the world about His love, compassion and grace.

EVANGELINE: (laughing) Well, I am kinda loud.

VISITOR TWO: Your whole life shall be a loud megaphone to your city and to those you know.

EVANGELINE: You mean, I'm goin' back? Now?

VISITOR ONE: Yes. The King desires that you return to the City of Doom to share the Good News. The King's plans for each pilgrim are different. From the Cross, He calls some to go further down the Heavenly Highway, and others he directs to go back home. You both must return.

EVANGELINE: Both? Oh, yes.

STORYTELLER: She put her hands around her belly.

EVANGELINE: I'm still not sure how to care for this thing.

VISITOR TWO: Thing? You are referring to your *baby*. Did you not know that the womb of a mother was the first earthly home of the King? The life within you is a miracle. Already, the King's Spirit is knitting your child together. Every fingerprint, brain cell, strand of hair and even the color of the baby's eyes are uniquely designed by the Artist of all artists—the King of kings. As He did with you, the King is engineering the baby in your womb for a purpose. You have no mere thing in your belly. You are his mother and you must bring him into the world by the King's grace.

EVANGELINE: Him? I'm havin' a boy?

VISITOR THREE: Yes. The King has given Him a name as well.

EVANGELINE: What is it?

STORYTELLER: The three Visitors stepped forward and placed their hands gently on her head.

VISITOR ONE: You will know what to name him when the time is right. Now go, child. Your city needs you and the King desires for you to move quickly.

STORYTELLER: Evangeline started to open her mouth, but there was a bright flash. When I saw her again, her eyes were still moist with tears. Her face was beaming with an unspeakable joy. She was alone and back on the Heavenly Highway.

SCRAPPIN' FOR PENNIES 17

17

STORYTELLER: Evangeline appeared radiant and overwhelmed with joy after making it to the Mountain of the Cross. Bird-ville was far behind her and looked like a small speck on the horizon.

It was now mid-afternoon. True to the instructions of the three Visitors, she set out to return to the City of Doom. Up ahead of Evangeline, I saw a circle of girls on the road. There was a lot of shouting and cursing. The girls were young, proba-bly no older than twelve or thirteen, and they were gathered in the middle of the Highway. Two girls in the center of the circle were fighting, screaming and rolling around on the ground. They were both exchanging savage punches and clawing at each other with their nails.

It was an ugly fight, as bits of hair and clothing were torn from their heads and bodies. The ones around the circle were cursing and cheering on the fight. Some of them had their cell phones out and were texting, updating their Spacebook status or taking video footage. One of the girls finally got on top and slapped the other one three times in the face. But as she did so, one of the other young ladies broke from the circle and kicked her in the ribs. She fell over, holding her side.

A few others jumped out of the circle and stomped her several times. The other girl, who had been on the bottom, climbed on top and started to punch and slap her as well. Evangeline hollered and raced up to the fight. The girls in the circle saw that she was older and that she was angry, so they cleared out of her way. The two fighters on the ground continued to tussle and scream until Evangeline yelled louder and pulled them apart.

PAYBACK: What'cha think ya doin'?

EVANGELINE: That's enough! Y'all fightin' out here like animals!

PAYBACK: That's 'cause this lil' tramp right here been runnin' her mouth and won't shut up!

STORYTELLER: Payback's crew mumbled their agreement and nodded their heads.

ANGRY: You started it! Makin' fun of those pictures I put on my Spacebook page. Sayin' I was ugly. Then you and ya homegirls started postin' mess on my page sayin' some nasty stuff 'bout me. Nah! I ain't gonna just sit 'round and let y'all say that stuff.

PAYBACK: Yeah. So then you just bumped me yesterday in the hallway. You been muggin' me in class and tellin' ya little clique that you was gonna beat me down and all that. Well, I just showed you who got beat down. We 'bout to put all this mess online anyway . . . put a lil' video clip up so er'body can see how I stomped you out.

CACKLE: It's done, girl. People already talkin' 'bout it.

STORYTELLER: Cackle smiled mockingly before getting back to the status updates that were coming in on her phone. Angry jumped to her feet and raced towards Cackle, but Evangeline grabbed her.

ANGRY: You better put that phone up before I smash it!

EVANGELINE: You need to chill out.

PAYBACK: You lucky this girl showed up and saved you before I could finish you off. C'mon, let's get outta here!

STORYTELLER: Angry lurched forward but Evangeline held her tight. Angry's eyebrows were drawn tightly. Hot tears ran down her face as she wiped her bloody cheek and lips with the back of her hands. Payback and her entourage of friends laughed and chattered as they walked away. They were looking at their phones and talking about the fight.

EVANGELINE: Just let 'em go, girl. Just let 'em go.

ANGRY: I ain't never gonna let this go. Payback thinks she can just do me like that. Never! I'm gonna get with my homegirls and we gonna stomp her and her ugly goons into the ground. Then we gonna tell the real story.

EVANGELINE: Stories like this one don't have no ending. At least, not a good one.

ANGRY: What'cha mean?

EVANGELINE: I'm guessin' that this fight here was like, what? Maybe chapter four or five of your story? You said somethin'. Then she said somethin'. Then you did somethin'. Then she did somethin'. She beat you down. Then you gonna beat her down. How does a story like that end?

STORYTELLER: Angry yanked the collar of her shirt up and wiped her eyes.

EVANGELINE: Girl, I used to be a fighter too. Look at this.

STORYTELLER: She turned her face to the side and pointed to a one-inch scar right next to her ear.

EVANGELINE: A girl I got to fightin' with gave me that scar. You know what I did to her? I ripped her hoop earrings out of her ears...broke her nose and put her in the hospital. She prob'ly woulda done worse to me, but she didn't have no friends like that girl back there.

STORYTELLER: Evangeline looked at Angry for a minute.

EVANGELINE: Well, she used to have friends. I used to be her friend, but then we got to arguin' 'bout a boy that we was both talkin' to. Words turned into angry words. Then angry words turned into angry mess. We started puttin' stuff on the computer and on our phones. That angry mess eventually turned into some angry fightin' and ended up with my friend lyin' in the hospital. Anger is a killer, for real.

ANGRY: Payback and I used to be cool too. But then she just started gettin' ugly and mean. We went from being friends to enemies. At least you stomped that girl you was fightin'. You won. Now everybody knows that you raw and won't mess wit you no more.

EVANGELINE: That's how I felt at the time. I was glad I messed up her and her face. She said some really nasty stuff 'bout me. But 'bout a week later, I realized that what I had really stomped out was my friendship with her. To this day, we don't even talk. She's got no love for me, for real. So, neither one of us won in the end. Fightin' didn't get us nowhere. It stomped us both and whatever good we actually had in our friendship.

STORYTELLER: Angry was done crying. Her shirt was ripped in several places and clumps of her hair were scattered on the ground.

EVANGELINE: Let me ask you somethin'. Would you fight a girl for a few pennies?

ANGRY: No! That'd be stupid!

EVANGELINE: What about for a million dollars?

ANGRY: Yeah. I'd be tempted to kill somebody for that.

EVANGELINE: Did you know that you owe someone more than you could ever repay and that they could stomp you flat in less than a second?

ANGRY: What'cha mean? I don't owe nobody nothin'!

EVANGELINE: We all do, girl. The One who made us, the King of kings, we owe Him a debt that we could never repay in a million lifetimes.

ANGRY: Huh?

EVANGELINE: You and me, we're sinners. We were born sinners. We do sin and we could die in our sin. Because of that sin, the King told us that we deserve death. It's 'cause the King is perfect and we're the opposite. Sinners like us can't live with this perfect King. He made us and He made the rules. And, according to Him and His rules, we're done for because of our sin.

ANGRY: So, how does this sin turn into a debt? I don't get it.

EVANGELINE: It's like when you commit a crime. They say you owe a debt to society. You pay that back by doin' community service, payin' a ticket or goin' to jail. Right? Those are the types of debts that we can pay with our time or out of our purse.

Because we *are* sinners and because we *do* sin, we owe a debt against our perfect King. He never sinned and our sinfulness is not just against our society, but against Him. The King said the only way to pay our sin-debt to Him is by death.

ANGRY: So, we can't pay that debt? We can't just tell this King we're sorry and we'll try harder?

EVANGELINE: It doesn't work like that. That'd be nice. But the only way to make this situation right is that someone has to die. In this case, the only thing that can die is us.

ANGRY: (frowning) Wow. Then we screwed.

EVANGELINE: Same thing I used to think, but there's Good News. This perfect King said He'd be willin' to be the One who has to die. Even though He didn't do a single thing wrong, He said He'd take the blame for all the sin-debt that we owe. He was willin' to die instead of us.

ANGRY: Nah. There's nobody who'd do that. Nobody would step up and die for nobody like that. I don't believe it! You lyin'!

EVANGELINE: Sounds crazy, I know. But it's true. I follow this King now. I gave Him my life. I told Him that He can take the blame for my sins, that He can cancel my debt and that He can set me free! I told Him that I'd follow Him no matter where He asked me to go.

ANGRY: What'cha mean, you *told* Him? He's dead, right?

EVANGELINE: (smiling) No. Death couldn't hold Him down. After gettin' stomped for our sins and dyin', He rose and stomped death itself. When He smashed death, He rose up and gave us life!

STORYTELLER: Angry stared at Evangeline in deep thought.

EVANGELINE: His death and resurrection are truly beautiful. The most beautiful thing I know.

ANGRY: Yeah. If that's really true, it's pretty amazin'.

EVANGELINE: I asked you a minute ago if you'd fight a girl for a few pennies and you said no. Well, all the drama and ugly that gets done to us by girls like Payback is just pocket change. When someone makes fun of us or threatens us, we keep a record of what they've done. It's like we keep a record of their debt against us. Then we keep track of that debt until we stomp 'em back with our fists or our words. We're basically willin' to fight over a few pennies of debt.

ANGRY: Pennies? That stuff Payback and those girls did to me is way too deep! That ain't no pennies.

EVANGELINE: Hold up! What 'bout what the King did? Every single ugly, evil, nasty thing we ever did or even thought about—we did against Him. Now how much debt is that?

ANGRY: That's a lot.

EVANGELINE: Yeah, it's a *whole* lot! But instead of stompin' us to death, He forgives us by takin' the blame for our sin. He cancels our debt and doesn't even remember it any more. Now if He's willin' to do that for me, what right do I have to fight a girl because she said somethin' 'bout me on the computer or in the school hallways? The King said this: If we want Him to cancel all our sin-debt to Him, then we need to be willin' to cancel the debts of everybody who owes us too. We can't keep our minds full of the pocket change people owe us.

ANGRY: That's so hard. Does He just expect me to ignore girls like Payback and just pretend like it ain't happenin'?

EVANGELINE: Sometimes. When we give our lives to Him, He gives us what we need most—His peace. He goes to work killin' all that meanness and anger in us. I'm a testimony to that. But He also gives us His Spirit to help us know how to handle each relationship. Sometimes it involves walkin' away from drama. Sometimes it means talkin' to the person who's makin' the drama and tryin' to make peace with them.

ANGRY: That sounds awfully hard. Maybe impossible.

EVANGELINE: I feel ya. It's real hard. Take me, I was one of the angriest girls in the City of Doom and I'd fight ya for some pennies any day. Matter of fact, I used to survive off of bein' angry and mean. But now, all that fightin' feels ugly. When I think about it, actin' mean makes me sick.

So anger don't rule me no more. Now, I'm just overflowin' with peace. Stuff that happened in the past could still make me mad, but I won't let it. Trust me, there's nothin' like the kinda peace the King gives.

When I look in ya eyes, I see the anger that's got ya all chained up inside. You beautiful, girl, but that meanness in ya face and in ya eyes has got you lookin' real ugly.

STORYTELLER: Angry let out a deep sigh. She looked at her hands for a moment. Her knuckles were bloody and her nails were chipped.

ANGRY: Peace sounds nice. I'm tired of bein' angry all the time. You right, I think this anger has got me in some serious chains, for real. But I still can't see myself just lettin' people talk all kinda mess about me and just do nothin'. I ain't no coward!

EVANGELINE: Most of the time, it takes more courage *not* to fight. The King tells us in His Book that it's actually to a man's glory to walk away from an offence, but it's the fool who's quick to run her mouth and swing her fists.

ANGRY: I don't get it. How's it courageous to walk away? Walkin' away just means you soft!

EVANGELINE: I'm learnin' from the King's Letters that a courageous person understands and believes some things. For one, she understands that she and er'body else are made in the King's image. Unlike animals and plants, the King made us to be like Him in a whole lotta ways. We have a lotta value to Him. So much value that He was willin' to die for us. Because of that, we should have a lot of value for other people, includin' our enemies.

For instance, He gave us a mind and a conscience. If you kick a dog, that dog is either gonna bite you or run away. That dog doesn't think, it just reacts. But you and me, we have a mind and we can *choose* what we're gonna do. We can fight, talk back or just walk away. But a person with courage also realizes that a lot of fires between two people can get put out by a kind word or a kind action.

Angry words and violence almost always make things worse. It doesn't take courage to act like an animal or to act like a fool. Any clown can do that. But it takes courage to make peace instead of war. It's the bigger person who says, "Ya know what? That mess you said 'bout me and your bad attitude ain't gonna have a hold on me. I'm not gonna let what you said define me or affect me." In fact, girl, a really strong person is actually willin' to put their pride aside and care more about their enemy than their own ego.

STORYTELLER: Angry listened intently to what Evangeline was saying.

ANGRY: It's like I hear what ya sayin', but I'm not sure I'm feelin' it, for real. I realize that I've got a lot of emotion inside of me and most of it's ugly and mad. I don't like that. But it also seems like everywhere I turn, there's someone talkin' 'bout me, botherin' me and gettin' in my way. I can only handle so much.

EVANGELINE: The Truth is that you and I can't handle very much at all. If we try to keep it cool for a while, sooner or later we crack. Then the monster comes out and people get hurt. I'm just tellin' you that until you give your whole life to the King, includin' your anger problem, then ya never gonna enjoy the peace and grace He has for ya.

ANGRY: Well, I appreciate you gettin' those girls off of me. That took some courage. Payback and her clique could have turned on you too.

EVANGELINE: (waving her hand and smiling) Nah. I wasn't worried 'bout them girls.

ANGRY: Thank you for talkin' with me. I like what you said. There's a peace in your face that I see and I'd like to have it too. I'm not sure that I wanna start lovin' my enemies just yet, but I'm gonna think 'bout what ya said.

EVANGELINE: Well, that's a start, ain't it? Let me pray for us.

STORYTELLER: Evangeline put her hands on Angry's shoulder and the two of them prayed right there in the middle of the blacktop on the Highway.

EVANGELINE: So, where ya from?

ANGRY: Down 'round the way in Pain Town.

EVANGELINE: Well, I hope ya find peace, and I hope you'll think hard 'bout the King. If He can turn an angry girl like me inside out, then He can do it for you too.

STORYTELLER: Angry grinned.

ANGRY: Yeah. I'll do that.

STORYTELLER: Evangeline gave Angry a hug before they parted ways. Having gained a friendship, Angry turned back down the road towards Pain Town with a lot to think about. Meanwhile, Evangeline moved swiftly towards the City of Doom.

THE REUNION 18

STORYTELLER: In my dream, I saw Evangeline walking down the Heavenly Highway. A quiet peace was settled in her eyes. There was even a noticeable change to her stride. She walked like one freed from bonds and burdens—like someone whose body was liberated from strain and oppression.

After some time passed, I spotted the City of Doom in the distance. Its buildings jutted from the earth like concrete monsters, veiled in ugly brownish smog. Evangeline stopped. The peace on her face was quickly replaced by a shiver of worry and doubt. As though by instinct, she wanted to have one last memory of the incredible journey she had undertaken.

Turning around with her back to the city, she stared at the landscape before her. Opposite the City of Doom were sprawling green fields, dotted here and there with gorgeous and radiant flowers. The melody of birds filled the air. There were tall and rambling groves of trees along with a quiet rippling stream that meandered close beside the Highway. Evangeline sighed and shook her head.

EVANGELINE: (to herself) Why, oh why, did I ever settle for the City of Doom for so long? I was convinced that life in the city was as good as it got. Now, just look at this beautiful open place.

STORYTELLER: With increasing despair over going back to the place of her birth, she inhaled a deep breath.

EVANGELINE: The air out here is...wonderful! It's so quiet. So clean! I could stay on this Highway forever—all the way to the City of Light.

VOICE: And you shall.

EVANGELINE: Who said that?

STORYTELLER: Evangeline swung quickly around. To her amazement, there before her on the Highway was a wondrous, glowing Being. Even in my dream I could not stare directly at Him because the light emanating from His countenance was so blinding. All at once, it became evident that she was in the presence of Someone powerful and beyond description. Evangeline cupped her hand over her mouth and immediately dropped to her knees.

EVANGELINE: (bowing) My King!

KING: It is I, My beloved.

EVANGELINE: Is it really You?

KING: Yes. Why is your face shrouded in doubt?

EVANGELINE: I have been told that I must return to the City of Doom, but I don't want to. I wanna stay out here...I love it out here.

KING: It is lovely, isn't it? But would you really keep all of this to yourself? Are there not many more people that you and I love who need to find their way down this road?

STORYTELLER: Evangeline nodded.

KING: You must remember, My beloved, the Heavenly Highway is now in your heart. The road to eternity is now paved in your soul. Do not forget that I am with you and that My Spirit is in you too. The stain of the City of Doom is washed away. In turn, I have filled your heart and soul with the fragrance and grace of Heaven. I have not just saved you, My child, *from your* doom. I have saved you *to join Me* in saving Doom itself.

EVANGELINE: But, my King, I was told that You are goin' to destroy the City of Doom.

KING: This is true. But not yet. There are many more who will believe. I desire to shine Heaven in that city and draw more men to Myself. My heart burns within Me for those who are perishing. Do you not feel that same burning in you too? Do you not also desire to share the gift of My love and My salvation with those who are lost without Me?

STORYTELLER: A small tear started to roll down Evangeline's cheek.

EVANGELINE: Yes, my King, I do. I do. But what do I have to offer? I'm a pregnant high school dropout. I got nothin' to offer and there's nothin' I can say. I'm saved. I know this. But I'm a saved failure.

KING: This also is true. And that is why I love you and long to use you. I did not come to recruit the healthy, the strong or the successful. I desire a broken heart and a contrite spirit. My power is made perfect in your weakness. You doubt, My beloved, that I find you wonderful and beautiful. Still, you doubt more that I can use you for beautiful purposes. Doubt is a poison. Humility is a gift. You bow before Me now in humility. But inside, your heart is reeling with doubt. I will fill you with more of My Spirit. I will purge and crush the doubt and shame that shackles your heart.

STORYTELLER: Just then, a flame burst forth from the King like an exploding star. It surrounded Evangeline and actually passed right through her—but it did not consume her. Then, to my surprise, the fire burned within her and she started to glow like a lantern. For a moment, she was as blinding as the King Himself.

This light passed as quickly as it came and afterwards the King was gone from sight. Evangeline slowly stood to her feet. She blinked and squinted several times. Finally, as she opened her eyes wide, I spotted a small fire raging within them. A broad and lovely smile started to emerge on her face.

Though the King was no longer visible, He spoke.

KING: Now go, My beautiful one. Return to the city. Return to help Kai'Ro. I am with you. You have all that you need.

STORYTELLER: Evangeline raised her eyes to the heavens.

EVANGELINE: I am sorry I doubted You and what You desire to do through me. I'm on my way...as long as You're with me. Here I go.

STORYTELLER: Evangeline took off again. Only this time there was a sense of strong purpose in her steps. She moved quickly and it wasn't long until the Highway took her up to the tall row of hedges. After taking a deep breath, she plunged back inside.

Once she was on the other side, the tranquility and quiet of the Heavenly Highway were immediately replaced with the grinding roar of the city. In fact, right after she passed through the hedges, three police cars raced down the street with sirens blaring. The flowers and open fields were no more. Instead, there was litter along the sidewalk and the curbs. The radiant colors that dotted the Highway were gone and loud angry smatterings of graffiti took their place along the sides of houses and buildings.

EVANGELINE: (with mixed feelings) Wow. It's good to be back.

STORYTELLER: She set off down the sidewalk. To her left was a small, brown brick building with darkly tinted windows. A thin woman in business attire stood outside the main entrance holding a cigarette in her slender fingers. She looked at Evangeline for a moment and then took a long gaze at Evangeline's pregnant belly.

MS. CHOICE: How far along are you, sweetheart?

STORYTELLER: Evangeline stopped.

EVANGELINE: Don't know for sure. Why?

MS. CHOICE: Did you want it?

STORYTELLER: Evangeline raised an eyebrow but said nothing.

MS. CHOICE: Does it have a daddy? I'm guessing you don't know who it is, do you?

EVANGELINE: You're askin' a lotta questions.

MS. CHOICE: Oh, don't get offended. You just look like someone who could use a *restart* button.

EVANGELINE: Excuse me?

MS. CHOICE: My guess is that you'd do just about anything not to have that thing in your belly.

EVANGELINE: You mean, my baby?

MS. CHOICE: (taking a long draw on her cigarette) If you want to call it that, yes. How old are you? Sixteen. Eighteen maybe? Are you ready to be a mama? Are you employed? How are you going to take care of that thing once it's born? In this neighborhood, it will be like a piece of raw meat left to the dogs. It won't stand a chance.

EVANGELINE: What do you want from me?

MS. CHOICE: I can offer *you* a restart button. A chance to literally start over. You can get back to life the way you want it. Life free from the burden and responsibility that little parasite in your belly is imposing on you. Wouldn't that be nice?

EVANGELINE: Parasite? Thing? You have a strange bunch of names for a baby.

MS. CHOICE: That thing makes you tired and sick, doesn't it? It invaded your belly against your will. It takes your energy...makes you fat and ugly. It doesn't give you anything in return. It was uninvited and it won't leave. That's my definition of a parasite. When I call it a thing, I'm being nice. Really, it's just a blob of tissue...kind of like a cancer.

EVANGELINE: (laughing) This baby that's growin' in my belly right now is a boy. I can feel him kick and move inside me. You're right. He makes me tired. He makes me fat and, early on, he made me sick too. But he gives me great joy. He's a miracle of life. That's what he is.

MS. CHOICE: Child, that thing is the result of an accident. One hot night of pleasure and look what you're left with. That isn't right. You shouldn't have to pay the price for an accident. Maybe you didn't use protection. Maybe your protection didn't work. Either way, does that mean you should be stuck with a moving, kicking tissue blob in your belly?

EVANGELINE: Accident? The only accident that happened was me havin' a baby *before* I was married. Had I waited 'til I was married, this baby wouldn't have a daddy—he'd have a father. But my boy ain't no accident. The King of kings is knittin' this child in my belly with His own amazin' hands. Every day that my boy will live has already been written in the King's book. Not only does the King know my baby, but this little one was made in His image.

This restart button you're offerin' me is nothin' short of murder. You're askin' me to snuff out a life. It ain't just pushin' a button. You want me to step inside ya clinic so you can chop my boy to pieces and suck him out of my womb.

STORYTELLER: Ms. Choice angrily flung what was left of her cigarette onto the pavement.

MS. CHOICE: Murder? Murder? What we do here is perfectly legal! It's been legal for over thirty years. Getting rid of a ball of tissue is not murder.

EVANGELINE: Now you trippin', for real. You put one of those ultrasound machines on my belly right now and you'll see a baby in there! A head with a brain in it! A beating heart! Two hands! Ten fingers! Two feet! Ten toes! Movin' arms and legs! Isn't that what a *baby* has? You can lie to me and all the sistas out here all you want, but I ain't buyin' ya mess! By the King's good grace, Ima have this baby boy and I'm gonna be the best mother for him that I can!

Now, lemme ask you somethin'. How come your clinic and all these kinda clinics are in poor neighborhoods like mine? I've been in the 'burbs and I don't see no murder clinics there. You got somethin' against poor people? You got somethin' against people of color? Seems to me like y'all have an agenda and it ain't just givin' girls a restart button!

STORYTELLER: Ms. Choice's face was covered with contempt but she said nothing.

EVANGELINE: Y'all hide back here on the corner offerin' hurtin' girls some hope. But what you're really doin' is givin' them scars that will never heal! My girl Drama came here like two years ago. She went in thinkin' she was gonna get a restart on life, for real. When she got out, the first thing she did was fall into my arms cryin, "What have I done? I just killed my baby!" Now she battles depression, has nightmares and is full of regret.

You and the doctors in there are gettin' rich off of murder. I can't put it any plainer than that. Life is sacred. Life is a gift from the King. Ima pray every day that the King shuts y'all down, and I'm gonna tell every pregnant sista I run into to steer clear of this place. But even more than that, Ima pray for you, ma'am. Ima pray that the King shows you that life is a gift. I hope that He breathes life back into your own heart, 'cause I'm afraid your heart is dead.

STORYTELLER: Evangeline stared at Ms. Choice but wouldn't back down. Her gaze was strong but there was love in her eyes. Ms. Choice stared back for a moment but then spun on her heels and went back into My Choice Clinic.

EVANGELINE: (to herself) Lord, have mercy. Can't believe I was thinkin' 'bout goin' there for a visit just a few weeks ago. King, please knock the walls of this place down like the walls of Jericho.

STORYTELLER: Evangeline looked to her left and to her right. She then set off down ANGER AVENUE. A few young men were gathered around a '64 Chevy, smoking and tinkering with the engine. One of them spotted Evangeline and nudged the others. In unison, they stared at her quietly as she approached them.

As she passed by, Crude whistled at her and made a comment about her pregnant belly. She continued on without saying a word. The young man's eyes hardened and he set out after her.

CRUDE: Aye, girl! Didn't you hear me? You can't just ignore a brotha like that and keep on walkin'. Nah!

STORYTELLER: Evangeline turned the corner and picked up her pace, but Crude was moving quickly with his two friends behind him.

CRUDE: Slow down! Slow down! I just wanna talk wit you, girl! Why ya in such a hurry? Where you goin'?

EVANGELINE: (to herself) King! I've been back for like ten minutes. Please don't let these boys get their hands on me or mistreat me. Please! I don't want no drama.

STORYTELLER: By now, Crude and his two companions were right at her heels. He reached out and grabbed her elbow but she shook free.

EVANGELINE: Leave me alone! I ain't playin'. Let me go!

STORYTELLER: Crude's two friends ran ahead and cut her off.

LEWD: You need to chill out, girl. You too cool to talk to some brothas?

RUDE: You might be one of our babies' mamas.

CRUDE: Matter a fact, that might be my baby you carryin' right now.

STORYTELLER: The three of them chuckled and looked at Evangeline with lustful eyes. Evangeline didn't look panicked, but I could tell she was growing more unsettled. There was nowhere to go and she couldn't see any help in sight.

Just in the nick of time, I spotted two young men rounding the corner. They were both decked out in hoodies. One of them had a silver cross dangling from a chain. It was Kai'Ro and Doulos.

When Kai'Ro recognized Evangeline, he ran as fast as he could and threw his arms around her in a giant hug. Evangeline's eyes erupted in surprise, but a peaceful smile slowly worked its way across her face. Realizing he had just rescued her, she wrapped her arms around him real tight. Kai'Ro wouldn't let her go either.

As though they were suddenly frozen in time, Crude, Lewd and Rude stood still. Watching such a tender embrace play out before their eyes, they looked shocked and confused. When Doulos jogged up to the circle, he nodded at the three strangers.

DOULOS: Sup, fellas?

CRUDE: W'sup.

EVANGELINE: (suddenly overjoyed) Kai'Ro. I didn't expect to see ya so soon!

STORYTELLER: When the three thugs heard Kai'Ro's name, their countenance changed and a look of worry crossed their faces. Almost in unison, all three of them took a step backwards.

Kai'Ro released Evangeline from his embrace and placed his hands gently on her face and looked into her eyes.

KAI'RO: You made it all the way to the Cross, didn't you?

EVANGELINE: (smiling) Yeah. How'd you know?

KAI'RO: 'Cause I can see it in ya eyes, girl. It's all over ya face. The peace of the King is all over you.

STORYTELLER: Lewd cleared his throat awkwardly and attempted to turn around and walk away.

KAI'RO: Aye, homie. Was there some kinda problem here or somethin'?

CRUDE: Ah, nah...dawg...

RUDE: We was just tryna make sure she got—

STORYTELLER: Kai'Ro turned to Evangeline and grabbed her hand.

KAI'RO: Did any of these cats put their hands on you, E.?

STORYTELLER: Crude, Lewd and Rude's eyes were nearly bugging out of their sockets with concern. They anxiously waited for Evangeline's answer.

EVANGELINE: Nah. Just let 'em go, Kai'Ro.

KAI'RO: (turning to Crude and his friends) Y'all better be treatin' the ladies in this community with some respect. Ya feel me?

LEWD: Yeah. We feel ya, dawg.

DOULOS: Then get to steppin', playa.

CRUDE: Yeah. C'mon, y'all. Let's bounce.

STORYTELLER: Crude, Lewd and Rude jogged back around the corner. Kai'Ro turned back to face Evangeline. She smiled from ear to ear and looked intently into Kai'Ro's eyes.

KAI'RO: So, you back already?

EVANGELINE: Yeah. The King told me to come back, to help you.

KAI'RO: For real?

EVANGELINE: Yeah. I was kinda disappointed, to be honest. I loved it out there!

KAI'RO: Yeah. I feel ya. I felt the same way when He called me back here too.

EVANGELINE: When that burden rolled off my back at the Cross, I never felt so alive and free. I just wanted to keep goin' all the way to the City of Light.

STORYTELLER: Kai'Ro took a look at Evangeline's belly and grinned happily.

KAI'RO: So how's ya, I mean, our...I mean, how's the baby?

EVANGELINE: He's good. I can feel him kickin' and squirmin' in there.

KAI'RO: (clapping his hands together) Him?

EVANGELINE: Uh-huh.

KAI'RO: How you know that?

EVANGELINE: The King let me know.

KAI'RO: For real? Shoot! That's amazin', girl. You got a name for him yet?

STORYTELLER: Evangeline nodded.

KAI'RO: Well, what is it?

EVANGELINE: (with a smile) Boy, I ain't tellin' you that yet!

KAI'RO: What? C'mon now! How 'bout Kai'Ro junior, but we call him Deuce?

STORYTELLER: Evangeline put her hands on her hips and frowned.

EVANGELINE: Boy. Quit playin'.

STORYTELLER: Doulos, who had been watching the whole time, cleared his throat and coughed.

KAI'RO: Oh, snap! Hey E., this is my boy, Doulos.

EVANGELINE: How ya doin'?

DOULOS: I'm straight.

KAI'RO: Yeah. Doulos is my boy. We been hangin' for a while . . . talkin' 'bout Life and talkin' bout the King, for real.

EVANGELINE: Ok. So you one of the King's soldiers then too?

DOULOS: Nah. Not yet. Ya man Kai'Ro has been teachin' me a lot 'bout Him, though. He's got me thinkin' I need to get out on that Heavenly Highway, for real.

EVANGELINE: Yeah. Kai'Ro can be pretty convincin'. But you oughta listen to him. I'm livin' proof that the Highway is just like he said. I went out there with a lotta guilt and a lotta questions. I came back feelin' free and with the answers I was lookin' for.

DOULOS: So, that's what up. I think ya boy is gonna battle Doc Destruction's goons in the War of the Words in a few nights.

EVANGELINE: For real?

DOULOS: There ain't no better platform for him to share what this King has put on his heart.

KAI'RO: Aye, come on, let's roll back to yo place, E. There's a lot I wanna hear about and talk about. Lot's happened since you been gone.

DOULOS: Aye, y'all, Ima bounce. I'll holler at you later, dawg.

STORYTELLER: Doulos took a turn at the end of the block, as Evangeline and Kai'Ro went back towards her place.

As they walked away, I watched Kai'Ro put his arm around her shoulder. I couldn't hear what they were saying, but I saw Evangeline throw her head back in a laugh. And, as they talked, I could see that both of their faces were glowing with joy.

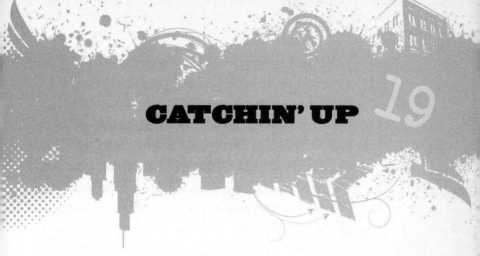

CATCHIN' UP

19

STORYTELLER: In my dream, I saw Kai'Ro and Evangeline sitting on the short set of stairs leading up to Evangeline's house. It was dusk and the sky around them was a dull dark orange. Kai'Ro had his hat in his hands.

EVANGELINE: (sighing) So, I'm back.

KAI'RO: Yeah. I'm glad ya back.

EVANGELINE: So, what now? We 'sposed to team up and save the city?

KAI'RO: (laughing) Ya mean like Batman and Robin or somethin'?

STORYTELLER: Evangeline offered a weak smile and shook her head.

EVANGELINE: I'm serious, Kai'Ro. I'm kinda confused. I mean, what does the King want us to do, for real? I'm a pregnant girl with no job. You got no education and no good job, for real. I mean, what're we 'sposed to do? It's not like people are gonna wanna listen to us. We look like everybody else on this block, washed up, used up...

KAI'RO: Aye, you need to chill out. I gotta believe you learned that the King can use anybody for His purposes.

EVANGELINE: Yeah, and I believe Him too. I guess I'm just wrestlin' with *how*. How're we gonna make a difference? What're we gonna do?

KAI'RO: Ya know, when I first came back, I felt overwhelmed too. I felt like the King sent me back here and wanted me to be Superman or somethin'. Like I was 'sposed to save the world, ya know? But it didn't go that way at all. He started showin' me it's all 'bout one life at a time. It's 'bout gettin' to know a few people...gettin' into their lives and their struggles and pointin' them to the King. *Only* the King can save the city. We're just His messengers. If we start takin' things one life at a time, it'll eventually turn into one street at a time—and then one block at a time—and then—

EVANGELINE: (laughing) And by then, we'll be ninety years old!

KAI'RO: Maybe, but the hope is that our kids and grandkids will get out on their grind for the King too. The King's soldiers don't die—they multiply. A while back, Preacher showed me that him and me aren't alone. There are a lotta people holdin' it down for the King here. Some of 'em are lawyers and some of 'em are bakers, but these people rep the King in their own way. That was encouragin' to me 'cause I knew then that I wasn't alone.

STORYTELLER: Evangeline grinned and shook her head.

KAI'RO: What? What's so funny?

EVANGELINE: Just look at us. Out on my mama's steps talkin' 'bout the King and bringin' the Good News of the King to the City of Doom. Two years ago, we'd be sittin' out here and you'd be drinkin' a 40. I'd be smokin' some cigarettes. We'd be talkin' mess...talkin' 'bout stupid stuff...even doin' stupid stuff and just actin' like there was no tomorrow...just livin' for the moment, you know.

KAI'RO: Yeah. I don't miss those days at all. Matter of fact, when I think 'bout 'em, it kinda makes me sick.

EVANGELINE: Me too. Makes me feel dirty and dumb. It was like I enjoyed livin' on a trash heap and callin' it home.

KAI'RO: That's a good way to put it.

EVANGELINE: It's funny 'cause my mom used to drag me to church when I was a young girl. You remember that church over on CRUSHED COURT? It was called For-Your-Good House of Faith?

STORYTELLER: Kai'Ro nodded.

EVANGELINE: I remember Sunday mornings hearin' Reverend Rich just straight hustlin' people with his religion. I mean, even I could tell everything the man said was so twisted. On Sunday mornin', he'd leave his mansion in the hills and roll on down in his big gold Cadillac. He always wore the nicest and most expensive suits. And he'd preach, and holler and sweat, telling everybody the same old story. His whole message was, if we'd just have more faith and if we'd just tithe more, God was gonna bless us!

You had moms who couldn't pay their power bills and put nothin' in the fridge for their babies, throwin' their last five dollars in the plate. Old ladies and broken people puttin' all their faith in that man. He'd take their money and cruise on back up the hill each evening. I watched my own mama put our last dime in the plate, just waitin' on her blessin' from the King.

I betcha she dragged me there for like five years. And you know what? I never saw a single thing change. I never saw nobody get outta the jams they was in. I never saw nobody get any lastin' hope. All I saw was Reverend Rich gettin' richer and usin' his own wealth as an example of how God wanted to bless other people.

But he and his sorry church did nothin' to make things better. The way they treated our community was like watchin' a helpless two-year-old kid drownin' in a pool and not doin' a thing 'bout it. By the time I was about twelve, I was done with *his* religion, *his* king and all that mess!

KAIRO: Yeah, that's all the dude was doin'. Instead of sellin' drugs, he was sellin' religion and false hope! Drugs and false hope will always sell to desperate and hurtin' people. Folks wanna snatch at that quick fix, for real!

EVANGELINE: Right. Dudes like Reverend Rich are sellin' that rock star gospel, ya know? They don't believe that the King is *the* King, for real. They don't know that the King ain't just any king—He's the *King of kings!* He demands and deserves all the glory and all the praise.

Reverend Rich has it twisted. He thinks the King's main interest is to be *his* costar. He wants people to believe that the King's main desire is makin' people's lives greater, easier, richer and all that. But I been readin' His Letters and that ain't the Gospel. The King's main interest isn't makin' our lives and our stories more impressive. In fact, it's just the opposite.

KAIRO: For sho, the King wants to invite us into *His* story. From the beginnin', He's been invitin' people to join *Him* in what *He's* doin' by bringin' the Good News to this dyin' world. You remember the Bible story about that rich cat, the one who came up to the King and asked what he needed to do to have eternal life?

EVANGELINE: Yeah. I read 'bout him in the Book not too long ago.

KAIRO: Uh-huh. The King told him to sell everything he had. The King said to give the money to the poor and then follow Him.

EVANGELINE: Yep. That dude couldn't do it. He was in love with his money. So he just walked away.

KAI'RO: Exactly. That rich man just wanted the King to come and be a part of *his* story. He was already grindin' and just wanted the King to join him in what he was already doin'.

EVANGELINE: (smiling) But the King was like "Nah. I came to this earth to invite you to join Me in what I'm doin'. Come and be a part of My story."

KAI'RO: That's right, girl. See, Reverend Rich and cats like him are completely ignorin' the warnings from the King's Letters. The King warns us that the love of guap is like the root of all evil. The King Himself said you can't serve both Him and that cash. He said you'd love one and hate the other. Those are some tough words, girl.

EVANGELINE: For real.

KAI'RO: But you gotta be careful. See, Reverend Rich sees money as a sign of the King's blessin'. He thinks poor people who don't have that queso are either short on faith or are on bad terms with the King. That's messed up. That message ain't nowhere in the King's Letters. Like you said, Reverend Rich has got it all twisted.

Now check this. There are some cats who have a lot of cash, but they don't see it as their own. They see themselves as stewards of the King's queso. In other words, the money that they got is His and they've got a big responsibility on how to use it. But Reverend Rich has got those Maybachs and Bentleys. He's convinced the King gave him the money so that he can roll big.

These other dudes believe the King gave them a lot of guap so they can give it out to others in need. Bein' rich ain't a sin, but it is when that money becomes your god and you serve it and worship it instead of the King.

STORYTELLER: Evangeline nodded in agreement.

KAI'RO: And, hey... let's be careful not to hate on the church as a whole. I mean, there's a lotta pastors and church folk who ain't no slave to money. They use what they have to care for their community and for those who are strugglin'. I got a lotta respect for dudes like Preacher and for his church. Folks like them keep me encouraged. Matter of fact... we need to get there this Sunday and start buildin' with them each week.

EVANGELINE: That's true.

STORYTELLER: Just then, she let out a giggle and put both of her hands on her belly.

EVANGELINE: Ooh! That boy just kicked me!

KAI'RO: For real? Lemme see.

STORYTELLER: Shortly after Kai'Ro placed his hand on her stomach, his eyes got real big.

KAI'RO: Hey! Lil' man is doin' some karate practice in there!

EVANGELINE: Maybe he's gonna be a dancer.

KAI'RO: Dancer? Nah, c'mon, girl. He's gonna be a ninja.

STORYTELLER: Evangeline smiled at Kai'Ro and gazed at him, while he remained transfixed on the baby in her belly.

EVANGELINE: So, where ya stayin'? At ya mama's?

KAI'RO: Nah. Lil' One turned my mama's crib into a drug den, for real. I can't stay there. I gave him a piece of my mind and tried to run him out. But then a few days later, I nearly got killed by some cats he's runnin' with. If I try to live at Ma's house, I'll either end up killin' him or somebody will end up killin' me.

EVANGELINE: I'm sorry. Lil' One was such a sweet boy. But after you left, he started followin' in your old footsteps, thuggin' and hustlin'.

STORYTELLER: Kai'Ro sighed and hung his head.

EVANGELINE: But it ain't over for him, Kai'Ro. If the King can rescue a no-good thug like you, I know He can rescue that lil' brother of yours too.

KAI'RO: Yeah, you right. I pray for Lil' One every day. I'm hopin' the King will give me an opportunity to share with him again.

EVANGELINE: So, where you stayin' then?

KAI'RO: Basically, I've just been sleepin' in Mr. Weary's garage for a while. He's got a little pull-out couch. He gave me a job at his shop too. That ol' dude's cranky, though...needs to drink more prune juice or somethin', for real. But he's been good to me...gave me a place to work and a place to crash. Sometimes he even let's me eat with him in the kitchen. I had nowhere to go and he took me in.

EVANGELINE: Look, I'm cool wit ya crashin' here, if you got no good place to stay. You can sleep on that bed in the extra room.

KAI'RO: I appreciate it, but nah. I don't want people to get the wrong idea.

EVANGELINE: What'cha mean?

KAI'RO: The King's Letters tell us to avoid every form of doin' evil. I mean, I'd be sleepin' in ya spare room, but it would have the appearance of bein' wrong. People would be convinced that I was sleepin' in ya bed.

EVANGELINE: (patting her stomach again) People already know ya been in my bed, boy.

KAI'RO: Yeah. I know. Now we gotta find out how to use lil' man as a way to proclaim the Truth.

EVANGELINE: What's that 'sposed to mean?

KAI'RO: What we did was wrong, girl. Havin' sex before marriage is wrong.

EVANGELINE: I know that, but it's a little too late now.

KAI'RO: It's too late in the sense that we havin' a baby, but it ain't too late to still teach the shorties out here that sex before marriage is wrong *one hundred* percent of the time. I'm just weary of people, even those up in the church, sayin' close to nothin' 'bout havin' babies outside of marriage. We got preachers' daughters gettin' knocked up. Folks will just run up and hug on the girl. Then they'll hold the baby when it's born, saying "Ah, look he's sooooo cute...just look at ya lil' boo!"

EVANGELINE: But babies are cute, Kai'Ro! Anybody knows that!

KAI'RO: True. True. But havin' babies in a broken home ain't cute at all. And sin ain't never cute!

EVANGELINE: Now, you startin' to sound like that lady I ran into at the abortion clinic!

KAI'RO: Hold up! I can't wait to hold my son, and I believe he's gonna be a blessin' from the King. The King is so amazin' that He can work out all things—*includin'* our sin and mistakes—for *good*! You and me producin' this baby boy out of wedlock was *sin* and a *mistake*. What I'm sayin' is that too many babies are bein' born into broken homes. Dad ain't around. Single moms tryna make ends meet. Kids growin' up thinkin' that a broken home is a normal home. Young girls convinced that if they got a baby or two then they're somehow desirable to men. Young men growin' up thinkin' sex is just a feel-good game and there's no responsibility that comes with it.

It's all part of a twisted circle that's gotta be broken. Someone's gotta tell people there ain't no such thing as safe sex. At least, not the way the world is teachin' about safe sex. The only safe sex the King is talkin' 'bout involves a wedding ring.

EVANGELINE: So, how do you see this workin' out then? You want me totin' 'round my baby, tellin' young girls that sex outside of marriage is wrong? What're you gonna do? Tell dudes to stay away from touchin' girls until they're married? You got no cred, boy! You already failed in that area. We both did.

STORYTELLER: Kai'Ro stared at the ground for a minute. Wrinkles formed on his forehead and his eyes narrowed.

KAI'RO: Look. I'm not sayin' that I have it all figured out just yet. But the King is in the business of takin' broken people, broken relationships and broken things—and usin' them for His glory. He knows how to use that kinda stuff and point people to a better way. He's passionate 'bout puttin' broken things back together again. He doesn't just want us to sit 'round and say "Oh well, we messed up. It's too late for us." I gotta believe He can use us, our mistakes and our future with this baby to do the same.

STORYTELLER: Evangeline exhaled a soft breath and put her hand on Kai'Ro's shoulder.

EVANGELINE: I believe you. You're right. I'm sorry for downin' what you been sayin'. The King has already shown me a love I didn't even think was possible, and He sent me back here to be with you. I'm kinda confused right now, but I believe that He has a plan and a purpose for me—for us—for all three of us.

STORYTELLER: Kai'Ro stood to his feet.

KAI'RO: I told you before you left for the Heavenly Highway that I wasn't gonna just be that baby's daddy. Ima be his *father*. I plan to take care of you too, E. Outside of the King, you've been the most important person in my life for the longest. Leavin' you for my own journey down the Heavenly Highway was the hardest thing I ever did. I felt like the King asked me to cut off my right arm when He told me to tell you goodbye and come follow Him.

But now He's given you back to me. And the connection that you and me have in Him is tighter than anything we ever had between us before. Plus, like I said a minute ago, I don't want our lil' man here thinkin' that it's normal to come from a broken home, where his dad is a dude who's just in and outta his life like a shadow. You and I grew up thinkin' that's just how it's 'sposed to be. But, by the King's good grace, I ain't gonna let my seed grow up that way.

STORYTELLER: Evangeline's eyes grew wider and wider the more Kai'Ro spoke. Like she was waiting for something special to come out of his mouth, she started to lean forward.

EVANGELINE: What're you tryna say to me, Kai'Ro?

STORYTELLER: Kai'Ro's face erupted into a big smile as he started to walk backwards down the steps and towards the sidewalk.

EVANGELINE: Hey! Where ya goin'?

KAI'RO: I gotta run. I'll holler at ya.

STORYTELLER: Evangeline called after Kai'Ro, but he took off down the sidewalk. His face was beaming and he was grinning from ear to ear.

MR. WEARY'S SECRET

20

STORYTELLER: My dream took me back to Mr. Weary's store. It was early morning. The sky was still a dusky grey but faint patches of sunlight pressed through the clouds.

The old storekeeper emerged from the storage room and walked down the center aisle, toiling with a heavy box full of laundry detergent in his hands. Kai'Ro was around the corner busily restocking the fridge with energy drinks when he heard Mr. Weary let out a slight moan. Kai'Ro raced from what he was doing and reached the older man just in time to catch the box of detergent before it crashed to the ground. Holding his back, Mr. Weary leaned forward and placed one hand on the younger man's shoulder.

KAI'RO: You all right, Mr. Weary? I told you that I can get those heavy boxes. You don't need to be carryin' all that weight.

MR. WEARY: Thank you, son. Give me just a minute. My old balky back has been givin' me fits lately.

STORYTELLER: Mr. Weary continued to lean on Kai'Ro for nearly two minutes before he finally straightened up. Kai'Ro waited patiently.

MR. WEARY: (sighing) There. That's better.

KAI'RO: You got any other heavy stuff back there? I'll take you out myself if I see you totin' another load like that.

MR. WEARY: Yeah. There's a few boxes of canned goods and a box of motor oil. Why don't you grab those and I'll finish stocking the fridge.

KAI'RO: Nah. How 'bout you just go sit behind the register and catch your breath. I got this.

STORYTELLER: Mr. Weary smiled and the wrinkles around his face were temporarily pushed away.

MR. WEARY: You're a good kid, Kai'Ro. Don't know what I would've done if you hadn't shown up in my store looking for work. These bones and joints of mine are starting to creak like old cupboard doors. Won't be too long before they just turn into dust and give out for good.

KAI'RO: Come on, Mr. Weary! You ain't that ol'. You gotta lot of years left in you. It wasn't so long ago that you used to chase me out of here with your old broom. You were quick too. I remember one time you sprang over the counter like a puma or somethin' and nearly caught me. You were growlin' and clawin' at me with that crazy look in your eyes. Nearly scared me half to death. I didn't know an ol' timer could move like that!

MR. WEARY: (chuckling) Boy, even an old snake like me can strike every once in a while. But, no. My time is coming to a close. I'm certain of it.

KAI'RO: What'cha mean?

STORYTELLER: Mr. Weary sighed and walked slowly back behind the counter. He opened the register, lifted up the money tray and pulled out an envelope. Placing it on the counter, he looked at Kai'Ro. Kai'Ro looked back at him for a moment before moving closer and picking up the envelope. When he opened it carefully and pulled out a thin sheet of paper, I watched as he read the news. Kai'Ro's face fell and he swallowed hard. His eyes slowly lifted from the paper to look at Mr. Weary.

MR. WEARY: Yes, son, death comes for us all. Came for me a little sooner than I bargained for. He's knocking on my door.

KAI'RO: Man, Mr. Weary, I'm sorry. I never knew. How come you never told me or anybody that you had cancer?

MR. WEARY: I don't know. Boy, you got enough weight on your shoulders. I don't want to burden nobody else with my pain. Besides, what can you do other than feel sorry for me?

KAI'RO: I woulda been prayin' for ya, for sure!

MR. WEARY: Huh! Prayer? I used to do that. Back in the day, I used to pray for a lot of stuff. But it seems like most of my prayers never left the room. It was like they got stuck in the ceiling or just fell back to the earth. Guess I gave up on prayer.

KAI'RO: So then, you didn't tell nobody?

MR. WEARY: Who was I going to tell? My wife has been dead for ten years. My only son died six years ago. I got a few relatives in town. Sure, I could tell them, but they'd just start bringing me casseroles and cakes and loving on me. At the same time, they'd be secretly hoping that I'd kick the bucket and leave them something in my will. My family? They're like blood-sucking mosquitoes—every last one of them.

KAI'RO: So, how much longer are they givin' you?

STORYTELLER: Mr. Weary shook his head and flicked a crumb off of the counter.

MR. WEARY: At the last visit, they said I got a month...maybe two, if I'm lucky.

KAI'RO: You know, Mr. Weary, you said that death was knockin' on your door.

MR. WEARY: Yeah? What about it?

KAI'RO: Well, death is knockin' on everybody's door. I mean, from the moment we're born, we're dyin'. You know, I may be young and look young, but I'm dyin' too. Every heartbeat and breath is just one more closer to my last.

MR. WEARY: What's your point?

KAI'RO: Well, death is knockin' on all of our doors, but so is Life.

MR. WEARY: Boy, don't start dropping all that religious stuff on me. You know I gave up on all that a long time ago.

KAI'RO: No, hear me out. This ain't no religious talk, for real. See, most people fear physical death. I mean, none of us wanna die. We worry about gettin' shot, gettin' a disease, gettin' hit by a car. But this is the great spiritual Truth. When we're born, we're already spiritually dead. I mean, we spiritually flatline the minute the doctor smacks our bottom in the hospital.

Yeah. We grow bigger and stronger and smarter physically. But spiritually, we're as dead as that cockroach over there on the floor. What I'm tryin' to say is most people go through their entire life fearin' physical death, not even knowin' they're already dead spiritually.

STORYTELLER: Mr. Weary opened his mouth as if he were going to say something, but then closed it and continued to listen.

KAI'RO: But here's the funny thing. See, we worry all the time 'bout tryin' to prevent somethin' that can't be stopped. I mean, look over here on aisle two.

STORYTELLER: Kai'Ro hurried over to the aisle and pulled some stuff off the shelf.

KAI'RO: See, you got "anti-wrinkle" creams and shampoo that's supposed to grow ya hair back—

MR. WEARY: Yeah. Those two products don't work. Trust me, I tried them.

KAI'RO: Here's some anti-aging makeup for the ladies...I mean, there's tons of stuff that's tryin' to slow down the unstoppable process of agin' and physical death. Imagine steppin' in front of a freight train that was movin' just five miles an hour. It's movin' slow, real slow, but could you really slow it down any more or stop it by just standin' in front of it with your arms stretched out?

MR. WEARY: No. You'd get smashed flat.

KAI'RO: Exactly. So why do we spend so much time and effort tryin' to stop somethin' we can't stop?

MR. WEARY: Probably because we're stupid.

KAI'RO: Yeah, maybe. But see, spiritual life is somethin' you can have in an instant. And it only grows stronger and more powerful as we live. It's almost like an anti-aging cream or a powerful vitamin for your soul.

MR. WEARY: You're losing me now.

KAI'RO: The King! I've told you 'bout Him. How He came not only to free us from the consequences of our sin, but He also came to give us new Life! When we give our lives to Him in return, He gives us His Spirit. Then His Spirit works powerfully in us and through us to give us more Life.

Take me, for example, you knew me as a shortie. I was angry, a liar, a thief and a thug. Every one of my decisions was hurtin' me and hurtin' others. But look at me now. Am I the same kid you knew a few years back?

MR. WEARY: No. The difference between what I saw then and what I see now is night and day.

KAI'RO: But see, that's 'cause I have Life now. I'm pretty sure that, deep inside of yourself, you've felt that spiritual death...that hollowness...that emptiness. Am I right?

STORYTELLER: Before answering, Mr. Weary stared at Kai'Ro in silence for a minute.

MR. WEARY: Sometimes. There have been times when I've felt depressed and miserable beyond words. If I'm honest, I've felt that way much more often than I've ever felt good about things.

KAI'RO: Well, there is Life the King wants to give you that will fill that emptiness. That Life is knockin' on ya door. Sure, you're dyin', but there's another part of you that the King longs to make alive forever! Not only that, the Life He wants you to have will be with you through this one and the Life to come!

STORYTELLER: Mr. Weary exhaled a long breath and put the envelope back in the register. He frowned.

MR. WEARY: I hear what you're saying, son, but I think it's too late for me. See, I've heard this message before. Not exactly the way you put it, but similar. I've just rejected it as a bunch of hooey. Believe it or not, I've been beyond the hedges there. Yeah, I stepped out there once back when I was close to your age. It was beautiful out there.

I almost kept going too, but there were too many things back here in the City of Doom that I wanted more. You might say I was hungrier for what this city had to offer. It wasn't long until I forgot about that Heavenly Highway...took my mind off of it and went on to school...wasn't too long before my heart grew old and cold.

STORYTELLER: Kai'Ro stepped forward and slapped the counter.

KAI'RO: Mr. Weary, it's *never* too late! Shoot! One of the dudes that got crucified next to the King cried out to Him and the King gave Him Life just before that dude gave up his last breath. Don't underestimate the King's love for you. He paid the biggest price there is to set us free and to give us new Life!

STORYTELLER: Mr. Weary's lower lip quivered slightly. His chin dropped on his chest and he stared hard at the floor. Moments later, he placed his hands on his hips and slowly raised his eyes to look at Kai'Ro.

MR. WEARY: Boy, what happened to you? Who are you? I've heard preachers and old timers share stuff with me since I was a child. But I don't know if I've ever heard someone like you before...don't know if I've ever seen anybody like you either. A lot of the religion some of the cats are peddling out here in these streets is a bunch of hooey.

But you, you're real, son. You walk the talk. You've been on time every morning. Every time I've counted the register it's been true down to the penny. You've treated every customer in here, even the ugly and nasty ones, with genuine respect. You've done everything I've asked you with a good attitude. And even the stuff I haven't asked you to do, you've done that too. I don't know how many kids your age would unclog a toilet, but you've done it many times with a smile.

I'd call you a good employee, but that wouldn't be the right way to put it. You've been a real bright spot in an old man's darkest days. I ain't gonna lie. I was scared to death the first week I let you sleep in my garage. I slept with a shotgun every night. But over time, it got to the point where I actually felt safer with you nearby—at my house and here at the store. I felt like maybe somebody sent me an angel to watch over me.

STORYTELLER: Kai'Ro stood there silently, listening.

MR. WEARY: (sighing) Maybe you're right, son. Maybe it ain't too late for me after all. If this King is as good as you say, I'd sure like to have that Life He has to offer. Maybe these old bones got enough strength for one more long walk before it's all over with.

STORYTELLER: Mr. Weary smiled a big smile and, for the first time, I saw a twinkle of light in his eyes.

MR. WEARY: Now, how about you go unpack those boxes. The customers are going to be rolling in here soon.

WAR OF THE WORDS

Rap lyrics written by Sho Baraka

STORYTELLER: My dream took me into a park that was packed with hundreds of people. It was nighttime and, through the dull glow of the yellowish street lights, I could see a massive crowd gathered around a stage. Some spotlights flashed on revealing a short fat man standing behind some turntables. He was wearing a dark gray T-shirt with a red-horned devil's face on the front. With a black ball cap cocked sideways on his head, he wore baggy jeans and some Timberlands.

Flipping some switches, the DJ started a track that blasted a slow-droning bass over the crowd like waves in the ocean. The audience pressed in around the stage until there was hardly any room to move. Like one massive living organism, the crowd moved to the beat of the music.

A few minutes went by before a fleet of Black Range Rovers appeared. As if on cue, the DJ addressed the crowd.

DJ GRIND: Aye, er'body, back on up! Make room for Doc Destruction and the Destroyas!

STORYTELLER: The crowd parted down the middle as the parade of vehicles drove right up to the front of the stage. Lil' Pain, Slice, Dice and Cutter jumped out of the first ride. Immediately, Lil' Pain's three comrades snarled and rushed up on some of the people in the crowd who were getting too close.

Lil' Pain was wearing dark designer skinny jeans, bright yellow Js and a crisp white beater. His eyes were hidden behind thick shades. There were two prominent tattoos on his forearms. One of them said VENGEANCE, with a long python coiled in and out of the letters. The other arm had the word TERROR on it, surrounded by nearly a dozen smoking bullet casings.

Young Sleazy got out of the second ride after a muscled chauffeur opened the door for him. Holding on to his arms were two beautiful girls. It was hard to tell whether or not they were wearing super-short dresses or just long, ultra-tight, low-cut shirts. Tattooed on the thigh of the girl on his right was the word PLEASURE. The girl on his left had IBGOOD2U tattooed along her swooping neckline. The eyes of nearly every man in the crowd wandered to Sleazy's two companions, whose outfits left nothing to the imagination.

Young Sleazy was dressed in designer jeans and some blue Chucks. He wore a plaid collared shirt that was unbuttoned at the top, revealing a flashy silver chain. A white ball cap rested precariously on his head and an iced-out watch draped his wrist.

Finally, King Ca$h and Doc Destruction emerged from the last vehicle. Both of them were quickly surrounded by bodyguards wearing dark suits and toting guns. King Ca$h was wearing an Armani suit. Two massive diamonds studded both of his ears. His head was neatly shaven, shiny and smooth.

Taking his time, Ca$h stopped and glared at the mob of people for a minute. Then he pulled a large wad of bills out of his breast pocket. In a dramatic gesture, he lobbed it over the circle of his bodyguards and out into the crowd. A cloud of hundred dollar bills floated down on the people as they cheered wildly, yelled, punched and fought like animals over the cascading money. Doc Destruction smirked and flicked the ash that was hanging from his fat cigar. The bodyguards nervously raised their guns as the crowd pressed in closer.

DJ GRIND: Yeeeaaah! That's what's up, y'all! The Destroyas are up in this joint! They 'bout to drop somethin' fierce on y'all tonight...'bout to bring that heat up in here!

STORYTELLER: My dream suddenly took me just outside the mob around the stage. I saw Kai'Ro standing on the sidewalk. To his left was Evangeline, and on his right were Preacher and Doulos. Kai'Ro was watching the rabid scene play out in front of him. He stood up straight with his hands in his pockets. Wearing a white tall-T, dark blue jeans, and some white and blue Airforce Ones, his tattered black Bible was stuck in his back pocket. His favorite chain with the cross hung round his neck. He looked calm and I noticed a quiet fire burning in his eyes.

DOULOS: You nervous, dawg?

EVANGELINE: You don't have to do this, Kai'Ro. Nobody's been on that stage and challenged those dudes before.

KAI'RO: (calmly) Nah. This is somethin' I gotta do, y'all. I feel like I was built to do this. There's a furnace ragin' inside of me that I can't explain.

EVANGELINE: They're goin' to tear you apart up there.

DOULOS: Every one of them three boys can spit, dawg. I've seen 'em straight clown some fools before. They're merciless. I know I gave you this whole idea in the first place. But if you back out I'll understand, homie.

KAI'RO: Y'all don't seem to understand. I can spit too. The King gave me a gift to rhyme just like those dudes. But it ain't 'bout me tonight. I've begged the King on my knees that He would spit through me tonight. Y'all right 'bout one thing. If all the crowd gets tonight is Kai'Ro, then I will fail.

But if the King shows up, then every ear will be opened and we'll beat the brakes off those cats. The King can silence those three clowns on the stage. He has the power to undress them, expose them as liars and then raise Himself up as the Truth. This is why I gotta go. He's called me as His messenger tonight. If I fall back, then I'm no better than a traitor.

PREACHER: This ain't just some rap battle here. This is a battle of the gods tonight. Those three men worship at the feet of their own gods—violence, pleasure, power, greed. They are fully convinced that their gods are great and worthy of their worship. Most of those people in the crowd feel the exact same way. They aren't here just for the music. They're here to worship those gods.

I believe the King has summoned Kai'Ro for a time such as this one. It's time for someone to introduce this city to the only One who can free them and save them and give them Life!

KAI'RO: All y'all know. That used to be me up there. I used to flow like those dudes 'cause that's how I was livin' back then. And like all those poor trapped zombies in the crowd, I used to worship what I was spittin'. But, now that I got the Truth. I mean, the *real* Truth, I just can't keep it shut up inside me. I gotta whole lotta light in me and I gotta let it shine!

STORYTELLER: Doulos took a deep breath and then nodded before patting Kai'Ro on the back. Evangeline stepped forward and grabbed his hand.

EVANGELINE: I believe in you, Kai'Ro.

STORYTELLER: Kai'Ro turned to Evangeline and placed his hands on her shoulders.

KAI'RO: Believe in the One who's in me and who's in you too.

EVANGELINE: (smiling) I do.

KAI'RO: Pray for me, y'all. Ima need it.

STORYTELLER: The music from the stage was almost deafening. The masses around the platform were nearly in a frenzy, pumping their fists, shouting and bobbing their heads. DJ Grind was working the turntables furiously. Pleasure and Ibgood2u were up there dancing seductively and vibing to the beat. Lil' Pain, Young Sleazy and King Ca$h had taken their places on the stage as well. They were pointing at the crowds and beating their chests.

Doc Destruction ordered a large leather sofa pulled out of a pickup truck and hauled onto the back of the stage for him to watch the festivities. He flopped down into the corner of it, crossed his legs and slowly bobbed his head, as he puffed his cigar and sipped from a glass.

DJ GRIND: All right! All right! Y'all ready for Doc Destruction and the Destroyas to get this place jumpin' tonight?

STORYTELLER: The crowd exploded in enthusiastic shouts.

DJ GRIND: Yeeeeah! Y'all know that Doc and his crew been layin' it down for us for the longest. They like the soundtrack to our souls. They like the heartbeat of this city. Our city! The City of Doooooooooooom!

STORYTELLER: His voice boomed and again the crowd erupted in shouts and cheers. But I noticed that some people stood there silently, particularly some of the older ones. Altogether, no one appeared to be older than forty.

DJ GRIND: Now let me hand the mic to the...Man with the Plan...The Sultan of Sexy...the Prince of Power...the Magi of Muscle...the Viceroy of Violence...the Count of Kush...the Duke of Diamonds and the King of Bling. The man who runs things up in here...Doc Deeeeeestruuuuuuctionnnnnn!

STORYTELLER: As his voice boomed once again, a third series of applause broke out. But, this time, it was nervous clapping. I noticed how those in the front row were clapping as loud as they could while eyeing Doc's thugs with their guns at the same time. Doc Destruction gave DJ Grind a slight shove and grabbed the mic.

DOC DESTRUCTION: (after a long pause of leering at the crowd) I know that y'all came tonight to be entertained...to be mesmerized...and to receive *true* enlightenment. Because y'all know how we do it up in here. Y'all know what we all about! If it feels good...then we *do* it! If it looks good...then we *got* it! If it speaks up or gets in our way...we *stomp* it! If you ain't rollin' large and rollin' hard, then you might as well roll over—'cause you nobody! We are the *heartbeat* of this city and tonight we gonna open our heart to you and let you vibe with us. But—

STORYTELLER: Doc held up one finger in the air and took a long puff on his cigar.

DOC DESTRUCTION: But you know, we ain't gotta keep this stage all to ourselves. Like we do every year, we open up a mic to a challenger. To someone who might feel just a little different, who might have the stones to step up here...and...get... destroooyed! No one has grabbed that mic in years, but maybe there's somebody out there tonight?

STORYTELLER: Doc Destruction sarcastically held his hand up to his eyes and squinted, as if he was looking to the very back of the crowd. As he did so, the crowd began to part and, in my dream, I saw Kai'Ro slowly making his way towards the stage.

One of the stage-crew members whipped his light around to shine it on Kai'Ro. But when he did, the bulb sparked and burned out. Then a light from above, from far beyond the building tops themselves, fell down on Kai'Ro with laser-like precision. The closer he moved to the front, the people in the crowd backed away. From my vantage point, the light on him was brilliant and Kai'Ro himself appeared like he was illuminated from within.

Just then, Lil' One jumped out of the crowd and grabbed his brother's arm.

LIL' ONE: (leaning into Kai'Ro's ear) Don't do this, bruh! I'm tellin' ya. This ain't gonna end good for you. They're gonna clown you off that stage and right outta town.

STORYTELLER: Kai'Ro grabbed his brother's shoulder and pulled him in close.

KAI'RO: The King is in the house tonight, lil' brother. Don't you feel Him? He's here. This is His stage. His mic. His night. It's time to get outta His way and let Him go to work. Open your heart to Him, bruh. He loves ya.

STORYTELLER: Kai'Ro jumped straight up onto the stage and snatched the extra mic out of DJ Grind's hand.

KAI'RO: I challenge these boys tonight.

DOC DESTRUCTION: (throwing back his head and laughing) You? Ain't you that lil' boy we slapped around a few weeks ago?

LIL' PAIN: That's the one. I slapped that boy around like an ugly dog.

YOUNG SLEAZY: Shoot! Toilet Boy wants to spit tonight? This is hilarious!

KING CASH: Somebody better call the police 'cause somebody's 'bout to get murdered on this stage tonight!

STORYTELLER: The crowd booed and called Kai'Ro names. Pleasure and Ibgood2u circled around Kai'Ro like two mean dogs, making ugly faces and pursing their lips at him.

IBGOOD2U: (in a hiss) You ugly, boy.

PLEASURE: You poor *and* you ugly. Get off this stage while you still can.

DOC DESTRUCTION: (growling into his mic) You don't stand a chance at this battle, boy. This is *real* war up here, son. You gonna get hurt. Baaaaad!

KAI'RO: You right. This is a real war up here. But I didn't come alone. I'm cliqued up with the King tonight. This ain't just words that we gonna be warrin' with. There's gonna be a war goin' on in heavenly places this evening.

DOC DESTRUCTION: (scratching his head) Huh? Somebody grab this clown off the stage and get him to a doctor. King? Boy, the four kings who run this town are standin' in front of you. You know that. Er'body knows that.

KAI'RO: After tonight, there will only be one King. The true King. The King of kings.

STORYTELLER: Doc Destruction's entire face wrinkled in anger.

DJ GRIND: (stepping between Kai'Ro and Doc Destruction) OK. OK. Let's do this thing. Let's do the toss. Let the coin decide who spits first.

STORYTELLER: DJ Grind pulled a silver coin out of his pocket. On one side was a skull and crossbones. On the other was an image of a scantily clad female.

DJ GRIND: The home team makes the call. Heads . . . or tail.

DOC DESTRUCTION: (pointing an imaginary pistol at Kai'Ro's face) Heads.

STORYTELLER: DJ Grind tossed the coin into the air. In my dream, it seemed to flip and spiral in the air forever before it fell to the ground. It spun and gyrated for a minute before lying flat. It was heads.

DJ GRIND: It's heads, y'all. Looks like the Destroyas are grabbin' the mic first tonight. Kai'Ro gets the last word.

KAI'RO: I ain't spittin' the last word. It's the *final* word!

KING CASH: Man, scratch this! Give me that mic. Let me start this thing off right. This boy won't know what hit him.

STORYTELLER: King Ca$h threw his suit coat at one of his body-guards. DJ Grind went back to the turntables and flipped on a track. It was an up-tempo beat. The crowd immediately threw their hands in the air and pumped them to the music.

KING CA$H:

Let's talk cash for a second, little man. Here we go . . .
This boy claims he got final word/
Talkin' 'bout King, don't this fool sound disturbed/
But he dress just like he can be my paper boy/
No one here cares what you think, you must be crazy, boy/
Don't come 'round here preachin', boy/
I got 'nough money to buy a church on Easter, boy/
Fool, you starin' at a real king/
Cars and cash, you see the way I bling/
Black and white diamonds, yeah, it's the real thing/
I'm the champ, go 'head 'n kiss the ring/
You a nine to five worker and toilet-seat cleaner/
I drive luxury Maybachs and Beamers/
Bentleys, Ferraris, Porsche two seaters/
This is my reality and you just a dreamer/
I stay with nicest things on da planet/
You look like ya can't afford a peanut butter jelly sandwich/
I throw away money, it's da thang that I do/
I got designer suits worth more than you/
But you can work for me and you can get paid/
You can be my trash man or you can be my maid/
Matter of fact, you can start today/
Since you trash, gon 'head and move yo' self off the stage!

STORYTELLER: When King Ca$h finished, the crowd burst into shouts. Those in the front row were jumping around and going absolutely crazy. Kai'Ro never once moved and hardly blinked, even though Ca$h had been up in his face and done his best to humiliate him.

LIL' PAIN: OK. I got this! Aye, DJ, hit me with somethin' that's bangin'.

STORYTELLER: DJ Grind threw on a track that was energetic and loud.

LIL' PAIN: (to the crowd below) Make ya hands into a fist. Then throw 'em in the air like this.

STORYTELLER: Immediately, the entire crowd did as they were told. They made their hands into fists and pumped them in the air in unison with Lil' Pain.

LIL' PAIN:

You a joke, little man, Imma killa/
City of Doom ain't seen one reala/
I come thru with a shottie and a nine/
Before you blink one time, I'll blow away yo' mind/
You keep talkin' 'bout some King in the sky/
Readin' fairytales books that teach you lies/
Dumb little kid, this is not a game/
We knew you was stupid, but now you insane/
But I got the medicine in my chamber/
One squeeze of the finger and you in danger/
Answer this . . . what kind of brother are you?/
We beat you down, yo brother sat there and watched you/
Plus we took over yo mom's crib/
Played a little house, that would make me yo dad, kid/
It's OK, baby, go 'head and cry/
You want revenge for yo beatin' go 'head and try/
If you had sense then you would realize/
We let you slide but next time you will not survive/
Cuz my goons just waitin' to end yo world/
Burn yo moms house down and take yo pretty girl/
Go 'head and admit you just scared of us/
I heard you were real but now you just a square punk/
By the way, what kinda name is Kai'Ro/

I jus' set you on fire er'body call you pyro/
Don't let me see you in da streets, lil' mane/
You'll find out again why they call me Lil' Pain/
Cuz out here, I take my respect, fool/
When I see you on the block, that King can't protect you!

STORYTELLER: During Lil' Pain's verse, several fights broke out in the crowd. I even heard a few gunshots. Kai'Ro looked back to see if Evangeline and his friends were all right. Still, just as before, he remained poised and waited for his turn to rhyme.

DJ GRIND: Daaaang! Y'all are puttin' the hurt on this poor dude. Somebody please call the medics. This boy is gettin' brutalized up here.

YOUNG SLEAZY: Hold up! We ain't done with him just yet. Yeaaah! You know how we do. Aye, DJ, play me somethin' real smooth that me and my girls can move to.

STORYTELLER: DJ Grind put on a track that was slow and sensual. The bass was deep and pronounced. Ibgood2u and Pleasure immediately started moving to the music. They got out on the front of the stage and teased some of the men in the crowd by pointing at them and pretending to draw them on stage with their fingers. Only the bodyguards and their guns kept the drooling men back. Then they circled around Young Sleazy and danced as he grabbed his mic and started to flow.

YOUNG SLEAZY:
Ask the girls, I get all the play/
Word on the street is that Kai'Ro is gay/
I get five or six different girls every week/
You got one girl and she a washed up freak/
I'm a player, homie, the game's too easy/
Go and ask your mom why they call me young sleazy/
Plus I drive a flashy car/
Pretty boy face, I'm like a Hollywood star/
Girls hit the dance floor when I start to rhyme/

I might steal yo girl and make her mine/
And I will keep her, if she acts all wild/
Look at her belly cuz that might be my child/
After this I may put your skull on my wall/
So when I bring the ladies home you can see it all/
Why you bring that ol' raggedy preacher/
My girls will turn him to a midnight creeper/
Nobody wants your church or religion/
We want the cars, and the cash, and the women/
Run to Heaven and go tell your King/
That He can call me if He's lookin' for His queen!

STORYTELLER: When all three of the Destroyers had finished their verses, I looked to Kai'Ro. There wasn't a man I knew who could have survived the first verse, let alone the three-fold verbal beatdown that he endured. I half-expected him to run off the stage and wouldn't have blamed him if he did.

The crowd was on the verge of insanity. Young Sleazy and his girls had brought out the worst in them. They cursed at Kai'Ro and threw bottles and trash at him. Doc Destruction was laughing almost hysterically on his couch. His eyes were brimming full of ridicule and scorn.

KAI'RO: (with his eyes closed and in a whisper) My King, You called me on this stage tonight. I'm only here to bring You glory. These men have stripped me down to my bones and humiliated me. But even more, they've attacked Your holy name. I ask You now to open my mouth and spit through me so that every deaf ear can hear. I ask You to shine bright through me so that every blind eye can see. Explode on this stage so that everyone will know tonight that You are King!

DJ GRIND: It's yo turn, boy. Ya ready?

KAI'RO: Yeah. Spin it.

STORYTELLER: DJ Grind flipped the switch but nothing came on. He tried a few more things but still nothing happened. With a puzzled look, he turned to Doc Destruction and shrugged. Bending down, he checked some plugs.

As he was stooped over searching for the problem, a powerful and beautiful track suddenly burst from the speakers. It was rhythmic and diverse. It startled DJ Grind and he stood up quickly and banged his head. Turning back to Doc again, he made a confused face and extended his arms in bewilderment. Kai'Ro smiled, grabbed the mic and started to flow.

KAI'RO:

The crowds cheerin' for you, but not much longer/
By the power of the King Ima come much stronger/
Ok, Ca$h, you got money. Pain, you got muscle/
Sleazy got women, the block respects the hustle/
But there were bruz before you who played the same game/
Like them, years from now, we'll forget yo name/
Y'all are just puppets, but you can't see the string/
But I've come to introduce you to a real King/
He's much greater than the stuff that y'all chasin'/
And His judgment is greater than the jail time y'all facin'/
I see all that y'all have and it's all temptin'/
But answer this . . . with all that, why are you still empty/
Give me a second I'll explain what I mean/
I see a nightmare in what you call a dream/
You always want more, you're never satisfied/
But you can't take that stuff wit you when you die/
But think about this, we don't own nothin'/
Who gives you sight, and breath and keeps your blood
   pumpin'/
You fightin' over streets and blocks that you ain't make/
The same corners and blocks that they sold slaves/
The same streets our grandparents fought to be on/
Fought for our schools but we rather be fools/
It's 'cause we love evil over good/
Instead of helpin' one another we steal in the hood/

That's all I see you three brothers doin'/
Do y'all have any idea how many lives you've ruined?

KAI'RO: (speaking to King Ca$h)
Yeah, you're a grown man who got a lotta toys/
But underneath all the money you a scared little boy/
Didn't get 'nough hugs, no pops to show love/
So now you hide your pain with money, clothes and drugs/
You ain't foolin' me, I was in the same boat/
Then it started drownin' and I know I wouldn't float/
No hearse will follow you to the grave/
Filled with all the stuff and the money you made/
So if you can't take it with you, why die for it/
So when you call me Paper Boy I just ignore it/
But like the paper boy I bring Good News/
Real soon the King returns to His throne and rules/
I had street money but I'm happier now/
I refuse to join this circus and play with you clowns/
Cuz the King got my riches on lock, He's the Savior/
I may look broke now but I will ball out later/
So take your crib, car, take your holiday bonus/
And I bet one percent of the King's wealth will make you look
    homeless/
Instead of buyin' a church on Easter, you need to attend/
Cuz even for those ugly suits you wear you need to repent/
So even though I look poor in your eyes I will manage/
I'm good with the King and my peanut butter and jelly sand-
    wich!

KAI'RO: (speaking to Lil' Pain)
Lil' Pain, yeah, you got guns and felony records/
But my King will smash you in a second/
I'm not scared of you, homie, I did this before/
No longer a goon on the streets, I thug for the Lord/
Pull out the 9 mil you won't see me jumpin'/
You shoot me today, and my life will mean somethin'/

But can you say the same thing, big brother/
Instead a hurtin' your neighbor can you love each other/
No, because you think that it's gay/
What you call bein' weak, is what we call bein' Saints/
I stand today willin' to die for the cause/
I'm not here to fight you or get their applause/
I'm here to rep the King, the One who knows it all/
You think you tough cuz you jumped me in a brawl/
Let me tell you a few things, I ain't no punk/
Sissy, scared little boy, or no chump/
Let me also tell you I ain't scared of your guns/
Or your three little flunkies over there lookin' dumb/
But you should be scared of the LORD when He come/
You can barely lift your arm, and He raises the sun/
I know your type, deep down you want someone to care/
About the sad little boy whose daddy wasn't there/
Cryin' to yo self thinkin' life ain't fair/
Brother, that's a story that we all can share/
So, as you can see I've changed, I'm a new man/
But I might just return, if you try to harm my fam!

KAI'RO: (speaking to Young Sleazy)
You get girls cuz you give them stuff, that's the truth/
But you sex to feel important so who's the real prostitute/
Just b'cuz I don't sleep around don't mean I'm gay/
I'm waitin' for my bride, that's the King's way/
And, yeah, back in the day I made some mistakes/
But I'll teach my child not to repeat the ones I make/
Usually the one who is gay tries to prove he's not/
And you sure do call other people gay a lot/
You were prob'ly hurt or misused/
Now you use sex as a tool to prove that you're cool/
See you think a real man is bein' sleazy/
Run 'round town sleep with girls that's easy/
Brother, you will wake up with an S.T. Deezy/

Then you'll pray to the King like, "LORD, please clean me"
But you will have to live with the conscious/
Of treating every single girl you know like some object/
But GOD made women from our flesh/
So we should treat them like ourselves, nothin' more, nothin'
    less/
Your body gets old and the girls get old too/
So when you get older, without sex, what you gonna do/
You wanna be known as the ol' man on the scene/
Sittin' back on his porch reading porn magazines/
And Evangeline is a jewel in this city/
Godly woman, classy, smart and pretty/
You wish you had a woman like that/
But the closest you'll get is a newspaper rack!

KAI'RO: (addresses the crowd and artists)
This was not to prove who is the best rapper/
I came here to bring the Truth of the matter/
That the City of Doom is a place in pain/
And the only One who can heal you is the true King/
As I stand here don't let these men here fool you/
They're just human so don't let these men rule you/
I hope y'all got Truth and love in the rhymes that you heard/
Cuz I'm here to rep the King and that's the final word!

STORYTELLER: When Kai'Ro was finished, I thought I saw a literal flame dancing in his eyes. The crowd around the stage was stunned to silence. Eyes were wide and mouths were open but a mesmerized hush was upon everyone. Young Sleazy, Lil' Pain and King Ca$h's faces were anguished with a look of defeat. Lil' Pain accidentally dropped his mic to the ground and clawed around awkwardly trying to retrieve it.

A strong gust of wind rushed across the stage that caught Doc Destruction by surprise and blew his cigar from his mouth. Then I heard a deep and frightening groan of thunder. There was a dazzling flash of lightning that hit DJ Grind's turntables.

They exploded into fire and all of the lights on stage spit sparks and went out.

The crowd fell back in shock, holding their hands in front of their faces. Some people took off running. Doc Destruction stood up from his couch and looked around him in disbelief. Young Sleazy jumped off the stage with Pleasure and Ibgood2u doing the same with a loud scream.

DOC DESTRUCTION: Somebody...grab that clown...NOW!

STORYTELLER: Doc's goons snapped out of their daze and whipped out their guns. They looked all around them and all through the crowd. But they were at a loss because Kai'Ro was nowhere to be found.

ABOVE AND BEYOND

STORYTELLER: After the rap battle ended, my dream took me beyond the park. Kai'Ro was standing near a curb next to Evangeline and Preacher. His face was wet with perspiration, and his eyes were aglow. Evangeline wrapped him in a hug and held him real tight. Preacher was speechless but kept smiling and shaking his head.

EVANGELINE: You were incredible up there, Kai'Ro! I didn't think you could still flow like that.

PREACHER: (finding his voice) Well done, son. Very well done.

KAI'RO: Aye, I appreciate it, y'all. But that was an amazingly unique experience. I gotta be real. I felt like my mind and heart were plugged into somethin' outside myself. It was like the King was flowin' and I was just His sound system. You know, He deserves all the credit for tonight.

EVANGELINE: You're right, but it took a lot of courage to get up on that stage. I don't know another man who woulda done that, for real.

STORYTELLER: Just then, in the distance, I heard a few loud popping sounds followed by loud shouting.

PREACHER: Is that fireworks?

STORYTELLER: Kai'Ro frowned.

KAI'RO: I don't think so.

STORYTELLER: Just then, Doulos came sprinting around the corner with a panicked look in his eyes.

KAI'RO: What up, homie? What's goin' on?

DOULOS: (hollering) Aye! You remember when I told you somethin' was gonna go down with Doc and that boy, Cut Throat?

KAI'RO: Yeah. W'sup?

DOULOS: Dawg, as soon as you finished flowin', some of Doc's goons and Cut Throat's goons started tusslin' in the crowd. Some shots started poppin' off. It's like world war three back there! I split as soon as I heard the first shot. But them dudes were shootin' right into the crowd! A few cats got dropped right beside me.

STORYTELLER: Kai'Ro's eyes widened.

KAI'RO: Lil' One!

EVANGELINE: No, Kai'Ro! It's too dangerous. You'll get killed!

DOULOS: You need to listen to ya girl, playa. The drama back there is thick.

STORYTELLER: Kai'Ro looked over at Preacher.

PREACHER: What's the King telling you to do, son? This ain't no time to try to be a hero. This is the time when you listen to what the King is speaking into your heart.

KAI'RO: Then I gotta go. Part of the reason the King sent me back was to bring Lil' One the Good News.

EVANGELINE: But you already told him 'bout the Good News and he tuned you out!

KAI'RO: You right, E. I *told* him 'bout the Good News, but now it's time to show him.

DOULOS: Dawg, you one craaazy fool.

KAI'RO: Preacher, please take E. back with you. If somethin' goes down, I need you to watch over her.

PREACHER: Like she's my own daughter.

STORYTELLER: Kai'Ro walked over to Evangeline and put both of his hands on her shoulders. She looked distraught and continued to shake her head in protest.

KAI'RO: The King has called me to do this. I need you to believe that and, even more, I need you to pray for me.

STORYTELLER: Tears pooled in Evangeline's eyes and slowly trickled down her cheeks.

EVANGELINE: I don't...we don't...wanna lose you, Kai'Ro.

STORYTELLER: Kai'Ro kissed her tenderly on her forehead before walking off in the direction of the gunfire and shouting.

PREACHER: (speaking loudly after Kai'Ro) For He will command His angels concerning you to guard you in all your ways. On their hands they will bear you up, lest you strike your foot against a stone.

KAI'RO: (whispering softly to himself) Because he holds fast to Me in love, I will deliver him; I will protect him, because he knows My name. When he calls to Me, I will answer him; I will be with him in trouble; I will rescue him and honor him. With long life I will satisfy him and show him My salvation.

STORYTELLER: As Kai'Ro drew closer, I could hardly believe what I saw before me. The field where the rap battle had taken place a few minutes before was littered with bodies. There were twenty to thirty men and women on the ground. Most of them lay still. A few cried out in agony.

Two of Doc Destruction's black SUVs were on fire. Large pillars of raging orange flames licked the sky. Three of Cut Throat's white Range Rover's were parked nearby. Goons in white beaters and white doo rags fired handguns and machine guns at a lone black SUV.

Kai'Ro walked slowly through the battlefield and wreckage. The loud rapid pops from the guns continued to echo through the night sky. Flashes of light burst forth from the open car windows while Doc's and Cut Throat's goons exchanged shots from behind the open car doors. There at the back of the stage lay Doc Destruction himself. He was slumped over on his couch with his chin resting on his chest. In his hand was a smoking gun. He was dead.

Not more than ten feet from him was King Ca$h. His body was surrounded by hundred dollar bills. Lying flat on his back, his eyes were wide open. But he too was gone.

Then I spotted Lil' One. He was on the ground holding his leg and crying out. Directly in the line of fire, bullets from both sides whizzed over his head and pattered the ground all around him.

KAI'RO: King, I need You now to be my rear Guard...my Shield...my Fortress...and my Strong Tower.

STORYTELLER: Lil' One turned his head and, through the smoke and dust, spotted Kai'Ro just on the edge of the deadly crossfire. His eyes widened in disbelief as his brother came racing towards him through the barrage of bullets. As he ran, I saw a circle of bright and powerful glowing figures surrounding Kai'Ro like a mighty wall. The stream of bullets pounded against them like hailstones storming a tin roof. But they quickly bounced away or fell to the ground as harmlessly as if they were wads of Styrofoam. Kai'Ro hunched down beside his brother as the chaos continued to erupt all around them.

LIL' ONE: What ya doin'? You craaazy!

KAI'RO: C'mon, we gettin' you outta here! You ain't 'sposed to die out here in this mess...not today!

STORYTELLER: With a great effort, Kai'Ro lifted his little brother off the ground and up onto his shoulder. Lil' Pain and two of Doc's body guards spotted them and redirected their fire towards Kai'Ro. But he lumbered to safety as fast as he could. Kai'Ro turned his head slightly and made eye contact as Lil' Pain squeezed off four shots from his handgun. But just as before, Kai'Ro was able to walk through the danger like he was bulletproof.

During Kai'Ro's brave rescue effort, Cut Throat and his squad poured a fresh volley of fire on Lil' Pain and the remaining two guards. One of the guards was hit and killed. The other one sprinted off and managed to find shelter behind a large dumpster. Lil' Pain took a shot in the shoulder and then in the leg. He let out an excruciating cry and fell to the ground.

At last, Kai'Ro was able to get Lil' One to safety well beyond the drama on the field. He gently set him down and rested him against a tree. Then he took off his shirt and tied a tight tourniquet around his brother's leg to slow the bleeding.

LIL' ONE: Why'd you do it, bruh? Why'd you come back for me like that?

KAI'RO: (smiling) I'd come back for you a hundred times if I had to, lil' bro. You been weighin' on my heart like a two-ton brick for the longest.

LIL' ONE: Dawg, you coulda died doin' what you just did!

KAI'RO: I know. But that was a risk I was willin' to take if it meant givin' you one more shot at Life.

STORYTELLER: Lil' One's emotions took over; his lower lip began to quiver and his eyes started to mist.

LIL' ONE: There ain't a single dude I know—not even one of my tightest homies—who would run through a wall of bullets to try to save me. Nobody would do that! That's real love, dawg, you willin' to lay down your life for me like that.

STORYTELLER: Kai'Ro grinned.

KAI'RO: Ya know, the King said the same thing once. He said there's no greater love than someone willin' to lay down their life for a friend. He laid down His life for you and me, for real. He actually died too. That's why I'm willin' to die daily, dawg.

STORYTELLER: Lil' One reached and grabbed Kai'Ro and pulled him into a powerful embrace. He held him for a minute as a stream of tears flooded down his cheeks.

Back at the fight, things had finally quieted down. With all of Doc's entourage dead or down, Cut Throat and his posse got back into their Range Rovers and drove away. Kai'Ro looked back towards the place where Lil' Pain had fallen. He was on the ground screaming in agony and holding his wounds with his hands. The guard who was hiding behind the dumpster reemerged once Cut Throat's vehicles were out of sight. He walked right up to Lil' Pain.

LIL' PAIN: C'mon, dawg... help me up! You gotta get me outta here, now!

SELFISH: (smirking) I ain't takin' you no where, playa. You think I wanna drive you around and risk gettin' myself arrested. Nah... you crazy!

STORYTELLER: Lil' Pain reached out and grabbed a hold of Selfish's pant leg. But Selfish shook off his arm, jumped into an SUV and fired up the engine. In an instant, he peeled away and disappeared down the block, leaving Lil' Pain cursing and crying out after him. Lil' One shook his head as he and Kai'Ro watched the whole scene.

LIL' ONE: Serves that dude right. Who knows how many people that clown has killed? He treated me and my boys like garbage every single day! I got no love for him!

KAI'RO: Can't leave 'em there like that, dawg.

LIL' ONE: Let him die, bruh! A dude like him ain't worth savin'. Besides, he just tried to kill us both like five minutes ago. And he beat you down a while back. He's an enemy, man. He don't deserve no love or second chances.

STORYTELLER: Kai'Ro stood to his feet.

KAI'RO: You right. I should despise him. I should let him bleed out over there on the ground. But killin' is no way to live. The King has said, if you take up the sword, you will die by the sword. So I can't give up on him, homie. He's as lost as they come. And if he dies in the next few minutes then things are gonna be even worse for him.

LIL' ONE: (clenching his fist) Dawg, scum like him deserves to die!

KAI'RO: We all do, bruh! He ain't no worse than you and me! The King died for all of us the same. Whether we merked a hundred dudes or just stole a candy bar—makes no difference. We've all fallen short in our sins!

STORYTELLER: Lil' One's angry countenance started to soften.

KAI'RO: I got love even for my enemies. It ain't my love, though, it's the King's love burnin' inside me.

STORYTELLER: Kai'Ro turned and walked back towards where Lil' Pain lay on the ground. As he drew closer, he stooped and picked up a gun from off the ground. When he got to him, Lil' Pain was lying on his back staring hopelessly up into the sky. He turned to see Kai'Ro and a strange combination of shock and terror passed over his face when he saw the gun in Kai'Ro's hand. He strained his arm and tried to grab his own gun, but it was out of reach. Kai'Ro stood over him.

LIL' PAIN: So, you gonna finish me off then, huh? I'm a true thug, dawg. I ain't afraid to die. Go on then! Pull that trigger!

STORYTELLER: Kai'Ro held the gun to Lil' Pain's head. Lil' Pain did all he could to look hard but fear was dancing across his face.

LIL' PAIN: Yeeah! See. I knew you was still a G. All that King stuff was just for show. You can't get that thuggery outta ya blood, dawg. Go on then! Pull that trigger!

STORYTELLER: Kai'Ro kept pointing the gun at him. For a split second, I thought he might pull the trigger. But then, he pulled his arm away and squeezed off a shot two feet from Lil' Pain's face.

KAI'RO: There. Now we even, homie. Vengeance ain't mine to take. It belongs to the King.

STORYTELLER: Lil' Pain looked confused.

KAI'RO: You deserve to die. Matter of fact, the whole hood would prob'ly feel relieved if I snuffed ya out right now, but this ain't my shot to take. Real talk? The King has given me a big burden for you, playa. About a year ago, I woulda put you in the ground no problem...wouldna cost me even a wink of sleep. But now if you was to die without knowing the King, I don't think I'd sleep for a week.

STORYTELLER: Far off in the distance, I could hear the shrill sound of sirens.

LIL PAIN: Look here, clown, I ain't goin' to no prison. And I ain't gonna live the rest of my life as no gimp. I'm hurt. Snuff me out. Let me go out like a G. Pull that trigger!

KAI'RO: Nah. It'd be better for you to limp into the King's arms as a gimp with a prison record than have your whole body thrown into hell. You afraid of standin' in front of a judge and havin' all your crimes against society held against you. I feel ya. But one day we all gonna stand in front of the Judge and it's gonna be a whole lot worse. He's got evidence of all the dirt we've done that nobody knows about—even every dirty thought we've ever had.

All of it has offended Him and He'll hold us accountable for every last detail. See, I could pull that trigger right now. It would keep you from goin' to prison and all that, but that would give you an immediate appointment with the Judge. And, dawg, you don't want that. Trust me. There ain't a lawyer in the world that could help you out. You'd get smashed and spend an eternity separated from your Creator—you'd be in an awful place.

LIL' PAIN: But prison *is* hell!

KAI'RO: (smiling) No, it isn't. It ain't even close. It's a bad scene. Trust me, I know, but it ain't hell.

STORYTELLER: The sirens were getting closer and sounded like they were about three blocks away.

KAI'RO: Look. In a few minutes, you're goin' to be under arrest and hauled away from here. Chances are almost certain they're gonna lock you away for a long time. But you get to decide if you wanna be free. See, the King that I love wants to arrest your heart. And despite the fact that you're gonna be locked up in a cell, He wants to give you freedom. Though you'll be put away for all the crimes and dirt you've done, He wants to wipe away your record and cover you with His righteousness. I know you feel dead and hopeless right now, but He longs to give you Life and hope, for real!

STORYTELLER: Lil' Pain's face was like that of a man drowning. He was clinging desperately to Kai'Ro's every word.

KAI'RO: Ima visit you in prison just like Preacher used to do for me. And by the King's grace, Ima introduce you to Life and Life *abundantly*.

STORYTELLER: Kai'Ro turned and walked slowly back to the tree where his brother was waiting. He gently helped Lil' One to his feet. Lil' One's face was covered in disbelief as he looked back over his shoulder at Lil' Pain.

Flashing blue and red lights danced around the park, as the approaching emergency vehicles came to a stop. Two police officers and a medic raced towards Lil' Pain. The wounded thug turned his head towards Kai'Ro and his brother but they had disappeared into the night like shadows.

SISTER COMPASSION 23

STORYTELLER: My dream took me to Preacher's church, Sanctuary of the Saints, where he and Evangeline were seated in a pew. The streetlights shone faintly through the stained glass windows. Their heads were bowed and they were praying for Kai'Ro and his safety. When they finished, Evangeline let out a big sigh.

EVANGELINE: I didn't realize followin' the King would have so much danger and drama. I thought all that was 'sposed to go away once we started followin' Him.

PREACHER: Not if we want to follow Him seriously. If you look at the King's life when He was on this earth, it was full of drama and danger. He was constantly harassed, misunderstood, verbally abused and finally beaten and killed for His message. He told His disciples that we should expect more of the same if we want to take what He said seriously and follow Him seriously.

EVANGELINE: So, does this mean Kai'Ro is gonna have to keep runnin' out in the streets like Batman every time he hears gun shots goin' off?

STORYTELLER: Preacher laughed.

PREACHER: No. Not necessarily. But maybe. See the King will always ask us to be willing to take a risk. Any time we risk danger for the King, we're putting aside our own agenda and plans and we're putting our trust in Him. We're stating with our very lives that we believe He's going to protect us and provide for us.

The risk we have to take sometimes means sacrificing our very lives and understanding that we could actually die for Him. But other times it means risking our reputation and being willing to be misunderstood and persecuted by friends and family for following Him.

EVANGELINE: Yeah. I've already run into that.

PREACHER: And maybe it means risking our finances by giving out of our own poverty or just giving in a way that's going to hurt us. We're tempted to only take a risk or to give—up to a point. It's rare that we'll risk or give until it could hurt us. But the King risked and gave everything He had to save us. Now, He's asked us to live the same way, by His grace.

EVANGELINE: I just don't wanna live in fear. I'm scared that Kai'Ro ain't gonna come back.

PREACHER: That's part of the risk. But the beautiful thing to remember is that the safest place you could ever find yourself is in the very center of His will.

EVANGELINE: What'cha mean?

PREACHER: We can insulate and isolate ourselves from risk. We can hide behind our doors or move to safer neighborhoods. We can also make certain choices with our money that will prevent us from being harmed, hurt or taken advantage of in any way.

You could call that the *safe* road. Sure, that road keeps you safe from a particular kind of harm. But in the end, it leads to rot and decay.

EVANGELINE: I don't know if I get it.

PREACHER: Well, picture having a monstrous pantry full of food. You could choose to keep all of it for yourself, but eventually it's going to rot. I mean, you can't eat it all by yourself, so it's going to go to waste. It's the same with our bodies. What happens when you don't exercise?

EVANGELINE: You get fat.

PREACHER: Exactly. See we're designed to exercise to burn off extra fat so we don't carry around all of that extra luggage. But if we sit on our behinds and don't do anything, it leads to flabbiness.

EVANGELINE: So, what you're sayin' is, we need to be givers and we need to stay active.

PREACHER: I couldn't have said it better myself. Whatever is in our pantry—be it money, food, possessions or talents—need to be distributed and shared with the world around us. Those things don't belong to us anyway. They belong to the King and He wants us to put them to good use. Hanging on to stuff just for ourselves and our own well-being is selfish and will eventually lead to rot.

EVANGELINE: So, the King wants us to be active and actually participate in what He's doin' in this fallen world. If we stay on the couch, then we'll grow spiritually flabby and start to rot away on the inside.

STORYTELLER: Preacher nodded.

PREACHER: Yes, it's about risk and also trust. We need to trust that He'll provide for us in every way. Otherwise, we end up trusting in our own abilities or trusting in what we've got tucked away in the pantry. We end up missing out on everything He's called us and equipped us to do, and we end up wasting our lives.

Your boy, Kai'Ro, has so many gifts. He's relevant to these streets because he's a product of these streets. When he shares about the King with some of the cats on the block, it connects with them on a deeper level. As a result, many of them will tune in and listen. He has the scars of the streets all over his body, but his soul is covered with the marks of the King. I believe the King is going to call Kai'Ro into some gritty and dangerous places, but I also believe the King will provide him with the protection and grace he needs to stay alive.

STORYTELLER: Just then, the church doors burst open. Both Kai'Ro and Doulos entered, propping up Lil' One between them. Evangeline leapt from where she was seated and ran over to Kai'Ro. After the two friends gently set Lil' One down on a pew, Evangeline threw her arms around Kai'Ro.

EVANGELINE: The King kept you safe! I'm so glad you're back!

DOULOS: Shoot! I saw the whole thing. Ya boy was like a superhero out there, racin' through walls of bullets and duckin' shots. It was amazin'!

KAI'RO: Nah. The King sent some angels to watch my back. It was real thick back there. Wasn't no way I coulda made it without Him. Hey, Preacher, we gotta find my brother a doctor. He's pretty messed up.

STORYTELLER: Preacher stood to his feet.

PREACHER: I had a feeling someone was going to come back in need of a doctor. I called Sister Compassion and told her to be ready. She lives two houses down from the church and she'll know what to do. I'll tell her to come right over.

STORYTELLER: Preacher pulled out his cell phone and disappeared around the corner.

LIL' ONE: (grimacing) I appreciate ya, Kai'Ro. I'd be dead for sure or dragged off to jail with Lil' Pain, if you hadn't showed up. I still don't know why ya did it. I mean, I love ya, dawg, but I don't think I'd race to my death for ya. You saved my life.

KAI'RO: I don't know if I really saved ya life, bruh. You didn't die tonight, but you're still dead. Your soul is as dead as some of those bodies back there in the park. If I did anything, I just hit ya soul with a defribulator and gave you another chance to hear about Life. But spiritually, you're dyin', dawg. And if you was to die tonight, you'd be lost forever.

LIL' ONE: I just want ya to know that I appreciate ya.

KAI'RO: Give thanks to the King. He's the One who protected us from all those bullets. Without Him, I woulda got dropped, for sure.

STORYTELLER: Lil' One stared off for a moment, like he was in deep thought. His eyes were fixed on an old wooden Cross at the front of the church. Minutes later, the doors opened and a middle-aged woman entered, carrying a black bag. She was tall and slender and had a pretty face.

PREACHER: Thank you for coming, sister. This is Lil' One and he was shot tonight.

SISTER COMPASSION: He should be at the hospital.

LIL' ONE: Nah. I can't go there.

SISTER COMPASSION: So, I take it you weren't an innocent bystander this evening?

LIL' ONE: I didn't shoot nobody. I was gonna, but I got hit before I could even squeeze off my first shot. I just don't wanna get mixed up in all that and spend time with the police asking all their questions.

STORYTELLER: Sister Compassion pulled some scissors out of her bag and cut away Lil' One's pant leg. She took a few minutes to examine the wound and then looked at Lil' One with a pleasant smile on her face.

SISTER COMPASSION: Do you realize how close to death you were this evening?

LIL' ONE: Yeah. There were bullets flyin' all 'round me. It was craaazy!

SISTER COMPASSION: That's not what I'm talking about. Surprisingly, the bullet that hit your leg missed your femoral artery by a fraction of an inch. Had it hit that artery, you would have bled out and died in a matter of minutes. Instead, the bullet passed through you and even the exit wound is quite small.

LIL' ONE: Guess I'm just lucky.

SISTER COMPASSION: Luck! Boy, open your eyes! How did you get out of that crossfire?

LIL' ONE: My brother ran and got me. He helped me get outta there.

SISTER COMPASSION: And you call that luck? Him running through bullets and chaos to save you? The bullet narrowly missed a major artery, and you call that luck too?

STORYTELLER: Lil' One sat there silently, taking in her words.

SISTER COMPASSION: Son, I heard that a lot of people died out there tonight. Why not you? Why are you still here? I will tell you why. The King has flooded His grace, love and mercy down upon you. He showed you that you have a brother who loves you so much that he was willing to give his very life for you tonight! The King has drenched you with compassion and covered you in it—and you have the nerve to call it *luck*! His goodness *should* lead you to repentance. You should be dead! But He chose to spare you tonight.

You need to figure out what you're going to do with this opportunity of a second chance. You aren't dead on that field back there for a reason. The King saved you because He loves you and desires to use you. Now, unless you're too thick-headed and stubborn, you should scream out to the King with a mighty "Hallelujah!" and "Thank You!" Then you should give your life to Him.

STORYTELLER: Sister Compassion thoroughly cleaned and dressed the wound. Lil' One winced in pain, but in his face I saw that something was stirring deep within him. When she finished, she gave some instructions to him and to the others on how to care for the wound in the days ahead.

SISTER COMPASSION: I've lost track of how many gun wounds I've had to work on in the last twenty years. But I will tell you that I have never seen one like this before. This could have been so much worse. It was truly a miracle. You'll heal up and be able to get around much sooner than you think.

Most importantly, I really hope that you start to wrestle with your soul tonight. Open the ears to your heart too. The King is screaming at the top of His lungs about how much He loves you. You need to open your heart to His love and then you need to surrender into His arms. Look at your brother, Kai'Ro, over here. I remember having to treat some gun wounds on him several years ago. You probably don't remember that, do you, Kai'Ro?

STORYTELLER: Kai'Ro shook his head.

SISTER COMPASSION: Well, you were just a no-good thug back then. I remember we'd clean you up and it wasn't more than a month before you were back with a new wound of some sort. It was like you couldn't see the King's love and mercy, even though it was right in front of your face. You should have died multiple times. I remember you being at the hospital with at least two friends who died from wounds on these streets, and you still didn't see it.

KAI'RO: I was blind. My heart was hard. I was a fool.

SISTER COMPASSION: (sighing) Well, we all were at one time. And apart from the King's grace, we still would be. Lil' One, I hope you'll hear what we're saying to you tonight. Your heart is still beating, but your soul is dead. One day, your heart will stop beating, whether it's a bullet that passes through it or it just stops on is own. But your soul? Well, son, your soul is forever.

STORYTELLER: Sister Compassion picked up her bag and prepared to leave. Lil' One grabbed her arm.

LIL' ONE: Thank you for bein' so kind to me. I didn't deserve any of what I got tonight . . a brother riskin' his life for me . . . a doctor gettin' up in the middle of the night to take care of my wound. You all are right. I see it now. I been runnin' my whole life from the King's love and it's like He hasn't given up chasin' me. Tonight, I feel like I got tackled by His love—and it feels great! I want more of it!

DOULOS: Look! I been playin' 'round too long myself. I've come up with like a thousand reasons for why I don't wanna give my life to the King, but every one of 'em is a lame excuse. I'm ready for Life too! I'm ready to follow this King, for real!

STORYTELLER: Before she moved towards the door, Sister Compassion put her hand on Lil' One's shoulder and touched Doulos's hand.

SISTER COMPASSION: (smiling gently at the two young men) Kai'Ro and Preacher can introduce you both to the King if you're ready. They'll tell you what you need to do next.

A BRIGHTER TOMORROW

24

STORYTELLER: In my dream, I saw Kai'Ro and Evangeline walking down the sidewalk towards Mr. Weary's store. The sun was still blanketed by the smog. But for the first time, I could see it glowing behind the grayish-brown clouds. Kai'Ro was holding Evangeline's hand and they both were smiling.

KAI'RO: Now, I've told Mr. Weary quite a bit about you. You gotta remember, he's a cranky ol' dude and he may ask you some annoyin' questions, give ya a hard time or just not even talk to ya.

EVANGELINE: Is he really that cranky?

KAI'RO: (laughing) Nah. He ain't bad. He's just kinda like a female...hard to predict.

STORYTELLER: Evangeline punched Kai'Ro in the arm in protest. As they reached the building, the faded black and orange sign in the window read "Open." Kai'Ro gave the door a tug but it was locked.

KAI'RO: Huh. That's funny.

STORYTELLER: Kai'Ro placed his hands up against the glass of the door and peered inside. Mr. Weary was nowhere to be seen. So he pulled some keys out of his pocket, opened up the store and they walked inside.

KAI'RO: Aye! Mr. Weary!

STORYTELLER: Kai'Ro called out and waited for a response, while he and Evangeline glanced around the store.

KAI'RO: Maybe he's in the back.

STORYTELLER: Kai'Ro was about to start down the aisle towards the back room when he spotted a large envelope with his name on it next to the cash register. He walked over and picked it up. Opening the packet, he found a letter along with a few other sheets of paper. The letter read:

Kai'Ro,

As I write you this letter, I must admit that I'm a ball of nervous energy. I've decided to leave and get out on that Heavenly Highway. Only this time I plan on making it all the way to the Cross. Our conversation a few weeks ago really stuck with me.

I lied awake a lot of nights, unable to shake the reality that I had spent almost my whole life missing out on having a relationship with the King. I was missing out on the love and Life He longed to give me. I was a doubter. But the King used you to change my mind.

Until I met you, I planned on going to my grave as a hopeless old man. Then the King brought you into my life and gave me a hope I did not expect to find. If the King can change the thug who robbed from me and trashed my store into the responsible, caring, honest and loving young man that I've come to know, then I am convinced that He's real and that He's willing to love a crotchety ol' fool like me too.

As I told you, my time on this earth is about done. I'm dying. I look forward to making it to the Cross, losing my burden and spending my last few days on the road with Him. Finding Life right before you die is a beautiful thing.

During my sleepless nights, I also wrestled with what I should do with my business. I am fully convinced that I'm supposed to leave the few things that I've owned in this life to you. As you know, my wife and my son are dead. I can think of no one better than you, Kai'Ro, to leave my business and my home. For the few months that I've known you, you've been like a son to me.

But there are some conditions for those things to become yours. I worked this out with my lawyer in the will that you'll also find in this envelope. And you better meet my conditions if you want anything! For one, I don't want no baby's daddy running my business or living in my home. You better marry that girl you got pregnant and you better treat her like a queen.

Two, I don't want no high school dropout running my business either. You're smart, son, but you need to finish what you started. You'll need to get your GED at the very least. But I hope you'll consider getting yourself a college degree. I'm already assuming that it's in your heart to do all of these things, but none of this stuff becomes yours until you finish my requirements.

Once the store becomes yours, you can run it or sell it or do whatever the King leads you to do with it. I'm quite certain that you'll put it to good use one way or the other.

I want to thank you again, Kai'Ro. You have brightened up my life in my final days, and you've pointed me to the true Source of Life. The King used you to refresh my old and weary bones for this final walk.

I love you, son.

Mr. Weary

STORYTELLER: Kai'Ro's face was covered in disbelief. He slowly folded up Mr. Weary's letter and placed it back in the large envelope. Evangeline stared at him curiously.

EVANGELINE: So?

KAI'RO: He's gone.

EVANGELINE: What'cha mean, gone?

STORYTELLER: Kai'Ro clapped his hands together in joy and then grabbed Evangeline by the shoulders.

KAI'RO: Don't you get it? He's gone. He left for the Heavenly Highway and the Cross! He's givin' his life to the King! He's been real sick and he wanted to spend his last days on the Highway. And—

STORYTELLER: Kai'Ro's face brightened even more.

EVANGELINE: And what?

KAI'RO: You're not gonna believe this, but he left me everything!

EVANGELINE: What?

KAI'RO: Yeah. It's all in his will, and a copy of it is here in this envelope. He left me this little convenience store and even his crib. It's a tight little place. He's kept it up real nice.

EVANGELINE: I'm speechless, Kai'Ro!

KAI'RO: But, he said there's some things I gotta do before it becomes official.

STORYTELLER: Evangeline narrowed her eyes for a moment.

EVANGELINE: Like what?

KAI'RO: Well, he said I need to get a GED and think about goin' to college. In his own "Mr. Weary way" he said he didn't want no dummy runnin' his business.

EVANGELINE: That ain't a bad idea. You've always been smart, Kai'Ro. Plus, you'd be the first one in your family to finish high school. I can't see how that'd hurt anything.

KAI'RO: Yeah. The idea had kinda bounced 'round in my head some too. It makes good sense. I mean, education can only provide more ways for the King to use me, right?

STORYTELLER: Evangeline nodded.

EVANGELINE: So, what else did he say?

STORYTELLER: Kai'Ro cleared his throat, removed his ball cap and nervously ran his hand over his head. He inhaled a deep breath and exhaled it slowly. Then he half-grinned and put a hand in his pocket.

KAI'RO: I...uh...well...I was meanin' to ask you...uh...

EVANGELINE: What? What is it?

KAI'RO: Look. Ima just come out with it. What Mr. Weary told me I had to do is what I've wanted to do. It's been burnin' in my heart to do it. You've been my girl for like five years now, and you've been my best friend. I thought I lost you forever when I left for the Heavenly Highway. I never thought I'd find a bigger love, but my crush on the King was the only thing that I found to be greater than the love I've had for you, girl. I prayed for you every day out on that Highway and you was in my thoughts constantly.

I never thought I'd get you back, but then the King gripped your heart too. When I saw you for the first time, after you came back from the Mountain of the Cross, I could see the joy of the King all over you. It's funny, but I immediately fell in love with you all over again. Only this time, it was a deeper love, a love I'd never felt for you before. I knew right then that the King answered the desire of my heart by giving you back to me. I knew right then that I wanted to spend the rest of my life with you.

STORYTELLER: Kai'Ro got down on one knee. As he did so, Evangeline cupped a hand over her mouth. He pulled a shiny ring from out of his pocket. It was silver and in the center was a beautiful blue stone.

KAI'RO: E., I'd like to ask you to marry me. I want to be your husband...wanna take care of you...raise a family with you...follow the King together...and grow old together.

STORYTELLER: Kai'Ro held the ring up and placed it near her hand.

KAI'RO: I love you, Evangeline. Will you marry me?

STORYTELLER: Happy tears brimmed in Evangeline's eyes.

EVANGELINE: I can't believe this...

KAI'RO: (smiling) I know, right?

EVANGELINE: (bursting out in laughter) I can't believe you asked me to marry you in the middle of the candy aisle in an old raggedy convenience store.

STORYTELLER: Kai'Ro looked surprised for a moment and then he too burst out in laughter.

EVANGELINE: Get up off ya knee, boy.

STORYTELLER: Kai'Ro stood to his feet and Evangeline threw her arms around his neck.

EVANGELINE: Of course, I'll marry you!

STORYTELLER: They held each other for a moment and then Kai'Ro carefully slid the ring on her finger. Then they embraced again. Kai'Ro's eyes were filled with light and joy.

EVANGELINE: You've always been the bravest and most amazin' man that I've ever known. And I've loved you for the longest. But now that you serve the King, I don't think I could find a greater man to spend my life with. And I don't think I could find a better father for our little son, Kai'Non.

STORYTELLER: Kai'Ro gently released Evangeline from his grip.

KAI'RO: So, you have his name? I like it. What does it mean?

EVANGELINE: It means "new." The King has done so many new things in our life...new opportunities...a new relationship between us...new hope. And I really believe He's brought us back, as a family, to participate with Him in doin' somethin' new in this city.

KAI'RO: I hear that.

STORYTELLER: The two of them held hands and gazed into each other's eyes. They spoke to each other. But I couldn't hear their words, for I was suddenly being pulled away until I could only see their silhouettes through the shop window. Soon, they and Mr. Weary's store faded altogether into the distance.

As my dream took me away, I noticed that the day was creeping quickly towards evening at an unusual pace. I could literally see the faint glow of the sun moving rapidly behind the clouds and heading towards the horizon. I too was moving down the street rather suddenly.

Before long, I found myself at the tall wall of hedges on the edge of town and my dream pulled me right through them. I was taken down the dirt road a short distance until I passed Lil' One and Doulos. They were walking and talking together on their journey towards the Mountain of the Cross.

I was carried along a bit further until I spotted Mr. Weary also walking down the dirt road. The anger in his eyes was gone and I noticed instead a quiet peace. Then my dream suddenly took me off the ground itself. I found myself hurtling into the sky like a rocket leaving the earth. Looking below, there lay the City of Doom, sprawling beneath as a massive stretch of orange glowing buildings and shadows.

To my surprise, I spotted a few tiny lights popping up in random places. Like fireflies in the dark of night, they glowed and even seemed to move about amidst the otherwise bleak and darkened cityscape below. I knew then that these were the King's lights—men and women who were shining His light for the city to see.

I found myself smiling in my dream and feeling overwhelmed with a sharp jolt of hope.

Then there was a bright flash and I awoke.

ACKNOWLEDGMENTS

This book would not have been possible without a host of fellow Christian soldiers who willingly loaned me their talents and time.

I am so grateful and humbled by the team the Lord assembled for this latest project. Big thanks to Ray Causly. You started this project with me as my editor and ended it as my brother and friend.

I'm grateful to Sho Baraka. I appreciate you sharing your gifts on chapter 21. Kai'Ro could have never spit for the King without you. I owe you lunch at that Cuban joint next time I'm in Atlanta.

I have to give a shout out to my wifey, Sara. Thank you for all the time you spent listening to me read my manuscript and for all the time you spent critiquing and editing it. I'm grateful for the encouragement you give and also for your honesty. You are my Evangeline and I couldn't have completed this journey without you.

Big thanks to Restoration Academy and my students and colleagues there. Kai'Ro was born in your hallways and will always belong to you. And then, in no particular order, I have to say thanks to Kids Across America for getting behind this project and for pubbing it.

Thanks to my "big" brother Jason Williams and to my man Tracy Hipps. You two have have been behind this project from day one and have done so much to get it into the hands of laborers in our urban fields.

Shout out to my lil' brother, Geoff. Thanks for sharing your ridiculous gift on both covers. Glad we got to do these two books together.

I appreciate my father-in-law, Dan. I'm grateful for all the time you gave to the project identifying Scriptures and formulating questions for the Leader's Guide.

Got to holler at my friends at Reach Records. Your music inspired me a great deal on this project. I appreciate you.

Lastly, thanks to everyone who is intentionally following Jesus' beautiful feet into our cities and prisons, seeking to reach our young people with the Gospel. Your labor is not in vain.

KAI'RO

978-0-8024-0729-0

Kai'Ro: The Journey of an Urban Pilgrim chronicles the epic quest of a young man named Kai'Ro. In jail. Beat down. Hopeless. Kai'Ro is overcome with his own guilt and failure and has nowhere to turn. But then the Preacher shows up with Good News. There is One who can free him from the burden of his sin, guilt, and pain and give him hope, life, and peace. He is the King. Leaving the City of Doom and his friends behind, Kai'Ro sets out on the Heavenly Highway on a journey of temptation, peril, and adventure in search of this King.

> *"I'm personally excited about the work Judah Ben has done. To see his years of influence in the urban context fleshed out in writing is priceless. I'm honored to support him."*
> **—Lecrae, Hip Hop recording artist**

> *"Kai'Ro has the special ingredients of realness and truth. Its content is relevant to the inner city core, while still maintaining biblical authenticity that any seminary student could appreciate."*
> **—Sho Baraka, Hip Hop recording artist, actor, writer, director**

MOODY
PUBLISHERS
www.MoodyPublishers.com